DEATH TIMES THREE

BITTER END
FRAME-UP FOR MURDER
ASSAULT ON A BROWNSTONE

"Each piece in this volume is carefully wrought, each is from a period when Stout was in top writing form, each contains incomparable moments, insights, and sallies of wit that will take their place in the memories of devotees of the saga."—from the Introduction by John McAleer

REX STOUT'S
NERO WOLFE

"It is always a treat to read a Nero Wolfe mystery. The man has entered our folklore; he is part of the psyche of anybody who has ever turned over the pages of a mystery novel. Like Sherlock Holmes . . . he looms larger than life and, in some ways, is much more satisfactory."
—*The New York Times Book Review*

"Nero Wolfe is one of the master creations."
—James M. Cain, author of *The Postman Always Rings Twice*

"The most interesting great detective of them all."
—Kingsley Amis, author of *Lucky Jim*

"This fellow is the best of them all."
—Supreme Court Justice Oliver Wendell Holmes

Bantam Books offers the finest in classic and modern American murder mysteries. Ask your bookseller for the books you have missed.

Rex Stout

Broken Vase
Death of a Dude
Death Times Three
Fer-de-Lance
The Final Deduction
Gambit
The Rubber Band
Too Many Cooks
The Black Mountain

Max Allan Collins

The Dark City

A. E. Maxwell

Just Another Day in Paradise
Gatsby's Vineyard
The Frog and the Scorpion

Joseph Louis

Madelaine
The Trouble with Stephanie

M. J. Adamson

Not Till a Hot January
A February Face
Remember March

Conrad Haynes

Bishop's Gambit, Declined
Perpetual Check

Barbara Paul

First Gravedigger
But He Was Already Dead When
  I Got There

P. M. Carlson

Murder Unrenovated
Rehearsal for Murder

Ross Macdonald

The Goodbye Look
Sleeping Beauty
The Name Is Archer
The Drowning Pool
The Underground Man
The Zebra-Striped Hearse
The Ivory Grin

Margaret Maron

The Right Jack
Baby Doll Games
One Coffee With

William Murray

When the Fat Man Sings

Robert Goldsborough

Murder in E Minor
Death on Deadline
The Bloodied Ivy

Sue Grafton

"A" Is for Alibi
"B" Is for Burglar
"C" Is for Corpse
"D" Is for Deadbeat

Joseph Telushkin

The Unorthodox Murder of
  Rabbi Wahl
The Final Analysis of Doctor Stark

Richard Hilary

Snake in the Grasses
Pieces of Cream
Pillow of the Community

Carolyn G. Hart

Design for Murder
Death on Demand
Something Wicked
coming soon: Honeymoon With
  Murder

Lia Matera

Where Lawyers Fear to Tread
A Radical Departure
The Smart Money
coming soon: Hidden Agenda

Robert Crais

The Monkey's Raincoat
coming soon: Scarecrow Falling

Keith Peterson

The Trapdoor
There Fell a Shadow
coming soon: The Rain

David Handler

The Man Who Died Laughing

Carolyn Wheat

Where Nobody Dies

Death Times Three

Three

Rex Stout

A Nero Wolfe Mystery

**With an Introduction
by
John J. McAleer**

BANTAM BOOKS

NEW YORK • TORONTO • LONDON • SYDNEY • AUCKLAND

DEATH TIMES THREE

A Bantam Book / December 1985
6 printings through September 1988

PRINTING HISTORY

"Bitter End" first appeared in the November 1940 issue of
The American Magazine, *and later in a limited edition volume*
entitled CORSAGE.

"Framed-Up for Murder" originally appeared in the June 21st,
June 28th, and July 5, 1958 editions of The Saturday Evening
Post.

"Assault on a Brownstone" appeared in substantially differ-
ent form as "The Counterfeiter's Knife" in the January 14th,
January 21st, January 28th issues of The Saturday Evening
Post *in 1961, and as "Counterfeit for Murder" in* HOMICIDE
TRINITY.

ISBN 0-553-27828-2

Published simultaneously in the United States and Canada

Bantam Books are published by Bantam Books, a division of
Bantam Doubleday Dell Publishing Group, Inc. Its trademark,
consisting of the words "Bantam Books" and the portrayal
of a rooster, is Registered in U.S. Patent and Trademark Office
and in other countries. Marca Registrada. Bantam Books,
666 Fifth Avenue, New York, New York 10103.

PRINTED IN THE UNITED STATES OF AMERICA

KR   15   14   13   12   11   10   9

Contents

Introduction

During the last years of Rex Stout's life, as his author-
ized biographer, I received numerous letters from well-
wishers and, on occasion, not-such–well-wishers, offering
me advice. "Is it true," one of the latter asked, "that
Stout has a secretary who writes all his stuff for him?" I
showed the letter to Rex, then in his eighty-ninth year.
He scanned it and said, "Tell him the name is Jane
Austen, but I haven't the address." The joke was on the
letter writer. Rex was classing himself with the best.
Not long before that he had told me, "I used to think
that men did everything better than women, but that
was before I read Jane Austen. I don't think any man
ever wrote better than Jane Austen."

It was no coincidence that, when I asked after
Wolfe a few days before Rex died, Rex confided, "He's
rereading *Emma*." Rex ranked *Emma* as Jane Austen's
masterpiece. In the last weeks of his life he also reread
it. That a book could be reread was to him solid proof of
its worth. Thus it pleased him when P. G. Wodehouse,
whom Rex admired, declared, at ninety-four, in a letter

that he wrote to me, "He [Rex Stout] passes the supreme test of being rereadable. I don't know how many times I have reread the Nero Wolfe stories, but plenty. I know exactly what is coming and how it is all going to end, but it doesn't matter. That's *writing*."

Since Rex's death, on October 27, 1975, the radiant host that constitutes his loyal following has reread many times the thirty-three novels and thirty-eight novellas believed to make up the entire corpus of the Wolfe saga. How jubilant must be this worldwide audience to learn now that many new pages of reading pleasure await it—a thirty-ninth novella, "Bitter End," known only to a smattering of readers; "Frame-up for Murder," a substantially expanded rewrite of "Murder Is No Joke," the existence of which has gone unsuspected by most Stout readers since it has never before appeared in book form; and a fortieth novella, the original version of "Counterfeit for Murder," which, after the first seven pages, pursues a plot line that differs markedly from that followed in the version eventually published in *Homicide Trinity* (1962). The existence of this unpublished manuscript was unknown, even to members of Rex Stout's own family, until 1972, when Rex furnished me a handwritten copy of his personal "Writing Record," in which the facts relating to its composition were recorded. A diligent search among his voluminous papers, at Boston College's Bapst Library, when they were delivered to the college following his death, disclosed that, contrary to his remembrance, he had not destroyed this manuscript and that there was, therefore, a seventy-third Nero Wolfe story that had never seen print. This discovery surpasses in significance the publication—in 1951, for the first time in the United States—of the fifty-first Father Brown story, "The Vampire of the Village," and the publication—in 1972, for the first time anywhere—of "Talboys," a hitherto unknown Lord Peter Wimsey story; it is on a par only with the discovery of an eightieth Sherlock Holmes story—an event which has not yet occurred.

For admirers of Nero Wolfe and Archie Goodwin, in the years between 1934 and 1975, the advent of a new Nero Wolfe story was ever an occasion for rejoicing. However, because the stories appeared with unfailing regularity (save for the years of World War II, when Rex Stout was heading up America's propaganda effort as chairman of the Writers' War Board), the thrill probably came to be regarded by many as theirs by right of entitlement. For a bona fide new story to come to light, after every legitimate hope for such an event had been relinquished, constitutes an occasion that must set the firmament ablaze with pyrotechnical wonders. What a windfall! What a gift from the stars! Yet, here we have, in this single volume, not only such a treasure, but two other Nero Wolfe tales largely new to us. None of the three, moreover, can be dismissed as a mere practice exercise, sketched out and flung aside by Rex Stout as beneath his standards. Each piece is carefully wrought; each is from a period when he was in top writing form; each contains incomparable moments, insights, and sallies of wit that will take their place in the memories of votaries of the corpus as new pinnacles in a landscape already wondrously sown with pinnacles. Let us consider each in its turn.

"Bitter End," published in *The American Magazine* in November 1940, was the first of what we now know to be forty Nero Wolfe novellas. But it began life not as a Nero Wolfe novella but as a Tecumseh Fox novel. In 1939, to accommodate his publishers, who had asked him to create another detective to spell Wolfe, Rex introduced Tecumseh Fox in *Double for Death*. Fox was not the superman Wolfe was, nor did he have

Archie's panache, but he did have brains and muscle and, without the advantage of a dogsbody to assist him, he worked out the solution to an intricate case. Rex's friends thought Fox was rather like Rex himself. Certainly, like Rex, he was on the move a lot. That was inevitable. Rex said he had made Wolfe housebound because other people's detectives "ran around too damn much." Yet he realized that two sedentary detectives would be too limiting.

In the summer of 1940 Rex was ready with a second Fox novel—*Bad for Business*. Farrar & Rinehart scheduled it for publication in November of that year in its *Second Mystery Book*, where it was to be the culminating tale in a volume that would include stories by Anthony Abbot, Philip Wylie, Leslie Ford, Mary Roberts Rinehart, and David Frome (a Leslie Ford alias) —*Bad for Business* though, weighing in at two hundred and five pages, was far and away the longest. As was customary, the story was offered to *The American Magazine* for abridged publication before the book itself appeared. To Stout's surprise, Sumner Blossom, publisher of *The American Magazine*, refused to pursue the Fox piece but offered Stout double payment if he would convert the story into a Wolfe novella. To Blossom's surprise, and maybe his own, Rex effected the transformation in eleven days. As he explained to me later, by then he had already become deeply committed to the war against Hitler and needed the money.

Thus "Bitter End," Rex's first Wolfe novella, appeared in *The American Magazine* in November 1940— and on November 28, *Bad for Business* appeared in the *Second Mystery Book*. Those who read both stories at that time must have been perplexed. The plot was basically unchanged. The names of the principal characters likewise were the same. This was true as well of many lines of dialogue and of many crucial expository passages. Yet, Tecumseh Fox's labors had been portioned out between Wolfe and Archie; Fox's nemesis from Homicide, Inspector Damon, had been supplanted, inevitably, by Inspector Cramer; and Dol Booner, whose path occasionally crossed Fox's in *Bad for Business*, had been dispensed with entirely.

These changes were by no means matter-of-fact substitutions. Although the new story was only a third as long as the original, compactness actually gave it a snap and purpose that it lacked before. Most of the members of the supporting cast were enhanced. They were not on stage as long as they had been before, so the moment an opportunity came their way, they made their presence felt. By dividing Fox's responsibilities between Wolfe and Archie, Rex showed how incomparable and how indispensable were the distinctive attributes of each member of his sublime duo. Each does superbly what Fox was able to do merely adequately. Working once again with the characters he loved best, Rex found ways to involve them intimately in events as they unfolded.

In *Bad for Business*, Tecumseh Fox learns secondhand that someone (in a prefiguration of the Tylenol tragedy of later times) is adulterating, apparently with sinister intent, Tingley's Tidbits, a liver paté. In "Bitter End," Nero Wolfe actually partakes of the paté, which is laced with quinine, and all but explodes at the dinner table, splattering a landscape that includes Archie. Predictably, and reminiscent of his duel to the death with Arnold Zeck, he commits himself to seeking out and revenging himself on the adulterator. Furthermore, Cramer abducts a guest from Wolfe's brownstone, simultaneously giving new scope to Wolfe's vendetta and a scope to Cramer's own performance that, by contrast, diminishes Inspector Damon's role. In *Bad for Business*, Tecumseh Fox learns secondhand of a bloody murder.

In "Bitter End," Archie arrives on the murder scene as one of the first witnesses. Surprisingly, though Fox openly romances the heroine in *Bad for Business*, in "Bitter End," Archie, though solicitous, keeps his distance. This enables Archie to give needed support to Amy's true suitor, the inept Leonard Cliff.

The viewpoint in *Bad for Business* is that of the omniscient author. In "Bitter End," naturally, Archie is the narrator. Rex Stout had proven that he could bring startling piquancy to a plot by relinquishing control of it to Archie, and we must concede that Stout showed excellent judgment in letting Archie be his spokesman throughout the Wolfe saga. When "Archie took control of the narrative," he said, he himself was no longer responsible for what Archie said and did. And he meant it. So successful were the results in "Bitter End" that we must regret that Rex was never motivated to rewrite each of the Fox stories as Wolfe stories, with Archie narrating. Let those who may undertake to continue the saga not leave that avenue unexplored. In "Bitter End," Rex Stout showed that it can be done with complete success.

It was not by chance that *Bad for Business* was never given separate hardcover publication in the United States or that Rex Stout dropped Fox after a few appearances. "Fox wasn't a created character, like Wolfe," Rex conceded. "He was put together piece-by-piece and wasn't worth a damn." Nonetheless, Fox's precedence as the sleuth who unknotted the tangled Tingley fortunes (in *Bad for Business*) made Rex reluctant to include "Bitter End" in his volumes of Wolfe novellas. Stout never went back and reread the story because he could not forget that Wolfe had been called in on the case as someone from whom a second opinion was sought. It was not becoming to Wolfe's dignity to sit him down to another man's leavings.

Rex ought to have remembered that a good story always stands the test of rereading. And "Bitter End," like the other seventy-two stories in the corpus, passes that test beyond quibble or sneer. Perhaps if Rex had remembered that it was this story that had shown him that Wolfe and Archie could thrive in a novella quite as well as in a novel, he would have given it due acknowledgment. Actually, in the last year of his life he may have come to that realization when he gave Michael Bourne permission to bring the story out in a limited edition of five hundred copies. Bourne conceived of this edition as a tribute to mark, in 1976, Rex's ninetieth birthday. Plans for it were still afoot when Rex died. In 1977, it appeared instead in the volume called *Corsage*, as a memorial tribute. Although its publication brought joy to those who were aware of it, the restriction Rex had placed on the number of copies to be printed resulted in a volume known to few readers who were not avid bibliophiles.

The entry in Rex Stout's Writing Record for "Murder Is No Joke," appears between the entries for *If Death Ever Slept* and *Champagne for One*. It reads: "Murder Is No Joke"—48 pp. Began 8/5/57, finished 8/15/57. 1 day out, 10 days writing time." Rex's breakdown, reporting his day by day output, shows that he worked on the story on eleven different days but counted two days as half days because he did not put in a full nine hours at his desk. On the thirteenth he had been interrupted by the arrival of a visitor. On the fifteenth he quit early because half a day's work brought him to the end of his labors. As usual, of course, he did no revision. Whatever had to be done was always done in his head. The first draft was always the only draft. "Murder Is No Joke" was the fourth story Rex worked on that year, because, in addition to *If Death Ever*

Slept, which he had begun in mid-May and finished in mid-June, he had finished "Easter Parade" in the first days of the new year, and then in March, in nine days, had written "Fourth-of-July Picnic." All were Nero Wolfe stories. Indeed, after World War II he wrote nothing else.

Notations in Rex's file on "Murder Is No Joke" disclose further writing labors for that year that were not entered in the Writing Record. On November 23, to oblige *The Saturday Evening Post*, he began work on an expanded version of "Murder Is No Joke." Taking only two days off, Sunday the twenty-fourth and Saturday the thirtieth, to celebrate his seventy-first birthday (when family and friends gathered at High Meadow, his eighteen-acre domain at Danbury, Connecticut), he completed the rewrite in thirteen days, having increased the original forty-eight pages to seventy-nine. Characteristically (Rex found holidays disruptive and, within reasonable limits, preferred to ignore them), he had written five pages on Thanksgiving Day and four on his birthday. Typically, also, he had not merely padded the old manuscript. He had thought the story through again, adding much that was new and enhancing what he kept. Now two different versions of the story existed, the latter clearly the superior of the former. Since that fact was self-evident, it should logically have followed that the original was suppressed in favor of the rewrite.

Yet that is not what happened. On February 14, 1958, as "Murder Is No Joke," the original was published in *And Four to Go*. On June 21, June 28, and July 5, 1958, as "Frame-up for Murder," the rewrite was published in three installments in the *The Saturday Evening Post*. Those who owned the book probably never compared their version to the *Post*'s version. Those who read the *Post*'s version probably never compared it to the version in *And Four to Go*. Thus no one complained that thirty-one pages of vintage Stout were buried in back issues of *The Saturday Evening Post*. But they were, and that was deplorable. Here, after a twenty-eight-year delay, as "Frame-up for Murder" achieves publication in book form another injustice is swept away.

In the notes that Rex Stout kept for this story—as always, on 5½ by 8½ goldenrod sheets—he recorded the following facts about eight of the characters: "Alec Gallant, 38, of Gallant Inc., 54th St. East of 5th. Bianca Voss, 37, who has taken charge. Carl Drew, 40, business manager & buyer. Anita Prince, 34, designer & fitter. Emmy Thorne, 26, contacts & promotion. Flora Gallant, 26, Alec's sister & handy woman. Sarah Yare, 35, has-been actress. Doris Hoft, 29, at phone." To readers of either version of the story the name Doris Hoft will come as a surprise. While Doris does have a small part to play in both versions, in neither does Rex mention her by name. More surprising to readers of "Murder Is No Joke" must be the revelation that Flora Gallant is twenty-six. In that story we are assured that she was twenty-five when she came to the United States from France, twenty years earlier, in 1937, and thus is forty-five. Rex's initial description of Flora bears this out. Archie relates, "When I opened the door to admit his sister Flora that Tuesday morning, it was a letdown to see a dumpy middle-aged female in a dark gray suit that was anything but spectacular. It needed pressing, and the shoulders were too tight, and her waist wasn't where it thought it was." In short, Flora is a frump who has seen her best days and these not lately. Nor does the ensuing dialogue encourage us to mellow toward her. She seems to be a bitter, spent woman who has outlived whatever romantic feelings she once had. With clinical detachment she dismisses the possibility of Wolfe's having a mistress, almost as one might rule out the likelihood of his catching whooping cough or breaking out in pubescent acne. We resent this woman who addresses Wolfe as though she were a case-hardened clinician talking to a eunuch. And Flora is similarly dispassionate when she says of brother Alec, " 'He has an *amie intime,* a young woman who is of importance in his establishment.' " The name Flora Gallant has encouraged us to expect something more. In "Murder Is No Joke" Flora is no flower. She is more of a nettle. That fact serves at least one good purpose. It makes it easy to believe that she is capable of skulduggery or even murder.

In "Frame-up for Murder" we must begin all over with Flora. She first catches Archie's eye in the lobby of the Churchill "because she rated a glance as a matter of principle—the principle that a man owes it to his eyes to let them rest on attractive objects when there are any around." Her chin was, Archie acknowledged, "slightly more pointed than I would have specified if I had had her made to order," but otherwise her ranking is high among the women who have intrigued Archie Goodwin over the years. A shoulder spread of mink, a floppy-brimmed hat, which is at Archie's ear level—so that, as he notes, her hair might graze his chin if she removed it—and a trace of a beguiling foreign accent, are all that this Flora needs, in addition to her beauty, to intrigue Archie. When she accosts him on the uptown side of Thirty-eighth Street, he confesses, "If she had been something commonplace like a glamorous movie star," he might have gone on his way without further interest. But that does not happen. Flora's game is to get to know Archie so that he will gain her an audience with Nero Wolfe. She dines with him and dances with him to assure the success of this strategem. Her kisses are prologue to inquisitions. Yet, she is naively obvious in her intrigues, and Archie, never for a moment taken in, finds her simple, obvious machinations (embarked on for no more sinister a purpose than to protect her brother and his business) a source of unmitigated delight. This new Flora burgeons in the opening pages of "Frame-up for Murder." Her subsequent pursuit of Archie through the streets of Manhattan and her success in bringing him down, on the wing, so to speak, stirs our interest in a way that totally eclipses the opening of "Murder Is No Joke."

Rex Stout enjoyed portraying beautiful foreign women of fierce integrity whose hearts are set on realizing some laudable goal that they pursue with a tenacity that gives consequence to their obvious ploys when they try to enlist the services of those who can get them the results they want. In his beautiful wife, the Polish-born Pola Hoffman, their friends recognized the prototype of these women. Here, in a story set in the world of high fashion, the identification is more easily made, for Pola Stout was one of America's foremost designers of woolen fabrics and her fabrics were much in favor with top fashion houses both in the United States and Europe. It was Pola's calling that gave Rex the setting and plot for several other stories, most notably *The Red Box* and *Red Threads*, and made him always attentive to the clothes his characters were wearing.

In "Murder Is No Joke," Flora Gallant offers Nero Wolfe a hundred dollars as a retainer. In "Frame-up for Murder," as befits her upgraded status, the sum increases to three hundred, still not a princely offering from someone swathed in mink, but enough, Archie says, either to pay his salary for two days or to keep Wolfe in beer for three weeks. That Archie has mellowed toward Flora since her transformation from frog to princess is evident. In "Murder Is No Joke" he had calculated that her hundred-dollar deposit would, at most, buy beer for Wolfe for four days. But more than pecuniary advantages attach to Flora's new appearance. Her metamorphosis generated most of the new pages that expanded "Murder Is No Joke" from forty-eight pages to seventy-nine. In "Murder Is No Joke," after murder was committed it was not worth anyone's bother to bring Flora on the scene when Archie visited the offices of Gallant, Inc., to interview the chief suspects. In "Frame-up for Murder" Flora is prominently visible, and her presence makes Archie's day. At the close of this interlude, moreover, Archie struts into Alec Gallant's office and speaks his mind with a bravado remarkable even for Archie. One has to assume that his recent smooching with Flora has produced such a rush of adrenaline that he is ready to take on the world. Perhaps that also accounts for his boast to Emmy Thorne that he can chin himself twenty times.

Nero Wolfe likewise appears to better advantage in the rewrite of "Murder Is No Joke," and not solely because a younger, demure Flora declines to speculate in jaded tones on his sex life. A vital Flora generates more excitement all around. Archie cares more about the case that evolves out of her visit to the brownstone, and so, inevitably, does Wolfe. Wolfe's speculations concerning the authenticity of the phone call made to Bianca Voss come forth more promptly and do not seem, as in "Murder Is No Joke," arrived at through the instigation of Inspector Cramer. The lively exchange of comments between Wolfe and Archie when Bianca's visit ends is also one of the high moments of the rewrite since it has no counterpart in "Murder Is No Joke." One detects, too, that, once drawn into the case, Wolfe becomes, on learning of Alec Gallant's resistance activities in World War II, allied to him in sympathies. Certainly Rex's own commitments in the war years assured both his allegiance to Gallant's principles and his tacit approval of Gallant's initiative taken when the niceties of the law raised the possibility that heinous crimes against humanity would go unpunished.

At one point in "Murder Is No Joke," Nero Wolfe is grossly insulted. He is told, " 'You are scum, I know, in your stinking sewer! Your slimy little ego in your big gob of fat!' " Even Cramer is nonplussed when these phrases are repeated to him. It is easier to believe that the drab and hostile Flora scripted these lines in "Murder Is No Joke" than to attribute them to the vivacious Flora of "Frame-up for Murder." But happily they survived the rewrite, and that kept in the marvelous scene in which Wolfe shows how the word "gob" made him aware that "the extraordinary billingsgate . . . spat at me" was a prepared text. To know the words were spoken only for calculated effect makes everyone feel better—Wolfe as well as the reader. And, really, we could not spare that moment when, after Wolfe's explanation is forthcoming and he gestures at the conclusion, Archie complacently observes, "He waved 'gob' away."

In "Frame-up for Murder," Inspector Cramer is given more to do than he was given in "Murder Is No Joke." We may commend him, perhaps, for his restraint in not pointing out that this attempt to deceive Wolfe repeats an episode from *The Rubber Band*. Perhaps it was Cramer's prudence on this occasion that induced Rex Stout to allow him to speak the words "Murder is no joke," which gave the story its title and accounts, as well, for Wolfe's generous reiteration of these words at a crucial moment in the story. It is surprising to observe, in scrutinizing the original manuscript, that Rex Stout once marked these words for excision. It is more surprising yet, to discover from his notes that originally he had settled on a different murderer. No harm can come from mentioning the name now, because no reasonable reader will see him as a possible suspect. We are referring to Carl Drew! It was a good day's work when Rex changed his mind.

While odd circumstances attended the writing of "Bitter End" and "Frame-up for Murder," the history of one other Wolfe novella is even more unusual—that is, the story serialized as "The Counterfeiter's Knife" in *The Saturday Evening Post*, in the issues for January 14, 21, and 28, 1961. Unaltered, the same story was published the following year as "Counterfeit for Murder" in *Homicide Trinity*, one of the tripartite Wolfe volumes. Rex's Writing Record for this story reads: "73 pp. Began 3/6/59, finished 3/31/59. 9 days out, 17 days writing time." His breakdown of days shows that he actually worked on it on twenty-three different days, but sometimes only for short intervals, which he recorded as fractions of days. Only on the nineteenth and twentieth, when he was in New York, and on the twenty-ninth, Easter Sunday, was he away from his desk entirely. For Rex to give so much time to a single novella was unusual. But we do not have to look far for an explanation. As he noted in his writing record, underlining the word twice for emphasis, the story he wrote in that twenty-six-day interval was a "Rewrite." Just ahead of the entry given above he had recorded these particulars concerning the original version of the story: " 'Counterfeit for Murder'—74 pp. Began 1/22/59, finished 2/11/59. 3 days out, 18 days writing time." Only on two days did he do no writing at all, the twenty-ninth and thirtieth of January, when he had to be in Providence. Fractions of days show that he could have reduced the total of working days by another three, making, in all, five days out. But, all things considered, the work had gone well; so that, quite up to his usual average, he had written four or five pages on twelve of the nineteen days he had written. Nothing in his notes suggests that he was dissatisfied with the results. Yet, less than a month later, he discarded all but the first seven pages of this story and, starting again at that point, took events in a direction so contrary to that in which they had moved before, that the lady who quickened Archie's heartbeat in the original is here hastily dispatched with a bread knife, and the dowdy boardinghouse keeper, who had promptly fallen prey to a hit-and-run motorist in the first version, here escapes with a grazing, is reanimated, and given liberty to engage Wolfe as well as Archie in some of the liveliest dialogue to be found anywhere in the corpus. She, Anthony Boucher said of Miss Hattie Annis, "is the most entertaining client to visit West Thirty-fifth Street in some time." And indeed she was.

A perusal of the two versions of "Counterfeit for Murder" shows that Hattie Annis's reappearance is so thoroughly desirable that it completely justifies Rex Stout's repudiating his folly in snuffing out a character that was endowed with her remarkable vitality. But was that the actual reason for his decision? We can only conjecture because, on July 11, 1972, when I asked Rex why he had rewritten this story, he said, "There must be a reason, but I have forgotten what it was." We know, at least, that Rex was not acting on the advice of anyone else, either editor or friend, because, in the twenty-three-day interval that elapsed between his completing the original and beginning the rewrite, he had shown the manuscript to no one. He arrived at the decision entirely on his own. Only one possible explanation can be offered. In that interval Rex had spent a fishing holiday, at Paradise Island, Florida, with his friend Nathaniel Selleck (the second of the three Nathaniel Sellecks who were Rex's physicians successively over a forty-five-year period). On the day that Rex returned from Florida, word reached him that Dr. Selleck had dropped dead moments after his departure. On receipt of the news Rex resumed writing at once, perhaps, in the creative act of calling back to life someone who had died, resorting to a form of therapy mysterious to some but not at all mysterious to those who write.

Hattie Annis is the most successful of several characters Rex based on his mother's sister, Alice Todhunter Bradley, who as a young woman, in the 1880s, traveled through the West alone, lecturing, serving as schoolmistress to Brigham Young's kin and, eventually, as a confidante to Eugene Debs. In the original "Counterfeit for Murder" Hattie does not meet Nero Wolfe. In the rewrite she not only meets him, she flabbergasts him by asking him for "lamb kidneys *bourguignonne*" when he invites her to lunch. This scene alone justifies the rewrite. Rarely is Nero Wolfe ever put out of countenance by anyone. By story's end Wolfe is won over by Hattie's homely candor and integrity. No mistake about it, Hattie is a straight-arrow.

If it is incumbent on us to ask what else readers gain in the rewrite of "Counterfeit for Murder," the question can at least be speedily answered. Wolfe is given more to do here. Once again he is able to utilize, to good advantage, the services of Saul, Fred, and Orrie, and to stage one of his revealing assemblies. We also learn the source of the counterfeit bills, a detail skimped on in the original story. And, finally, Wolfe is able to compromise severely the dignity of Albert Leach (that his surname recalls a parasite is not accidental), a T-man whose patronizing attitude has awakened his indignation. This scene foreshadows Wolfe's brilliant coup in humbling J. Edgar Hoover, six years later, in *The Doorbell Rang*.

We need not suppose that the rewrite of "Counterfeit for Murder" cannibalized the original, stripping from it its most meritorious parts. Tamaris Baxter, who changes roles with Hattie in the rewrite, to become the needed corpse, is intelligent and resourceful but a bit starchy, probably because she is not the person she pretends to be. To dispense with her is no hardship. But the original story has several wonderful scenes that can ill be spared. The restoration of them to a place in the corpus is a gain that all discriminating Neronians will applaud. Early in the story tensions run high between Wolfe and Archie. Archie comes upon Wolfe studying a terrestrial globe, "probably picking out a place for me to be exiled in." Wolfe fires Archie, and Archie reports, "I turned and marched out, chin up, with my ego patting me on the back, and mounted the stairs to my room." It is a joy to see Wolfe later weasel out of this commitment when he realizes he needs Archie after all.

Midway in the story we are treated to two superb scenes, one treading close on the heels of the other. Albert Leach, accompanied by a team of four other T-men, invades the brownstone and conducts an inch-by-inch search, even to sifting through the files in Wolfe's office and the osmundine in his plant rooms. " 'My house has been invaded, my privacy has been outraged, and my belongings have been pawed,' " Wolfe declares. He locks himself in his bedroom and refuses to emerge until the T-men are gone. Unfortunately, for himself, Inspector Cramer chooses this disagreeable hour—it is eleven thirty at night—to call, and Wolfe, with unprecedented vigor, uses his physical bulk to block his entrance, in what surely is one of the great moments of the saga.

Archie's witty sallies and disclosures, as usual, are sprinkled through the story and add to its zest. It is intriguing to learn that he once spent nine rainy hours in a doorway on a stakeout. At one point he tells us, too,

"I no longer had any illusions about dimples. The most attractive and best-placed ones I had ever seen were on the cheeks of a woman who had fed arsenic to three husbands in a row." The invasion of the brownstone by the T-men sparks some of his most audacious quips. He asks one of them, " 'Did you find the snow in the secret drawer?' " And he also asks the man to turn his mattress because it's due for a turning. He explains further that FBI stands for "Foiled By Intelligence." We cannot pass from the subject of Archie without noting one curious detail attaching to the original manuscript. Archie's crucial maneuver of leaving his hat and coat in Hattie's parlor was, for Rex, an afterthought. He actually taped that detail over the passage it replaced. For Rex such backtracking in his manuscripts was unprecedented.

William S. Baring-Gould surmised that the events recounted in "Counterfeit for Murder" occurred on a Monday and Tuesday in the winter of 1960–1961. He was wrong. Rex's notes show that they occurred in 1959, on Monday, January 26, and Tuesday, January 27. These dates, used in the original, were retained in the rewrite.

The year in which Rex wrote his two versions of "Counterfeit for Murder" was, for him, an annus mirabilis. He wrote three stories in 1958 and three again in 1960. In 1959 he worked on five. "Eeny Meeny Murder Mo," was finished in January. Between January and March he produced his two versions of "Counterfeit for Murder." *Plot It Yourself* was begun in May and finished in July. "The Rodeo Murder" was begun in September and finished in October. A suggestion that he wrote "Counterfeit for Murder" twice because he was unsure of himself can have no validity. Rex was far from being written out. Indeed, he would write another seventeen Nero Wolfe stories, eleven of them novels, before he racked up his quill at eighty-nine. That he could do a second version of "Counterfeit for Murder" and come within ten lines of making it exactly the same length as its predecessor bespeaks a virtuosity that confirms that his mastery over his material was unimpaired.

While Rex was writing "Counterfeit for Murder," his grandsons, Chris and Reed Maroc, aged three and five, were living at High Meadow. When their mother, Rex's daughter Barbara, told them not to bother their grandfather because he was "busy with a counterfeiting plot," they took this literally and invaded Rex's study to confront him with drawn, toy pistols. "They had a point," Rex conceded. "It could be argued that all fiction writing is counterfeiting." When "The Counterfeiter's Knife" was published in *The Saturday Evening Post*, the boys, clad in, respectively, Superman outfit and western gear, restaged their stickup for a photograph to accompany the story. This, Rex explained, did not make them liable to charges of false arrest. "A reconstruction," he said, "is no good as evidence." As encountered in this volume, Rex's own reconstructions, however, are excellent evidence of the fecundity of his genius.

John J. McAleer
Mount Independence
March 25, 1985

BITTER END

In the old brownstone house which was the dwelling, and also contained the office, of Nero Wolfe on West 35th Street near the Hudson River, in New York, heavy gloom had penetrated into every corner of every room, so that there was no escaping from it.

Fritz Brenner was in bed with the grippe.

If it had been Theodore Horstmann, who nursed the 3,000 orchids on the top floor, it would have been merely an inconvenience. If it had been me, Archie Goodwin, secretary, bodyguard, goad, and goat, Wolfe would have been no worse than peevish. But Fritz was the cook; and such a cook that Marko Vukcic of Rusterman's famous restaurant, had once offered a fantastic sum for his release to the major leagues, and met with scornful refusal from Wolfe and Fritz both. On that Tuesday in November the kitchen had not seen him for three days, and the resulting situation was not funny. I'll skip the awful details—for instance, the desperate and disastrous struggle that took place Sunday afternoon between Wolfe and a couple of ducklings— and go on with the climax.

It was lunchtime Tuesday. Wolfe and I were at the dining table. I was doing all right with a can of beans I had got at the delicatessen. Wolfe, his broad face dour and dismal, took a spoonful of stuff from a little glass jar that had just been opened, dabbed it onto the end of a roll, bit it off, and chewed. All of a sudden, with nothing to warn me, there was an explosion like the bursting of a ten-inch shell. Instinctively I dropped my sandwich and put up my hands to protect my face, but too late. Little gobs of the stuff, and particles of masticated roll, peppered me like shrapnel.

I glared at him. "Well," I said witheringly. I removed something from my eyelid with the corner of my napkin. "If you think for one moment you can get away—"

I left it hanging. With as black a fury on his face as any I had ever seen there, he was on his feet and heading for the kitchen. I stayed in my chair. After I had done what I could with the napkin, hearing meanwhile the garglings and splashings of Wolfe at the kitchen sink, I reached for the jar, took a look at the contents, and sniffed it. I inspected the label. It was small and to the point:

TINGLEY'S TIDBITS—Since 1881—The Best
Liver Pâté No. 3

I was sniffing at it again when Wolfe marched in with a tray containing three bottles of beer, a chunk of cheese, and a roll of salami. He sat down without a word and started slicing salami.

"The last man who spat at me," I said casually, "got three bullets in his heart before he hit the floor."

"Pfui," Wolfe said coldly.

"And at least," I continued, "he really meant it. Whereas you were merely being childish and trying to show what a supersensitive gourmet you are—"

"Shut up. Did you taste it?"

"No."

"Do so. It's full of poison."

I regarded him suspiciously. It was ten to one he was stringing me, but, after all, there were a good many people who would have regarded the death of Nero Wolfe as a ray of sunshine in a dark world, and a few of them had made efforts to bring it about. I picked up the jar and a spoon, procured a morsel about the size of a pea, and put it in my mouth. A moment later I discreetly but hastily ejected it into my napkin, went to the kitchen and did some rinsing, returned to the dining-room and took a good large bite from a dill pickle. After the pickle's pungency had to some extent quieted the turmoil in my taste buds, I reached for the jar and smelled it again.

"That's funny," I said

Wolfe made a growling noise.

"I mean," I continued hastily, "that I don't understand it. How could it be some fiend trying to poison you? I bought it at Bruegel's and brought it home myself, and I opened it, and I'd swear the lid hadn't been tampered with. But I don't blame you for spitting, even though I happened to be in the line of fire. If that's Tingley's idea of a rare, exotic flavor to tempt the jaded appetite—"

"That will do, Archie." Wolfe put down his empty glass. I had never heard his tone more menacing. "I am not impressed by your failure to understand this abominable outrage. I might bring myself to tolerate it if some frightened or vindictive person shot me to

3

death, but this is insupportable." He made the growling noise again. "My food. You know my attitude toward food." He aimed a rigid finger at the jar, and his voice trembled with ferocity. "Whoever put that in there is going to regret it."

He said no more, and I concentrated on the beans and pickles and milk. When he had finished the cheese he got up and left the room, taking the third bottle of beer along, and when I was through I cleared the table and went to the kitchen and washed up. Then I proceeded to the office. He had his mass deposited in the oversized chair behind his desk, and was leaning back with his eyes closed and a twist to his lips which showed that the beer descending his gullet had washed no wrath down with it. Without opening his eyes he muttered at me, "Where's that jar?"

"Right here." I put it on his desk.

"Get Mr. Whipple, at the laboratory."

I sat at my desk, and looked up the number and dialed it. When I told Wolfe I had Whipple he got himself upright and reached for his phone and spoke to it:

"Mr. Whipple? . . . This is Nero Wolfe. Good afternoon, sir. Can you do an analysis for me right away? . . . I don't know. It's a glass jar containing a substance which I foolishly presumed to be edible. . . . I have no idea. Mr. Goodwin will take it down to you immediately."

I was glad to have an errand that would take me away from that den of dejection for an hour or so, but something more immediate intervened. The doorbell rang and, since Fritz was out of commission, I went to answer it. Swinging the front door open, I found myself confronted by something pleasant. While she didn't reach the spectacular and I'm not saying that I caught my breath, one comprehensive glance at her gave me the feeling that it was foolish to regard the world as an abode of affliction merely because Fritz had the grippe. Her cheeks had soft in-curves and her eyes were a kind of chartreuse, something the color of my bathroom walls upstairs. They looked worried.

"Hello," I said enthusiastically.

"Mr. Nero Wolfe?" she asked in a nice voice from west of Pittsburgh. "My name is Amy Duncan."

I knew it was hopeless. With Wolfe in a state of mingled rage and despondency, and with the bank balance in a flourishing condition, if I had gone and told him that a good-looking girl named Duncan wanted to see him, no matter what about, he would only have been churlish. Whereas there was a chance . . . I invited her in, escorted her down the hall and into the office, and pulled up a chair for her.

"Miss Duncan, Mr. Wolfe," I said, and sat down. "She wants to ask you something."

Wolfe, not even glancing at her, glared at me. "Confound you!" he muttered. "I'm engaged. I'm busy." He transferred it to the visitor: "Miss Duncan, you are the victim of my assistant's crack-brained impudence. So am I. I see people only by appointment."

She smiled at him. "I'm sorry, but now that I'm here it won't take long—"

"No." His eyes came back to me. "Archie, when you have shown Miss Duncan out, come back here."

He was obviously completely out of control. As for that, I was somewhat edgy myself, after the three days I had just gone through and it looked to me as if a little cooling off might be advisable before any further interchange of sentiments. So I arose and told him firmly, "I'll run along down to the laboratory. Maybe I can give Miss Duncan a lift." I picked up the jar. "Do you want me to wait—?"

*   *   *

"Where did you get that?" Amy Duncan said.

I looked at her in astonishment. "Get it? This jar?"

"Yes. Where did you get it?"

"Bought it. Sixty-five cents."

"And you're taking it to a laboratory? Why? Does it taste funny? Oh, I'll bet it does! Bitter?"

I gawked at her in amazement. Wolfe, upright, his eyes narrowed at her, snapped, "Why do you ask that?"

"Because," she said, "I recognized the label. And taking it to a laboratory—that's what I came to see you about! Isn't that odd? A jar of it right here—"

On any other man Wolfe's expression would have indicated a state of speechlessness, but I have never yet seen him flabbergasted to a point where he was unable to articulate. "Do you mean to say," he demanded, "that you were actually aware of this infamous plot? That you knew of this unspeakable insult to my palate and my digestion?"

"Oh, no! But I know it has quinine in it."

"Quinine!" he roared.

She nodded. "I suppose so." She stretched a hand toward me. "May I look at it?" I handed her the jar. She removed the lid, took a tiny dab of the contents on the tip of her little finger, licked it off with her tongue, and waited for the effect. It didn't take long. "Br-r-uh!" she said, and swallowed twice. "It sure is bitter. That's it, all right." She put the jar on the desk. "How very odd—"

"Not odd," Wolfe said grimly. "*Odd* is not the word. You say it has quinine in it. You knew that as soon as you saw it. Who put it in?"

"I don't know. That's what I came to see you for, to ask you to find out. You see, it's my uncle— May I tell you about it?"

"You may."

She started to wriggle out of her coat, and I helped her with it and got it out of her way so she could settle back in her chair. She thanked me with a friendly little smile containing no trace of quinine, and I returned to my desk and got out a notebook and flipped to a blank page.

"Arthur Tingley," she said, "is my uncle. My mother's brother. He owns Tingley's Tidbits. And he's such a pigheaded—" She flushed. "Well, he is pigheaded. He actually suspects me of having something to do with that quinine, just because—for no reason at all!"

"Are you saying," Wolfe demanded incredulously, "that the scoundrel, knowing that his confounded tidbits contain quinine, continues to distribute them?"

"No," she shook her head, "he's not a scoundrel. That's not it. It was only a few weeks ago that they learned about the quinine. Complaints began to come in, and thousands of jars were returned from all over the country. He had them analyzed, and lots of them contained quinine. Of course, it was only a small proportion of the whole output—it's a pretty big business. He tried to investigate it, and Miss Yates—she's in charge of production—took all possible precautions, but it's happened again in recent shipments."

"Where's the factory?"

"Not far from here. On West Twenty-sixth Street near the river."

"Do you work there?"

"No, I did once, when I first came to New York, but I—I quit."

"Do you know what the investigation has disclosed?"

"Nothing. Not really. My uncle suspects—I guess he suspects everybody, even his son Philip, his adopted son. And me! It's simply ridiculous! But chiefly he

7

suspects a man—a vice-president of P. & B., the Provisions & Beverages Corporation. Tingley's Tidbits is an old-established business—my great-grandfather founded it seventy years ago—and P. & B. has been trying to buy it, but my uncle wouldn't sell. He thinks they bribed someone in the factory to put in the quinine to scare him into letting go. He thinks that Mr.—the vice-president I spoke of—did it."

"Mr.—?"

"Mr. Cliff. Leonard Cliff."

I glanced up from my notebook on account of a slight change in the key of her voice.

Wolfe inquired, "Do you know Mr. Cliff?"

"Oh, yes." She shifted in her chair. "That is, I—I'm his secretary."

"Indeed." Wolfe's eyes went shut and then opened again halfway. "When you left your uncle's employ you came to terms with the enemy?"

She flared up. "Of course not!" she said indignantly. "You sound like my uncle! I had to have a job, didn't I? I was born and brought up in Nebraska. Three years ago my mother died, and I came to New York and started to work in my uncle's office. I stuck it out for two years, but it got—unpleasant, and either I quit or he fired me, it would be hard to say which. I got a job as a stenographer with P. & B., and six weeks ago I was promoted and I'm now Mr. Cliff's secretary. If you want to know why it got so unpleasant in my uncle's office—"

"I don't. Unless it has a bearing on this quinine business."

"It hasn't. None whatever."

"But you are sufficiently concerned about the quinine to come to me about it. Why?"

"Because my uncle is such a—" She stopped, biting her lip. "You don't know him. He writes to my

8

father, things about me that aren't so, and my father writes and threatens to come to New York—it's such a mess! I certainly didn't put quinine in his darned Tidbits! I suppose I'm prejudiced, but I don't believe any investigating he does will ever get anywhere, and the only way to stop it is for someone to investigate who knows how." She flashed a smile at him. "Which brings me to the embarrassing part of it. I haven't got much money—"

"You have something better," Wolfe grunted.

"Better?"

"Yes. Luck. The thing you want to know is the thing I had determined to find out before I knew you existed. I had already told Mr. Goodwin that the black-guard who poisoned that pâté is going to regret it." He grimaced. "I can still taste it. Can you go now with Mr. Goodwin to your uncle's factory and introduce him?"

"I—" She glanced at her watch and hesitated. "I'll be awfully late getting back to the office. I only asked for an hour—"

"Very well. Archie, show Miss Duncan out and return for instructions." . . .

It was barely three o'clock when I reached the base of operations, and the jar in my pocket was only half full, for I had first gone downtown to the laboratory and left a sample for analysis.

The three-story brick building on West 26th Street was old and grimy-looking, with a cobbled driveway for trucks tunneled through its middle. Next to the driveway were three stone steps leading up to a door with an inscription in cracked and faded paint:

TINGLEY'S TIDBITS OFFICE

As I parked the roadster and got out, I cocked an admiring eye at a Crosby town car, battleship gray, with license GJ88, standing at the curb. "Comes the revolution," I thought, "I'll take that first." I had my foot on the first stone step leading up to the office when the door opened and a man emerged. I had the way blocked. At a glance, it was hard to imagine anyone calling him Uncle Arthur, with his hard, clamped jaw and his thin, hard mouth, but, not wanting to miss my quarry, I held the path and addressed him: "Mr. Arthur Tingley?"

"No," he said in a totalitarian tone, shooting a haughty glance at me as he brushed by, with cold, keen eyes of the same battleship gray as his car. I remembered, just in time, that I had in my pocket a piece of yellow chalk which I had been marking orchid pots with that morning. Circling around him, I beat him to the car door which the liveried chauffeur was holding open and with two swift swipes chalked a big X on the elegant enamel.

"Don't monkey with that," I said sternly, and, before either of them could produce words or actions, beat it up the stone steps and entered the building.

It sure was a ramshackle joint. From a dingy hall a dilapidated stair went up. I mounted to the floor above, heard noises, including machinery humming, off somewhere, and through a rickety door penetrated a partition and was in an anteroom. From behind a grilled window somebody's grandpa peered out at me, and by shouting I managed to convey to him that I wanted to see Mr. Arthur Tingley. After a wait I was told that Mr. Tingley was busy, and would be indefinitely. On a leaf of my notebook I wrote, "Quinine urgent," and sent it in. That did it. After another wait a cross-eyed young man came and guided me through a labyrinth of partitions and down a hall into a room.

Seated at an old, battered roll-top desk was a man talking into a phone, and in a chair facing him was a woman older than him with the physique and facial equipment of a top sergeant. Since the phone conversation was none of my business, I stood and listened to it, and gathered that someone named Philip had better put in an appearance by five o'clock or else. Meanwhile I surveyed the room, which had apparently been thrown in by the Indians when they sold the island. By the door, partly concealed by a screen, was an old, veteran marble-topped washstand. A massive, old-fashioned safe was against the wall across from Tingley's desk. Wooden cupboards, and shelves loaded down with the accumulation of centuries, occupied most of the remaining wall space.

"Who the hell are you?"

I whirled and advanced. "A man by the name of Goodwin. Archie. The question is, do you want the *Gazette* to run a feature article about quinine in Tidbits, or do you want to discuss it first?"

His mouth fell open. "The *Gazette*?"

"Right. Circulation over a million."

"Good God!" he said in a hollow and helpless tone. The woman glared at me.

I was stirred by compassion. He may have merited his niece's opinion of him, expressed and implied, but he was certainly a pathetic object at that moment.

I sat down. "Be of good cheer," I said encouragingly. "The *Gazette* hasn't got it yet. That's merely one of the possibilities I offer in case you start shoving. I represent Nero Wolfe."

"Nero Wolfe, the detective?"

"Yes. He started to eat—"

*   *   *

11

The woman snorted. "I've been expecting this. Didn't I warn you, Arthur? Blackmail." She squared her jaw at me. "Who are you working for? P. & B.? Consolidated Cereals?"

"Neither one. Are you Miss Yates?"

"I am. And you can take—"

"Pardon me." I grinned at her. "Pleased to meet you. I'm working for Nero Wolfe. He took a mouthful of Liver Pâté Number Three, with painful consequences. He's very fussy about his food. He wants to speak to the person who put in the quinine."

"So do I," Tingley said grimly.

"You don't know. Do you?"

"No."

"But you'd like to know?"

"You're damn' right I would."

"Okay. I come bearing gifts. If you hired Wolfe for this job, granting he'd take it, it would cost you a fortune. But he's vindictive. He wishes to do things to this quinine jobber. I was sent here to look around and ask questions."

Tingley wearily shook his head. He looked at Miss Yates. She looked at him. "Do you believe him?" Tingley asked her.

"No," she declared curtly. "Is it likely—?"

"Of course not," I cut her off. "Nothing about Nero Wolfe is likely, which is why I tolerate him. It's not likely, but that's how it is. You folks are comical. You're having the services of the best detective in the country offered to you gratis, and listen to you. I'm telling you, Wolfe's going to get this quinine peddler. With your co-operation, fine. Without it, we'll have to start by opening things up with a little publicity, which is why I mentioned the *Gazette*."

Tingley groaned. Miss Yates's shrewd eyes met mine. "What questions do you want to ask?"

"All I can think of. Preferably starting with you two."

"I'm busy. I ought to be out in the factory right now. Did you say you had an appointment, Arthur?"

"Yes." Tingley shoved back his chair and got up. "I have—I have to go somewhere." He got his hat from a hook on the wall beside his desk, and his coat from another one. "I'll be back by four-thirty." He struggled into his coat and confronted me. His hat was on crooked. "If Miss Yates wants to talk to you, she can tell you as much as I could. I'm about half out of my senses. If this is an infernal trick of that P. & B. outfit—" He darted to his desk, turned a key in a bottom drawer, pocketed the key, and made for the door. On the threshold he turned: "You handle it, Gwen."

So her name was Gwendolyn, or maybe Guinevere. It certainly must have been given to her when she was quite young—say sixty years ago. She was imperturbably and efficiently collecting an asortment of papers Tingley had left scattered on his desk and anchoring them under a cylindrical chunk of metal with a figure 2 on it, a weight from an old-fashioned balance scale. She straightened and met my gaze:

"I've been after him to get a detective, and he wouldn't do it. This thing has got to be stopped. It's awful. I've been here all my life—been in charge of the factory for twenty years—and now—" She squared her jaw. "Come along."

I followed her. We left by another door than the one I had entered by, traversed a hall, passed through a door at the end, and there we were, in the Tidbits maternity ward. Two hundred women and girls, maybe more, in white smocks, were working at tables and benches and various kinds of vats and machines. Miss Yates led me down an aisle and she stopped beside a

13

large vat. A woman about my age who had been peering into the vat turned to face us.

"This is Miss Murphy, my assistant," Miss Yates said brusquely. "Carrie, this is Mr. Goodwin, a detective. Answer any questions he wants to ask, except about our formulas, and show him anything he wants to see." She turned to me. "I'll talk with you later, after I get some mixes through."

I caught a flicker of something, hesitation or maybe apprehension, in Miss Murphy's eyes, but it went as fast as it came, and she said quietly, "Very well, Miss Yates." . . .

Wolfe was sticking to his accustomed daily schedule, in a sort of stubborn desperation in spite of the catastrophe of Fritz's grippe. Mornings from 9 to 11 and afternoons from 4 to 6 he spent up in the plant rooms. When he came down at six that afternoon I was in the office waiting for him.

He stopped in the middle of the room, glanced around, frowned at me, and said, "Dr. Vollmer states that Fritz can get up in the morning. Not today. Not for dinner. Where is Mr. Tingley?"

"I don't know."

"I told you to bring him here."

He was using his most provocative tone. I could have put quinine in his food. I said, "It's a good thing Fritz will be up tomorrow. This couldn't go on much longer. Tingley is on the verge of a nervous breakdown. He went out soon after I got there. Miss Yates, whose name is Gwendolyn, the factory superintendent, and her assistant, Miss Carrie Murphy, showed me around. I have just finished typing a detailed report, but there's nothing in it but facts. Tingley returned about four-thirty, but when I tried to see him he was having a talk with his son and I was thrown out on my ear. I'm going back in the morning if I'm still working for you. Those in favor of my resigning, raise their hand." I stuck my hand up high.

"Pfui!" Wolfe said. "A man sells poisoned food—"

"Quinine is not poison."

"A man sells poisoned food and you leave him sitting comfortably in conversation with his son. Now I'm going to the kitchen and try to prepare something to eat. If you care to join—"

"No, thanks. I've got a date. Don't wait up for me."

I went to the hall and got my hat and coat and beat it. From the garage on Tenth Avenue I took the sedan instead of the roadster, drove to Pietro's on 39th Street, and operated on a dish of spaghetti and half a bushel of salad. That made me feel better. When I reached the sidewalk again it was raining, with cold November gusts whipping it around, so I skedaddled around the corner into a newsreel theater. But I was not at peace. There had been enough justification for Wolfe's crack—say one percent—to make it rankle.

My watch said a quarter to eight. I went to the lobby and got out my memo book and turned to the page where, following habit, I had entered the names and addresses of persons connected with the current proceeding. Tingley lived at 691 Sullivan Street. There was no point in phoning, since the idea was to get him and deliver him. I went to the sedan and headed downtown in the rain.

It was an old brick house, painted blue, probably the residence of his father and grandfather before him. A colored maid told me that he wasn't home, hadn't shown up for dinner, and might be at his office. It began to look like no soap, but it was only a little out of the way, so when I got to 26th Street I turned west. Rolling to the curb directly in front of the Tingley

Building, it looked promising; lights showed at a couple of the upstairs windows. I dived through the rain across the sidewalk, found the door unlocked, and entered.

A light was on there in the hall, and I started for the stairs. But with my foot on the first step I stopped; for I had glanced up, and saw something so unexpected that I goggled like a fish. Standing there halfway up, facing me, was Amy Duncan, Her face was white, her eyes were glassy, and she was clinging to the rail with both hands and swaying from side to side.

"Hold it!" I said sharply, and started up. Before I could reach her she lost it. Down she came, rolling right into me. I gathered her up and went back down and stretched her out on the floor. She was out cold, but when I felt her pulse it was pretty good. Routine faint, I thought, and then took it back when I saw a large lump on the side of her head above her right ear.

That made it different. I straightened up. She had unquestionably been conked.

I ascended the steps one at a time, looking for the birdie. There was a light in the upper hall also in the anteroom. I called out, and got no reply. The door leading within was standing open, and I marched through and kept going through more open doors and down the inside hall to the entrance to Tingley's office. That door too stood open and the room was lit, but from the threshold no one was in sight. It occurred to me that the screen, at right angles to the wall, would do nicely for an ambush, so I entered sideways, facing it, and circled around the end of it for a survey just in case.

A mouse ran up my backbone. Tingley was there on the floor alongside the screen, his head toward the marble washstand, and if the head was still connected with the body it must have been at the back, which I couldn't see. There was certainly no connection left in front.

16

I took a couple of breaths and swallowed saliva, as a sort of priming for my internal processes, which had momentarily stopped.

The blood from the gash in his throat had spread over the floor, running in red tongues along the depressions in the old warped boards, and I stepped wide of it to get around to the other end of him. Squatting beside him for an inspection, I ascertained two facts: He had a lump at the back of his skull and the skin had been broken there, and he was good and dead. I straightened up and collected a few more items with my eyes:

1. A bloody towel on the floor by the washstand, sixteen inches from the wall.

2. Another bloody towel on the rim of the basin, to the right.

3. A knife with a long, thin blade and a black composition handle on the floor between the body and the screen. In the factory that afternoon I had seen girls slicing meat loaves with knives like it.

4. On the floor between the two front legs of the washstand, a cylinder of metal with a "2" on it. It was Tingley's paperweight.

5. Farther away, out beyond the edge of the screen, a woman's snakeskin handbag. I had seen that before, too, when Amy Duncan called at Wolfe's office.

Circling around the mess again, I picked up the handbag and stuffed it in my pocket, and took a look at the rest of the room. I didn't touch anything, but someone else had. A drawer of the rolltop desk had been jerked out onto the floor. The door of the enormous old safe was standing wide open. Things on the shelves had been pulled off and scattered. Tingley's felt hat was on the wall hook at the left of his desk, but his overcoat was in a heap on the floor.

I looked at my watch. It was 8:22. I would have liked to do a little more inspecting, but if Amy Duncan should come to and beat it . . .

She hadn't. When I got back downstairs she was still there stretched out. I felt her pulse again, buttoned up her coat, made sure her hat was fastened on, and picked her up. I opened the door and got through without bumping her, navigated the steps, and crossed the sidewalk to the car, and stood there with her in my arms a moment, thinking the rain on her face might revive her. The next thing I knew I damn' near needed reviving myself. Something socked me on the side of the jaw from behind.

I went down, not from compulsion but from choice, to get rid of my burden. When I bobbed up again I left Amy on the sidewalk and leaped aside as a figure hurled itself at me. When I side-stepped he lost balance, but recovered and tore at me again. I feinted with my left and he grabbed for it, and my right took him on the button.

He went down and didn't bounce. I dashed back to the stone steps and closed the door, returned, and opened the rear door of the car and lifted Amy in, and wheeled as he regained his feet, started for me, and yelled for help and police, all at once. He obviously knew as much about physical combat as I did about pearl diving, so I turned him around and from behind locked his arms with my left one and choked his throat with my right, and barked into his ear, "One more squawk and out go the lights! You have one chance to live. Behave yourself and do what I tell you to." I made

18

sure he had no gun before I loosened the hook on his neck. He didn't vocalize, so I released him. "Open that car door—"

I meant the front door, but before I could stop him he had the rear one open and most of himself inside and was bleating like a goat, "Amy! Good God, she's—Amy—"

I reached in for a shoulder and yanked him out and banged the door and opened the front one. "She's alive," I said, "but you won't be in five seconds. Get in there and fold yourself under the dash. I'm taking her to a doctor and you're going along."

He got in. I pushed him down and forward, disregarding his sputtering, wriggled back of him to the driver's seat, pulled the door to, and started the car. In two minutes we were at 35th Street, and in another two we rolled to the curb in front of Wolfe's house. I let him come up for air.

"The program," I said, "is as follows: I'll carry her, and you precede me up those steps to that door. If you cut and run I'll drop her—"

He glared at me. His spirit was 'way ahead of his flesh. "I'm not going to cut and run—"

"Okay. Me out first."

He helped me get her out and he wanted to carry her, but I shooed him on ahead through the rain and told him to push the button. When the door opened Wolfe, himself, stood there. At sight of the stranger his colossal frame blocked the way, but when he saw me he fell back and made room for us to enter.

The stranger began, "Are you a doc—?"

"Shut up!" I told him. I faced Wolfe, and observed that he was sustaining his reputation for being impervious to startlement. "I suppose you recognize Miss Duncan. She's been hit on the head. If you will please

phone Doc Vollmer? I'll take her up to the south room."
I made for the elevator, and when the stranger tagged
along I let him. In the south room, two flights up, we
got her onto the bed and covered up.

The stranger was still standing by the bed staring
down at her when Doc Vollmer arrived. After feeling
her pulse and glancing under her eyelid, Doc said he
thought it would be a long time till the funeral and we
wouldn't be needed for a while, so I told the stranger to
come on. He left the room with me and kindly permitted me to close the door, but then announced that he
was going to stay right there outside the door until the
doctor had brought her to.

"You," I said, "might as well learn to face facts.
You know damn' well I could throw you downstairs. If I
do you'll have to go to bed, too. March!"

He marched, but he sure hated it. I followed him
down, and into the office. Wolfe was there at his desk,
looking imperturbable, but when he saw us he started
rubbing his chin, which meant he was boiling inside.

"Sit down," I told the stranger. "This is Mr. Nero
Wolfe. What's your name?"

"None of your damned business!" he informed me.
"This is the most outrageous—!"

"You bet it is. When you rushed me from behind,
you must have come from inside the building. Didn't
you?"

"That's none of your business, either!"

"You're wrong, brother. But I'll try again. Why did
you kill Arthur Tingley?"

He gawked at me. "Are you crazy?"

"Not a bit. Stop me if you've heard it before. I
went there to get Tingley and bring him here to see
Mr. Wolfe. Amy Duncan was there on the stairs looking doubtful. She fell and I caught her, and left her on
the hall floor while I went up to investigate. Tingley

was on the floor of his office with his throat cut. After a brief inspection I returned to Amy and carried her out, and was putting her in the car when you attacked me from behind. You must have come from somewhere. Why not from inside the building? The idea appeals to me."

The stranger had decided he could use a chair, and sank into one. "You say—" He swallowed. "Are you telling the truth?"

"Yes, sir."

"Tingley—with his throat cut? Dead?"

"Very dead." I turned to Wolfe: "He pretended to be going on the theory that I was kidnapping Amy. He's all for Amy. I brought him along because I thought you might need him."

Wolfe was glaring at me. "And why should I need him?"

"Well, he was there. He must have come out of that building. He probably murdered Tingley—"

"And what if he did?"

"Oh. So that's how you feel about it."

"It is. I am under no obligation to catch murderers indiscriminately. Phone the police. Tell them Miss Duncan and this gentleman are here and they can—"

"No!" the stranger blurted.

"No?" Wolfe lifted a brow at him. "Why not?"

"Because it's—Good God! And Amy— You can't—"

"Hold it," I commanded him. "I'm doing this." I grinned at Wolfe. "Okay, boss; I'll call the cops. I merely thought you might like to chat with this bird first, since it seemed likely that whoever killed Tingley also put quinine in your food."

"Ah," Wolfe murmured. "That abominable—" He wiggled a finger at the victim. "Did you poison that liver pâté?"

"I did not."

"Who are you? What's your name?"

"Cliff. Leonard Cliff."

"Indeed. You're a vice-president of the Provisions & Beverage Corporation. Mr. Tingley, himself, suspected you of adulterating his product."

"I know he did. He was wrong. So is this man wrong when he says I must have come out of that building. I wasn't inside the building at all."

"Where were you?"

"I was in the driveway. There's a driveway tunnel near the door. I was in there."

"What were you doing there?"

"Keeping out of the rain. Look here," Cliff said appealingly. "I can't think straight. This is terrible! If Tingley has been murdered the police have to be notified, I know that, but for God's sake don't get them here now! With Miss Duncan—Let me get her to a hospital! And get a lawyer—"

Wolfe cut him off: "What were you doing in the driveway?"

He shook his head. "It had no connection—"

"Pfui! Don't be a fool. If you adulterated Mr. Tingley's product, or cut his throat, either or both, I advise you to get out of here at once. If you didn't, I advise you to answer my questions promptly and fully. Not to mention truthfully. Well, sir? . . . Archie, call police headquarters. I'll talk."

I dialed the number, and when I had it, Wolfe took it at his instrument. "Hello. . . . This is Nero Wolfe, Write this down: Arthur Tingley. His office at his place—"

"Wait!" Cliff blurted. "I'll answer your questions—" He started from his chair, but I got in between him and the desk and he subsided.

Wolfe continued: "—his place of business at Twenty-sixth Street and Tenth Avenue. He's there dead. Murdered. . . . Let me finish, please. My assistant, Archie Goodwin, was there and saw him. Mr. Goodwin had to leave, but he will be here at my home later. . . . No. I have no idea."

He pushed the phone away, and regarded Cliff with his eyes half closed. "You had better make it as succinct as possible. What were you doing in the driveway?"

Cliff was on the edge of his chair, straight, rigid, meeting his gaze. "I was waiting for Miss Duncan to come out. I had followed her there."

"Followed? Without her knowledge?"

"Yes."

"Why?"

Cliff's jaw worked. "I had a dinner engagement with her, and she phoned me at six o'clock and broke it. The reason she gave sounded phony, and I was—damn it, I was jealous! I went to where she lives, on Grove Street, and waited across the street. When she came out it had started to rain, and she took a taxi, and I managed to grab one and follow her. She went straight to Tingley's and dismissed her cab and went in. I did the same, but I went in the tunnel entrance and waited there. I couldn't imagine what she was doing there."

"What time did she arrive?"

"A few minutes after seven. It was one minute to seven when she left her place on Grove Street. When I saw a man drive up and go in, and a little later come out carrying her and start to put her in his car, naturally I went for him."

"Naturally," Wolfe said. "Were you in the tunnel while Miss Duncan was inside?"

"Yes. And I saw three men come and go in and leave again. Goodwin was the last one. There were two others before that."

*   *   *

Wolfe shook his head. "I doubt if that's a good idea. If you invent a constant stream of visitors, and it develops—"

"I'm not inventing, damn it! I saw them!"

"Tell me about them."

"The first one was at seven-thirty. A big, gray town car stopped at the curb, and the driver got out and held an umbrella over another man as he crossed the sidewalk to the entrance. In five minutes the man came out again and ran to the car and got in, and the car drove off. The license was GJ88."

I grunted. They looked at me. "Nothing," I said, "go ahead."

"I nearly missed seeing the second one go in, because he was walking. He had on a raincoat. It was seven-forty when he entered, and he was inside seven or eight minutes. When he came out I got a pretty good view of his face by a street light. He walked off to the east."

"Did you recognize either of the men?"

"No. But that license number—"

"Do you know it?"

"No, but I can guess, on account of the GJ. I think it belongs to Guthrie Judd. It can be checked."

"Guthrie Judd, the banker?"

"He calls himself a banker, yes. He's more of a promoter. He's been boosting an outfit he calls Consolidated Cereals. Recently he's been after the Tingley business. He's shrewd and unscrupulous—and tough."

"Was it Judd who entered the building at seven-thirty?"

"I couldn't tell. The driver was holding an umbrella over him."

Wolfe grunted. "That's prudent. Should you claim to have recognized Judd, and he is able to prove—"

"I'm telling the truth!" Cliff got spirited again. "I'm telling you exactly what happened! Do you think I'm a damned idiot?" He stood up. "I'm going upstairs."

A voice behind him asked, "May I come in?"

It was Doc Vollmer. At Wolfe's nod he entered, his bag in his hand, and spoke professionally: "She'll do all right. She got a bad knock on the head, but there's no fracture. It seems to be nervous shock more than anything. After a night's rest—"

"Is she conscious?" Cliff demanded.

"Oh, yes." Cliff was darting off, but the doctor grabbed his arm. "Now, wait a minute—just take it easy—"

"Can she be moved?" Wolfe inquired.

"I wouldn't advise it. Not tonight."

"I want to ask her some questions."

"Now? Is it urgent?"

"Fairly urgent. The police will be here pretty soon."

"I see. All right, I'd better go up with you. You'll have to go easy with her."

We moved. Wolfe headed for the elevator and the rest of us walked up the two flights. We got there first. Amy, lying on her side, opened her eyes at us, with no indication of interest for Doc or me, but when they lit on Cliff they opened wide and she made a noise.

"Amy!" Cliff squawked. "Thank God! Amy—"

Vollmer held him back.

"You—" she said weakly. "Where—you—I don't—"

"Take her hand," Vollmer said judiciously. "Hold her hand. Don't talk."

Wolfe came in, and Amy moved her head enough to get him in view. "Hello, there," she squeaked.

"Good evening, Miss Duncan," he said politely. "Does it hurt much?"

"Not—well—it aches."

"I suppose so. Can you understand words?"

"Yes—but I don't understand—"

"Please listen. You said nothing this afternoon of any intention to go to your uncle's place this evening. But at seven o'clock you went. Why?"

"He phoned—and asked me to come. Soon after I got home from work."

"What for? Did he say?"

"He said it was something about Phil. My cousin." She went to move her head, and a little moan came out of her. "He wouldn't say what it was on the phone."

"But when you got there? What did he say then?"

"He didn't—oh—"

"Take it easy now," Doc Vollmer warned.

"I'm all right," Amy declared. "I'm not going to faint again. But when I shut my eyes I see it. The door of his office was open and the light was on, but he wasn't there. I mean—I didn't see him. I went right on in."

"Go ahead."

"That's all I remember. The next thing I remember was my head. I thought something was on it holding it down. I tried to lift myself up and then I saw him. Oh!" Her brow creased. "I thought I saw him—my uncle—there with the blood—"

"That's all right. Don't worry about that. What happened next?"

"Nothing happened. I don't remember anything."

"Didn't you see anyone at all when you went in? Or hear anyone?"

"No. I don't think—I'm sure I didn't—"

"Excuse me," I said. "The doorbell's ringing. If it's city employees do I ask to see a warrant?"

"No." Wolfe scowled at me. "Take them to the office. . . . Wait a minute. Dr. Vollmer, if this young woman is in no condition to leave my house it would be cruel and dangerous for her to undergo a police grilling. Do you agree?"

"I do."

"Good . . .. Miss Duncan, when a policeman comes up here to look at you, keep your eyes closed and moan. Will you do that?"

"Yes. But—"

"No buts. Don't overdo it, and don't speak." He moved. "Come, gentlemen."

When we got downstairs I waited until they were in the office before opening the front door. There I was greeted by a surprise. It was no squad lieutenant, but Inspector Cramer himself, who shoved in rudely over the sill, with a pair of dicks on his heels. All he had for me was a discourteous remark about answering doorbells as he made for the office. Having to shut the door, I brought up the rear.

Cramer appeared to be having an attack of gout. Not bothering to pass the time of day, he barked at me like a howitzer, "What were you doing down at Twenty-sixth Street?"

I looked at the boss. He murmured, "He's upset, Archie. Humor him."

"Humor hell! What time did you get there?"

I looked thoughtful. "Well, let's see . . ."

"Quit clowning! You know damn well you've always got a timetable!"

"Yes, sir," I said abjectly. "Arrived at 8:08. Left at 8:24."

"You admit it!"

"Admit it? I'm proud of it. It was quick work."

"Yeah." If glares could kill, I would have been awful sick. "And Wolfe phoned from here at five after nine! You didn't see the phone right there on Tingley's desk? I've warned you about that. Now, talk! Fast!"

Having received no flag from Wolfe to retain any

items for our personal use, I gave Cramer the crop, as far as my activities and observations were concerned, omitting the crumbs that had been gathered in conversation with Cliff and Amy. My candor didn't seem to make him any more friendly.

When I finished he grunted vulgarly. "So you stood there in that room with a man lying there murdered; and a phone right there and you didn't use it. . . . Where's the woman?"

"Upstairs in bed."

"You can check her out. Doyle, stay here with Mr. Cliff. Foster, come with me—well?"

Doc Vollmer blocked the way. He said firmly, "Miss Duncan should not be disturbed. I speak as her physician."

"You do." Cramer eyed him. "I'll take a look at her. Come, Foster."

Doc Vollmer, leading the way, went with the forces of law and order. Wolfe heaved a sigh, leaned back, and closed his eyes. Pretty soon steps were heard descending the stairs, and Cramer and Vollmer entered. Wolfe opened his eyes.

"She's faking," Cramer declared. "Sure as hell. I'll send a police doctor."

"Dr. Vollmer," Wolfe murmured, "is a competent and reputable physician."

"Yeah, I know. And a friend of yours. I'll send a police doctor. And I'm taking Goodwin and Cliff downtown."

"Where's that man you had with you?"

"Upstairs. On a chair outside Miss Duncan's door. He's going to stay there. And no one but the doctor is going either in or out."

Wolfe's bulk became upright. "This is my house, Mr. Cramer," he said icily, "and you can't use it for the persecution of innocent and battered females. That man can't stay here."

"Try and put him out," Cramer said grimly. "Next time Goodwin stumbles on a man with his head cut off, maybe he'll let us know the same day. . . . Come on, you two." . . .

At ten o'clock the following morning we didn't have a guest any more, but we had a client. Having been kept at headquarters until three A.M., I was peevish from lack of sleep. Fritz was on his feet again, but unstable from his grippe. Wolfe was a seething volcano from a sense of outrage. He had had the minor satisfaction of refusing admission to the police doctor the night before, but at eight in the morning they had come with a warrant for Amy Duncan as a material witness and carted her off, and all he could do was grind his teeth. So when I told him, as he sat propped up in bed sipping chocolate and glowering like a thunderhead, that down at headquarters Leonard Cliff had hired him, through me, to go to work, he didn't even blink an eye. His method of starting the job was customary and characteristic:

"Have Mr. Guthrie Judd here at eleven."

Before leaving the office I typed what seemed to me to be a nifty visiting card:

Mr. Judd: I respectfully submit the following schedule of events last evening at the Tingley Building:

7:05: Amy Duncan arrives; is knocked on head.
7:30: Guthrie Judd arrives.
7:35: Guthrie Judd leaves.
8:08: I arrive, find Tingley dead.
            May I discuss it with you?
                        Archie Goodwin.

I phoned his office in the financial district a little after nine, but was unable to extract any information from anyone even about the weather, which was fine, so I got out the roadster and drove down there.

After a supercilious receptionist condescended to phone someone, and a sap with slick hair made sure I wasn't Jesse James, I got the envelope dispatched. Then I waited, until finally a retired prize fighter appeared and conducted me through doors and down corridors, and ushered me into a room about the size of a tennis court; and he stayed right at my elbow for the trip across a couple of acres of rugs to where a man sat at an enormous flat-topped desk with nothing on it but a newspaper. On the man's face was the same totalitarian expression that had goaded me into chalking an X on the door of his car the day before. The corner of the card I had typed was held between the tips of a finger and thumb to avoid germs.

"This impertinence," he said, in a tone he must have been practicing from boyhood, in case he had ever been a boy. "I wanted to look at you. Take him out, Aiken."

I grinned at him. "I forgot to bring my chalk. But you're already down. You'll discuss it either with me or the police—"

"Bah. The police have already informed me of Mr. Cliff's false and ridiculous statement. Also, they have just told me on the phone who you are. If you annoy me further I'll have you jailed. Take him out, Aiken."

The ex-pug actually put his hand on my arm. It was all I could do to keep from measuring one of the rugs with him. But I merely set my jaw and walked back across the carpet department to the door. He accompanied me all the way to the elevators. As the elevator door opened I said in a kindly tone, "Here, boy," and flipped a nickel at his face. It got him on the tip of the nose, but luckily his reflex was too slow for him to thank me properly before the door closed.

For the second time in twenty-four hours I had failed to fill an order, and as I went back to where I had parked the roadster and started uptown I was in no mood to keep to the right and stop for lights. It was more than likely that Judd would get away with it. If a man in his position maintained that Cliff had either misread the license number of the car or was lying, there wasn't much the cops could or would do about it. They might have a try at the chauffeur, but of course Judd would have attended to that.

It was with the idea in mind of a substitute for Judd that I turned west on 26th Street and drove to the Tingley Building. Not something just as good, but anyhow something. But that was a dud, too. The place was silent and deserted, which I suppose was natural in view of what had happened.

I thought I might as well proceed with my search for a substitute, and, after consulting my memo book, drove to 23rd Street and turned east and stopped in front of an old brownstone. The vestibule was clean, with the brass fronts of the mailboxes polished and shining, including the one which bore the name of Yates, where I pressed the button. I entered on the click, mounted one flight, and had my finger on a button at a door in the rear when the door was opened by Gwendolyn herself.

"Oh," she said. "You."

Her face was moderately haggard, and her lids were so swollen that her eyes didn't seem anything like as keen and shrewd as they had the day before.

I asked if I could come in, and she made room for me and then led the way into a large living-room. Sitting there was Carrie Murphy. She looked as if she had been either crying or fighting; with an Irish girl you can't tell.

"You folks look kind of all in," I said sympathetically.

Miss Yates grunted. "We didn't get much sleep. They kept us up most of the night, and who could sleep, anyway?" She gazed at me curiously. "It was you that found him."

"It was," I agreed.

"What did you go there for?"

"Just to invite him to call on Nero Wolfe to discuss quinine."

"Oh. I was going to phone you. I want to see Amy Duncan. Do you know where she is?"

That made her a pushover. "Well," I said, "she spent the night up at our place under the care of a doctor. I left early this morning, so I can't guarantee that she's still there, but I suppose she is."

"The paper says," Carrie Murphy put in, "that she's going to be detained for questioning. Does that mean that she's suspected of killing her uncle?"

"Certainly."

"Then—"

"We want to see her," Miss Yates interposed.

"Okay, come along. I've got a car."

It still lacked a couple of minutes till eleven when we got there, so Wolfe hadn't come down from the plant rooms, and the office was empty. I got the visitors arranged in chairs and then beat it to the roof. Wolfe was at the sink in the potting room washing his hands.

"The baboon named Judd," I reported, "is going to have me jailed for annoying him. Probably you, too. He's the kind you read about, made of silk reinforced with steel, very tough. He has informed the police that Cliff is a liar. I went to Tingley's and found no one there. I found Miss Yates at her apartment, and Carrie

Murphy there making a call, and they said they wanted to see Amy Duncan, so I told them she was here and brought them along."

I made myself scarce before he could make what he would have regarded as a fitting comment on my failure to get Judd. On my way down I stopped at my room to powder my nose, and heard the elevator start its descent, so I hurried along.

He acted fairly human when I introduced the two callers. After ringing for beer and heaving a sigh of pleasure when Fritz brought it in, he leaned back and slanted his eyes at Gwendolyn.

"Mr. Goodwin tells me you wish to see Miss Duncan. She's not here. The police came with a warrant and took her."

"A warrant?" Carrie Murphy demanded. "Do you mean she's arrested?"

"Yes. As a material witness. They took her from my house. I don't like people being taken from my house with warrants. Her bond is being arranged for. Are you ladies friends of hers?"

"We know her," said Miss Yates. "We're not enemies. We don't want to see her unjustly accused."

"Neither do I. I think it very unlikely that she had anything to do with that quinine. What do you think?"

"The same as you do. Will they let us see her?"

"I doubt it."

"You see," Carrie blurted, "there's something we didn't tell the police! We didn't want them to know about the quinine!"

Wolfe shrugged. "That's absurd. They already know. Not only from Mr. Goodwin, from Mr. Cliff, too. What was it that you didn't tell them?"

"We didn't—" Carrie checked herself and looked at her boss. Miss Yates compressed her lips and said nothing. Carrie transferred back to Wolfe. "We don't know," she said, "whether it's important or not. From what it says in the paper we can't tell. That's what we want to ask Amy. Can we ask you?"

"Try."

"Well—Amy was there, wasn't she?"

"At the Tingley Building last evening? Yes."

"What time did she get there?"

"Five minutes past seven."

"And what happened?"

"As she entered the office someone who was hiding behind the screen hit her on the head with an iron weight and knocked her unconscious. She remained unconscious for an hour. When Mr. Goodwin arrived, at eight minutes past eight, she was trying to descend the stairs, but collapsed again. He brought her here, after investigating upstairs and finding Tingley's body. She says that when she entered the office her uncle was not in sight, so it is supposed that he was already dead."

Carrie shook her head. "He wasn't."

Wolfe's brows went up. "He wasn't?"

"No. And Amy didn't kill him."

"Indeed. Were you there?"

"Of course I wasn't there. But if she had been knocked unconscious, could she have murdered a man? Even if she would?"

"Probably not. But you are postulating that she is telling the truth. The police aren't so gallant. What if she's lying? What if someone hit her after she had killed her uncle? What if she killed him soon after her arrival?"

"Oh, no," Carrie declared triumphantly, "she couldn't! That's just it! Because we know he was alive at eight o'clock!"

Wolfe gazed at her, with his lips pushed out. Then he poured beer, drank, used his handkerchief, leaned back, and leveled his eyes at her again. "That's interesting," he murmured. "How do you know that?"

"He was talking on the telephone."

"At eight o'clock?"

"Yes."

"To you?"

"No," Miss Yates interposed. "To me. At my home. Miss Murphy was there and heard it."

"Are you sure it was Mr. Tingley?"

"Certainly. I've known him all my life."

"What were you talking about?"

Gwendolyn answered, "A private matter."

Wolfe shook his head. "The police will soon pull you off that perch, madam. It's murder. I, of course, have no authority, but, since we've gone this far . . ."

"It's about the quinine. One of the girls reported to me that she had seen Miss Murphy doing something suspicious. Yesterday afternoon, just before closing time. Sneaking some of a mix into a little jar and concealing it. I asked Miss Murphy for an explanation and she refused to give any. Told me that she had nothing to say—"

"I couldn't—"

"Let me finish, Carrie. After she had gone home I went to Mr. Tingley's office and was going to tell him about it, but I don't think he even heard what I said. I had never seen him so upset. Philip, his adopted son, had just been there, and I suppose that was it, but he didn't say anything about Philip. I left at a quarter after six and went home to my flat on Twenty-third Street. I always walk; it's only a seven minutes' walk. I took off my hat and coat and rubbers and put my umbrella in the bathtub to drain, and ate some sardines and cheese—"

She stopped, and grunted. "The police asking me

questions all night seems to have got me into a habit. I don't suppose you care what I ate. About half past seven Miss Murphy came. She said she had been thinking it over and had decided she ought to tell me about it. What she told me made me madder than I've ever been in my life. Mr. Tingley suspected me of putting that quinine in! Me!"

"That isn't fair, Miss Yates," Carrie protested. "It was only—"

"Rubbish!" Gwen snapped. "He had you spying on me, didn't he?"

"But he—"

"I say he had you spying on me!" Miss Yates turned to Wolfe. "Since this trouble started, we've kept a sharp eye on the mixers and filling benches, and I've sent a sample of every mix in to Mr. Tingley, including even Carrie's. And, behind my back, she was sending him samples of my mixes!"

"I was obeying orders," Carrie said defensively. "Could I help it?"

"No. But he could. If he were alive I'd never forgive him for that—but now—I'll try to. I've given my whole life to that factory. That's the only life I've got or ever have had, and he knew it. He knew how proud I was of every jar that left that place, and yet he could set a spy on me—"

"So," Wolfe said, "you phoned Mr. Tingley to give him the devil."

She nodded.

"How do you know it was eight o'clock?"

"Because I looked at my watch. I called his home first, but he wasn't there, so I tried the office."

"Did he corroborate Miss Murphy's story?"

"Yes. He admitted it. He didn't even apologize. He said he was the head of the business, and no one, not even me, was above suspicion. He told me that to my face!"

"Not precisely to your face."

"Well, he said it!" She blew her nose again. "I hung up. I had a notion to go and have it out with him, but I decided to wait till morning. Anyway, I was played out—I had been under a strain for a month. Carrie stayed and I made some tea. I couldn't blame her, since she had only done what he told her to: We were still there talking at ten o'clock when a policeman came."

"With the news of the murder."

"Yes."

"But you didn't tell about the phone call."

"No," Miss Yates said. "I didn't want them to know about the quinine."

"But we'll have to tell them now," Carrie said. She was sitting on the edge of her chair with her fingers twisted into knots. "Since they've arrested Amy. Won't we?"

Wolfe grimaced. "Not for that reason," he said grumpily. "It would do Miss Duncan more harm than good. They think she's lying, anyhow. Do as you please. For myself, I shall tell them nothing."

They discussed it. Wolfe drank more beer. I covered a yawn, feeling that my substitute for Guthrie Judd had turned pretty sour on us. If Tingley had been alive at eight o'clock, Judd couldn't very well have killed him between 7:30 and 7:35, nor could the other man, the one in the raincoat, between 7:40 and 7:47. Of course, either of them could have returned just after eight, but, since I arrived at 8:08, that would have been cutting it fine, and besides, Cliff would have seen them unless they entered by another way. Unless Cliff was lying, or Amy was, or these two tidbit mixers were . . .

When they finally left, their intentions still appeared to be in a state of heads or tails. I offered to take them back to 23rd Street, which seemed only fair under the circumstances, and they accepted. That is, Gwendolyn did; Carrie said she was bound for the subway, so with her I went on to 34th and unloaded her at the express station.

When I got back I found that company had arrived. Leonard Cliff and Amy Duncan were there in the office with Wolfe. Cliff looked so grim and harassed. Amy was worse, if anything. She was puffy under the eyes and saggy at the jaws. The soft in-curves I had liked in her cheeks weren't there. Wolfe, himself, turned a black scowl on me.

I sat down. "My God," I said, "it could be worse, couldn't it? What if they charged you and tossed you in the coop?"

"Miss Duncan," Wolfe growled, "is under bond. The thing has become ridiculous. Mr. Cramer states that the knife handle bears her fingerprints."

"No!" I raised the brows. "Really? How about the chunk of iron? The weight."

"None. Clean."

"Ha. I thought so. She forgot to remove her prints from the knife, but after banging herself on the bean with the weight she carefully wiped it off—"

"That will do, Archie! If you insist on being whimsical—"

"I am not being whimsical. I'm merely agreeing with you that it's ridiculous." I sent him back his glare. "I know what you're doing, and so do you! You're letting it slide! Your performance with those two women I brought here was pitiful! I've got legs and I'm using them. You've got a brain and where is it? You're sore at Tingley because he got killed before you could shake your finger at him and tell him to keep quinine out of his liver pâté. You're sore at Cramer because he offended your dignity. You're sore at me because I didn't get Judd. Now you're sore at Miss Duncan because while she was lying there unconscious she let someone put her prints on that knife."

I turned to Amy: "You shouldn't permit things like that to happen. They annoy Mr. Wolfe."

Wolfe shut his eyes. There was a long silence. The tip of his forefinger was making little circles on the arm of his chair. Finally his lids went up halfway, and I was relieved to see that the focus was not me but Amy. He leaned back and clasped his fingers above his breadbasket. "Miss Duncan," he said, "it looks as if we'll have to go all over it. Are you up to answering some questions?"

"Oh, yes," she declared. "Anything that will—I feel pretty good. I'm all right."

"You don't look it. I'm going on the assumption that you and Mr. Cliff are telling the truth. I shall abandon it only under necessity. I assume, for instance, that when you left your uncle's employ and later became Mr. Cliff's secretary you were not coming to terms with the enemy."

"You certainly may," Cliff put in. "We knew she had worked in Tingley's office, but we didn't know she was his niece. That's why I was so surprised when I saw she was going there last evening, I couldn't imagine what she was doing there."

"Very well. I'll take all that." Wolfe went on with Amy: "What would you say if I told you that Miss Murphy was responsible for the quinine?"

"Why—" Amy looked astonished. "I wouldn't know what to say. I'd ask you how you knew. I couldn't believe that Carrie would do a thing like that."

"Did she have a grudge against your uncle?"

"Not that I know of. No special grudge. Of course, nobody really liked him."

"What about Miss Yates?"

"Oh, she's all right. She's a kind of a holy terror with the girls in the factory, but she's certainly competent."

"Did you and she get along?"

"Well enough. We didn't have much to do with each other. I was my uncle's stenographer."

"How were her relations with Tingley?"

"As good as could be expected. Of course, she was a privileged character; he couldn't possibly have got along without her. He inherited her from my grandfather along with the business."

Wolfe grunted. "Speaking of inheritance. Do you know anything about your uncle's will? Who will get the business?"

"I don't know, but I suppose my cousin Philip."

"His adopted son?"

"Yes." Amy hesitated, then offered an amendment by a change of inflection: "I *suppose* he will. The business has always been handed down from father to son. But, of course, Philip—" She stopped.

"Is he active in the business?"

"No. That's just it. He isn't active in anything. Except—" She stopped.

"Except—?" Wolfe prodded her.

"I was going to say, except spending money, only for the past year or so he hasn't had any to spend. Since Uncle Arthur kicked him out. I suppose he's been giving him enough to keep him from starving. I thought—I had an idea, when my uncle phoned and asked me to come to his office yesterday, and he was so urgent about it, that it was something about Philip."

"Why did you think that?"

"Well—because the only other time he ever sent for me it was about Philip. He thought that I could— that I had an influence over him."

"Did you?"

"Maybe—a little."

"When was the other time?"

"Nearly a year ago."

"What did he want you to influence Philip to do?"

"To—well, to settle down. To take an interest in the business. He knew that Philip was—had wanted to marry me. Of course, Philip isn't really my first cousin, since he was adopted. He isn't any relation at all, but I didn't want to marry him. I wasn't in love with him."

"And your uncle tried to persuade you to marry him?"

"Oh, no. He was dead against our marrying—I thought that was odd—but anyway he thought I had enough influence with Philip to reform him."

"Had Philip, himself, abandoned the idea of marrying you?"

"Well, he—he had quit trying."

Leonard Cliff was scowling. "Look here," he blurted at her suddenly, "what does he look like?"

"Philip?"

"Yes."

"Why—he's tall. Tall and broad, with a bony face and deep-set eyes. He's cynical. I mean he looks cynical—"

Cliff hit the arm of his chair with his palm. "It was him! I saw him at police headquarters this morning. It was him!"

"What if it was?" Wolfe demanded impatiently.

"Because that's what I came to tell you about! He's the man I saw last night! The one in the raincoat!"

"Indeed," Wolfe said. "The one who arrived at seven-forty? After Mr. Judd left?"

"Yes!"

"How sure are you?"

"Damned sure. I was sure when I saw him there at headquarters, and I started to try to find out who he was, but they hustled me out. And now, from the description Amy gives—"

Wolfe snapped at Amy, "Do you know where he lives?"

She shook her head. "No, I don't. But, oh—I can't believe—you don't think—"

"I haven't begun to think. First I have to get something to think about." He turned to me: "Archie, do you know of anyone we might hire to find Philip Tingley and bring—"

That was all I heard. I was on my way out.

This was the third man I had been sent for in less than twenty-four hours. The first one had been dead when I got to him. The second one had threatened to have me jailed. I intended to get this one.

But first I had to find him, and that turned into a job. From the colored maid at Tingley's house I got the address easily enough, east of Second Avenue on 29th Street, but he wasn't there. It was a dump, a dingy, dirty, five-story walk-up. I pushed the button labeled "Philip Tingley," but got no answering click. The button's position showed that he was four flights up, and since the door was unlatched, I entered and climbed the dark and smelly stairs. There were no buttons on the inside doors, so at the fifth floor rear I knocked half a dozen times, but without result.

I sat down at the top of the stairs and tried not to stew for nearly two hours.

Up to five o'clock that was one of the most unsatisfactory afternoons I remember. The sensible thing would have been to get Fred Durkin, who works for Wolfe on occasion, and leave him on post while I explored, but I wanted to make the delivery without any help. After a dish of beans and a couple of glasses of milk at a joint on Second Avenue I tried again, with the same result. Inquiries of the janitor in the basement and some of the other tenants were a good language lesson, but that was all. At half past four I went out again and did some research from a phone booth and drew nothing but blanks. It was during that expedition that he flew back to the nest. When I returned, a little after five o'clock, and, just to be doing something, pressed the button in the vestibule, the click sounded immediately. I popped in and bounced up the four flights.

The door to the rear flat was standing open and he was there on the sill when I reached his level. My first glance at him showed me not only that Amy's description had been accurate, but that I was an unwelcome surprise. He didn't like me at all.

"What do you want?" he demanded as I appeared.

I grinned at him. "You, brother. I've been around here wanting you for five hours."

"Are you from the police?"

"Nope. My name's Goodwin. I—"

The ape was shutting the door. I got against it and slid inside.

"Get out!" he snarled. "Get out of here!"

"My goodness," I protested, "you haven't even asked me what I want! How do you know I'm not Santa Claus?" I kicked the door shut behind me. There was no hurry, since Wolfe wouldn't be available until six o'clock. "Let's go in and talk it over—"

I suppose I was careless but what he did was so unexpected that he had me before I knew it. Not only did he get his long, bony fingers around my throat, but the strength of his grip indicated that they weren't all bone. I grabbed his wrists, but that was no good; he had the leverage. I ducked and twisted, and broke his hold, but he pressed on in, clutching at me, scratching me on the cheek. I don't like to plug a guy who never learned what fists are for, but I don't like to be scratched, either, so I pushed him back with my left and hooked with my right. He staggered, but the wall kept him from going down.

"Cut it out," I said curtly. "I don't want to—"

He hauled off and kicked me! What with my throat hurting when I talked, and the scratch on my cheek, and now this, I hit him harder, the second time, than I intended to. He didn't topple over, he folded up. As if he had melted. Then he didn't move.

I stooped over for a look at him, and then slid past for an inspection of the premises. The only way I could account for his violent lack of hospitality before he ever knew what I came for was that there was someone else there who wasn't supposed to be. But the place was empty. All there was of it was a bedroom and kitchen and bath. I gave them a glimpse, including the closet and under the bed, and went back to the tenant. He was still out.

In view of his disinclination even to let me state my intentions, it didn't seem likely that I would get any kind of co-operation from him in my desire to escort him to Wolfe's house, so I decided to wrap him up. He was too big to do anything with in the narrow little hall, and I dragged him into the kitchen. With a length of old clothesline from a kitchen drawer and a roll of adhesive tape from the bathroom cabinet, I soon had him arranged so that he would at least listen to me without kicking and scratching. I was putting the third strip of tape crosswise on his mouth when a bell rang right behind me.

I jerked up. The bell rang again.

So that was it. Not that someone was there, but someone was expected. I found the button on the wall that released the door latch downstairs, pushed it several times, took a swift look at the job I had just completed, stepped out and closed the kitchen door, and opened the door to the public hall.

I heard faint and hesitating footsteps from below on the uncarpeted stairs. Before a head appeared above the landing I had decided it was a woman; and it was. When she got to my level she stopped again, glanced the other way, and then saw me. She was a new one on me. Fifty or maybe a little more, slim and slick, in a mink coat.

I said politely, "Good evening."

She asked, with a sort of gasp, "Are you—Philip Tingley?"

I nodded. "Don't you recognize me?"

That seemed to hit some mark. "How would I recognize you?" she demanded sharply.

"I don't know. From my statue in the park, maybe." I stood aside from her passage to the door. "Come in."

She hesitated a second; then pulled her shoulders up as if bracing herself against peril and swept by me. I followed her in and motioned her to the living-bedroom and shut the door. All was dark before me, figuratively speaking, but anyway I could try some fancy groping and stumbling.

I went up to her. "Let me take your coat. This isn't the sort of chair you're used to, but it'll have to do."

She shuddered away from me and glanced nervously around. When she sat she let just enough of her come in contact with the shabby, soiled upholstery to call it sitting. Then she looked at me. I have never regarded myself as a feast for the eye, my attractions run more to the spiritual, but on the other hand I am not a toad, and I resented her expression.

"It seems," I ventured, "that something about me falls short of expectations."

She made a contemptuous noise. "I told you on the phone that there can be nothing sentimental about me and never has been."

"Okay," I agreed. "I'm not sentimental, either."

"I wouldn't expect you to be." If the breath of her voice had dribbled off the edge of a roof it would have made icicles. "It's not in you from either side. Neither from your father nor from me. My brother says you're a blackguard. He also says you're a coward and a bluffer, but considering where your blood came from, I don't believe that. I tell you frankly, I think my brother is making a mistake." She was biting the words off. "That's why I came. He thinks you'll take what he has offered, but I don't. I know I wouldn't, and half of you came from me."

I was loping along behind trying to keep up. The best bet seemed to be that I was a blackguard, so I did as well as I could with a sneer. "He thinks I'm a coward, does he?" I emitted an ugly little laugh. "And he thinks I'll take his offer? I won't!"

"What will you take?"

"What I said! That's final!"

"It is not final," she said sharply. "You're making a mistake, too. You're a fool if you think my brother will give you a million dollars."

"He will, or else."

"No. He won't." She moved on the chair, and I thought she was going to slide off, but she didn't. "All men are fools," she said bitterly. "I thought I had a cool head and knew how to take care of myself, but I was doomed to be ruined by men. When I was a pretty little thing in that factory—that finished me with men, I thought—but there are more ways than one. I don't deny that you have some right to—something; but what you demand is ridiculous. What my brother offers is also ridiculous, I admit that. If I had money of my own but I haven't. You're obdurate fools, both of you. He has never learned to compromise, and apparently you haven't, either. But you'll have to on this; you both will."

I kept the sneer working. "He's a pigheaded blubber-lip." I asserted. "It takes two to compromise. How about him?"

She opened her mouth and closed it again.

"So," I said sarcastically. "It strikes me that you're not any too bright yourself. What good did you expect to do by coming here and reading me the riot act? Do you think I'm boob enough to say, okay, split the difference, and then you run back to him? Now, that would be smart, wouldn't it?"

"It would at least make—"

"No!" I stood up. "You want this settled. So do I. So does he, and I know it. All right, let's go see him together. Then you can tell both of us to compromise. Then we'll find out who's being ridiculous. Come on."

She looked startled. "You mean now?"

"I mean now."

She balked. She had objections. I overruled them. I had the advantage, and I used it. When I put on my coat she just sat and chewed on her lip. Then she got up and came along.

When we got downstairs and out to the sidewalk there was no car there but mine; apparently she had come in a cab. I doubted if Philip Tingley ought to own a car, so I snubbed it and we walked to the corner and flagged a taxi. She shoved clear into her corner and I returned the compliment, after hearing her give an address in the 70's just east of Fifth Avenue. During the ride she showed no desire for conversation.

She allowed Philip to pay the fare, which seemed to me a little scrubby, under the circumstances. Before the massive ornamental door to the vestibule she stood aside, and I depressed the lever and pushed it open. The inner door swung open without any summons, and she passed through, with me on her heels. A man in uniform closed the door.

She seemed to have shrunk, and she looked pale and peaked. She was scared stiff. She asked the man, "Is Mr. Judd upstairs?"

"Yes, Miss Judd."

She led me upstairs to a large room with a thousand books and a fireplace and exactly the kind of chairs I like. In one of them was a guy I didn't like. He turned his head at our entrance.

Her voice came from a constricted throat: "Guthrie, I thought—"

What stopped her was the blaze from his eyes. It was enough to stop anyone.

I walked over and asked him, "Is Aiken around?"

He ignored me. He spoke to his sister as if she had been a spot of grease: "Where did this man come from?"

"It's a long story," I said, "but I'll make it short. She went to Philip Tingley's flat and I was there and she thought I was him." I waved a hand. "Mistaken identity."

"She thought—" He was speechless. That alone was worth the price of admission. His sister was staring at me frozenly.

He picked on her. "Get out!" he said in cold fury. "You incomparable fool!"

She was licked. She went.

I waited till the door had closed behind her and

then said, "We had a good, long talk. It's an interesting situation. Now I can give you an invitation I was going to extend yesterday when you interrupted me. You're going down to Thirty-fifth Street to call on Nero Wolfe."

"I'll talk with you," he said between his teeth. "Sit down."

"Oh, no. I invited you first. And I don't like you. If you do any wriggling and squirming, I swear I'll sell it to a tabloid and retire on the proceeds." I pointed to the door. "This way to the egress." . . .

Wolfe sat at his desk. I sat at mine, with my notebook open. Guthrie Judd was in the witness box, near Wolfe's desk.

Wolfe emptied his beer glass, wiped his lips, and leaned back. "You don't," he said, "seem to realize that the thing is now completely beyond your control. All you can do is save us a little time, which we would be inclined to appreciate. I make no commitment. We can collect the details without you if we have to, or the police can. The police are clumsy and sometimes not too discreet, but when they're shown where to dig they do a pretty good job. We know that Philip Tingley is your sister's son, and that's the main thing. That's what you were struggling to conceal. The rest is only to fill in. Who, for instance, is Philip's father?"

Judd, his eyes narrowed, and his jaw clamped, gazed at him in silence.

"Who is Philip's father?" Wolfe repeated patiently. Judd held the pose.

Wolfe shrugged. "Very well." He turned to me. "Call Inspector Cramer. With the men he has, a thing like this— Did you make a noise, sir?"

"Yes," Judd snapped. "Damn you. Philip's father is dead. He was Thomas Tingley. Arthur's father."

"I see. Then Arthur was Philip's brother."

"Half-brother." Judd looked as if he would rather say it with bullets than words. "Thomas was married and had two children, a son and a daughter, by his wife. The son was Arthur."

"Was the wife still alive when—?"

"Yes. My sister went to work in the Tingley factory in 1909. I was then twenty-five years old, just getting a start in life. She was nineteen. Arthur was a year or two younger than me. His father, Thomas, was approaching fifty. In 1911 my sister told me she was pregnant and who was responsible for it. I was making a little more money then, and I sent her to a place in the country. In September of that year the boy was born. My sister hated him without ever seeing him. She refused to look at him. He was placed in a charity home, and was forgotten by her and me. At that time I was occupied with my own affairs to the exclusion of considerations that should have received my attention. Many years later it occurred to me that there might be records at that place which would be better destroyed, and I had inquiries made."

"When was that?"

"Only three years ago. I learned then what had happened. Thomas Tingley had died in 1913, and his wife a year later. His son Arthur had married in 1912, and Arthur's wife had died in an accident. And in 1915 Arthur had legally adopted the four-year-old boy from the charity home."

"How did you know it was that boy?"

"I went to see Arthur. He knew the boy was his half-brother. His father, on his deathbed, had told him all about it and charged him with the child's welfare— secretly, since at that time Thomas's wife was still alive. Two years later, after Arthur's wife had died, leaving him childless, he had decided on the adoption."

"You said you had a search made for records. Did Arthur have them?"

"Yes, but he wouldn't give them up. I tried to persuade him. I offered—an extravagant sum. He was stubborn, he didn't like me, and he was disappointed in the boy, who had turned out a blithering fool."

Wolfe grunted. "So you made efforts to get the records by other methods."

"No. I didn't." A corner of Judd's mouth twisted up. "You can't work me into a melodrama. I don't fit. Not even a murder. I knew Arthur's character and had no fear of any molestation during his life-time, and he conceded me a point. He put the papers in a locked box in his safe and willed the box and its contents to me. Not that he told me where they were. I found that out later."

"When?"

"Two days ago."

Wolfe's brows went up. "Two *days*?"

"Yes. Monday morning Philip called at my office. I had never seen him since he was a month old, but he established his identity, and he had copies with him of those records. He demanded a million dollars." Judd's voice rose. "A million!"

"What was the screw, a threat to publish?"

"Oh, no. He was smoother than that. He said he came to me only because his adopted father would allow him nothing but a pittance—he said 'pittance' —and had disinherited him in his will. Arthur had been fool enough to let him read the will, rubbing it in, I suppose, and the bequest of the locked box to me had made him smell a rat. He had stolen the box from the safe and got it open, and there it was. His threat was not to publish, but to sue me and my sister for damages, for abandoning him as an infant, which of course amounted to the same thing, but that put a face on it.

And was something we could not allow to happen under any circumstances, and he knew it."

Wolfe said, "So why didn't you pay him?"

"Because it was outrageous. You don't just hand out a million dollars."

"I don't, but you could."

"I didn't. And I wanted a guaranty that that would end it. For one thing I had to be sure I was getting all the original records, and Arthur was the only one who could satisfy me on that, and he would see me Monday. I put Philip off for a day. The next morning, yesterday, Arthur phoned me that the box was gone from the safe, but even then he wouldn't come to my office or meet me somewhere, so I had to go to him."

I looked up from the notebook with a grin. "Yeah, and I met you coming out. When I put that chalk—"

He rudely went on without even glancing at me. "I went to his office and told him of Philip's demand and threat. He was enraged. He thought Philip could be brow-beaten into surrendering the box, and I didn't. What I proposed—but I couldn't do anything with him. He would have it his way. It was left that he would talk with Philip that afternoon, and the three of us would have it out the next morning, Wednesday—that would have been today—in his office. I had to accept—"

"That won't do," Wolfe said bluntly. "Don't try any dodging now."

"I'm not. I am telling you—"

"A lie, Mr. Judd. It's no good. You three were to meet at Tingley's office Tuesday evening, not Wednesday morning. And you went there—"

I missed the rest. The doorbell rang, and I went to attend to it, because Fritz wasn't being permitted to exert himself. A peep through the glass showed me a phiz only too well known, so I slipped the chain on before I opened the door to the extent of the six inches which the chain permitted.

"We don't need any," I said offensively.

"Go to hell," I was told gruffly. "I want to see Guthrie Judd. He's here."

"How do you know?"

"So informed at his home. Take off that damn' chain—"

"He might have got run over on the way. Be seated while I find out."

I went to the office and told Wolfe, "Inspector Cramer wants to see Judd. Was told at his home that he had come here."

Judd, quick on the trigger, spoke up: "I want your assurance."

"You won't get it," Wolfe snapped. "Bring Mr. Cramer in."

I went back out and slipped the chain and swung the door open, and Cramer made for the office with me following.

After using grunts for greetings he stood and spoke down to Judd: "This is a confidential matter. Very confidential. If you want to come—"

Judd glanced at Wolfe from the corner of his eye. Wolfe cleared his throat.

Judd said, "Sit down. Go ahead."

"But I warn you, Mr. Judd, it is extremely—"

"He has answered you," Wolfe said. "Please make it as brief as possible."

"I see." Cramer looked from one to the other. "Like that, huh? Suits me." He sat down and placed the leather bag on the floor in front of him, and hunched over and released the catches and opened it. He straightened up to look at Judd. "A special-delivery parcel-post package addressed to me by name was delivered at police headquarters about an hour ago." He bent and got an object from the bag. "This was in it. May I ask, have you ever seen it before?"

Judd said, "No."

Cramer's eyes moved. "Have you, Wolfe? You, Goodwin?"

Wolfe shook his head. I said, "Not guilty."

Cramer shrugged. "As you see, it's a metal box with a lock. On the top the letters 'GJ' have been roughly engraved, probably with the point of a knife. The first thing about it is this: A box of this description, including the 'GJ' on its top, was left to you by Arthur Tingley in his will. The police commissioner asked you about it this afternoon, and you stated you knew nothing of such a box and had no idea what it might contain. Is that correct, Mr. Judd?"

"It is," Judd acknowledged. "Hombert told me the will said the box would be found in the safe in Tingley's office, and it wasn't there."

"That's right. The second thing is the lock has been forced. It was like that when the package was opened. The third thing is the contents." Cramer regarded Judd. "Do you want me to keep right on?"

"Go ahead."

"Very well." Cramer lifted the lid.

"Item one, a pair of baby shoes." He held them up for inspection.

"Item two, a printed statement of condition of your banking firm. As of June 30, 1939. A circle has been made, with pen and ink, around your name, and a similar circle around the sum of the total resources, $230,000,000 and something."

He returned the folder to the box and produced the next exhibit. "Item three, a large manila envelope. It was sealed, but the wax has been broken and the flap slit open. On the outside, in Arthur Tingley's handwriting, is this inscription: 'Confidential. In case of my decease, to be delivered intact to Mr. Guthrie Judd. Arthur Tingley.' "

Judd had a hand extended. "Then it's mine." His tone was sharp and peremptory. "And you opened it—"

"No, sir; I didn't." Cramer hung onto the envelope. "It had already been opened. It is unquestionably your property, and eventually no doubt it will be surrendered to you, but we'll keep it for the present. Under the circumstances. It contains the birth certificate of 'Baby Philip,' dated September 18, 1911, four pages from the records of the Ellen James Home regarding the sojourn in that institution of a young woman named Martha Judd, and a written statement, holograph, dated July 9, 1936, signed by Arthur Tingley. Also, a certificate of the legal adoption of Philip Tingley by Arthur Tingley, dated May 11, 1915. If you wish to inspect these documents now, in my presence—"

"No," Judd snapped. "I demand the immediate surrender of the box and its contents to me."

Cramer shook his head. "For the present, sir—"

"I'll replevy."

"I doubt if you can. Evidence in a murder case—"

"That has nothing to do with Tingley's murder."

"I hope it hasn't." Cramer sounded as if he meant it. "I'm only a cop and you know what you are. A man in your position and a thing like this. It was too hot for the district attorney and he wished it onto me. So it's a job, and that's that. You have a sister named Martha. Was she at the Ellen James Home in the year 1911?"

"It would have been sensible of you," Judd said icily, "to follow the district attorney's example." He aimed a finger at the box. "I want that, and demand it."

"Yeah, I heard you before. I can get tough, you know, even with you. Let's try this. You said it wasn't you that entered the Tingley Building at seven-thirty yesterday evening. Do you still say that?"

"Yes."

"We're taking your chauffeur down to headquarters."

Judd made a contemptuous noise.

"Also Philip Tingley. You might as well come down off your horse. Somebody's going to talk; don't think they won't. If you expect—"

The phone rang. I answered it, and learned that Sergeant Foster wished to speak to Inspector Cramer. Cramer came to my desk to take it. About all he did for two minutes was listen and grunt. At the end he said, "Bring him here to Nero Wolfe's place," and hung up.

"If you don't object," he said to Wolfe.

"To what?" Wolfe demanded.

"A little talk with Philip Tingley. They found him over in his kitchen tied up and gagged." . . .

I have got, and always will have, a soft spot in my heart for Philip Tingley. Consider the situation from his standpoint when he entered Nero Wolfe's office at seven o'clock that Wednesday evening. Two burly detectives were right behind him. He was surrounded by the enemy. His jaw was swollen, his head must have been fuzzy, and he was wobbly on his pins. He knew I was stronger than he was. And yet, by gum, the minute he caught sight of me he power-dived at me as if all he asked was to plant one bomb! That's the spirit that wins ball games.

The dicks jumped for him. I hastily arose, but they got him and held him.

"What the hell?" Cramer inquired.

"It's a private matter," I explained, sitting down. "It was me that fixed his jaw and tied him up. That has no bearing—"

I got on my feet again. With one mighty, spasmodic heave of his bony frame Philip had busted loose and was on the move. But not toward me; he had changed his objective. What he was after was the metal box on Cramer's knees. He not only grabbed for it, but he got it. The dicks went for him again, this time with more fervor. One of them retrieved the box and the other one slammed him down. I went to help, and we picked him up and shoved him into a chair. Panting like a polar bear on a hot day, he glared at us, but quit trying.

"Whistle for help," Cramer said sarcastically. He looked at me. "You say you fixed his jaw? Let's take that first."

I started to explain, but Philip took the floor again, this time verbally. He had seen Judd. "You!" he yelled. "You got it! You killed him and took it! And you framed me! You had her say she was coming to see me, and you sent that man—"

"Shut up!" I told him. "Judd never sent me anywhere and never will. She did come to see you, but she saw me instead."

"He got the box!"

"You damned idiot," Judd said bitterly. "You'll cook your goose—"

"That'll do," Cramer growled. "If—"

"You can't bully me, Inspector—"

"The hell I can't. If you don't like it, go hire a lawyer. Hang onto that box, Foster." Cramer regarded Philip. "You recognize it?"

"Yes! It's mine!"

"You don't say so. When and where did you see it before?"

"I saw it when I—"

"Don't be a fool," Judd snapped. He stood up. "Come with me. I'll see you through this. Keep your mouth shut."

* * *

"You're too late, Mr. Judd." It was Nero Wolfe taking a hand. "Either keep still or go home. You're licked."

"I have never been licked."

"Pfui! You are now. And this is my house you're in. If you try interrupting me, Mr. Goodwin will throw you out with enthusiasm." Wolfe turned to Philip: "Mr. Tingley, I'm afraid you're holding the short end of the stick. The police have got the box. Its contents are known, so you have no lever to use on Mr. Judd. And you're deep in another hole, too. Mr. Judd, who advises you to keep your mouth shut, has himself been talking. We know of your call on him Monday and the demands you made; and of the copies you showed him of the contents of that box; and of your talk with Arthur Tingley yesterday afternoon; and of the arrangement he made for you and Mr. Judd to come to his office last evening—"

Philip snarled at Judd. "You dirty rat—"

Wolfe sailed over it. "Also, we know that you went there. You walked to the building in the rain, wearing a raincoat, entered at twenty minutes to eight, and came out again seven minutes later. What did you see inside? What did you do?"

"Don't answer him," Judd commanded sharply. "He's only—"

"Save it," Philip told him in harsh contempt. He looked sullenly at Wolfe. "Yes, I went there, and I went in, and I saw him there dead on the floor."

"What—?" Cramer began blurting, but Wolfe stopped him: "I'll do this. . . . Mr. Tingley, I beg you to reflect. I may know more than you think I do. You got there at seven-forty—is that right?"

"About that, yes."

"And Tingley was dead?"

"Yes."

58

"What if I have evidence that he was alive at eight o'clock?"

"You couldn't have. He was dead when I got there."

"Was Amy Duncan there?"

"Yes. She was on the floor unconscious."

"Did you see anyone else anywhere in the building?"

"No."

"Where did you go besides Tingley's office?"

"Nowhere. I went straight there and straight out."

"You were there seven minutes. What did you do?"

"I—" Philip halted and shifted in his chair. "I felt Amy's pulse. I wanted to get her out of there—but I didn't dare—and she was breathing all right and her pulse was pretty good. Then I—" He stopped.

"Yes? You what?"

"I looked for the box. The safe door was standing open, but it wasn't in there. I looked a few other places, and then I heard Amy move, or thought I did, and I left. Anyway, I thought Judd had been there and killed him and taken the box, so I didn't hope to find it. So I left."

Wolfe was scowling at him. "Are you aware," he demanded, "of what you're saying? Are your wits working?"

"You're damned right they are."

"Nonsense. You had previously stolen the box from the safe and had it in your possession. How could you have been looking for it in that office last evening?"

"I didn't have it in my possession."

"Oh, come. Don't be ass enough—"

"I say I didn't have it. I had had it. I didn't have it then. He went to my place and found it and took it."

"Who did? When?"

"My half-brother. Arthur Tingley. He went to my

59

flat yesterday afternoon—I don't know how he got in—and found it."

So that, I thought, turning a page of my notebook, was the errand that had called Tingley away from his office when I had gone there to interview him about quinine.

Wolfe asked, "How do you know that?"

"Because he told me. He had the box there in the safe yesterday afternoon."

"Are you telling me that at five o'clock yesterday afternoon that box was in Tingley's safe in his office?"

"I am."

"And when you returned two hours later, at seven-forty, it was gone?"

"It was. Judd had been there. Judd had taken it. And if the lousy ape thinks he can—"

"Be quiet, please," Wolfe said testily. He closed his eyes.

We sat. Wolfe's lips were moving, pushing out and then drawing in again. Judd started to say something, and Cramer shushed him. The inspector knew the signs as well as I did.

Wolfe's eyes opened, but they were directed, not at Judd or Philip, but at me. "What time," he asked, "did it begin raining yesterday?"

I said, "Seven P.M."

"Seven precisely?"

"Maybe a little after. Not much."

"Not even a drizzle before that?"

"No."

"Good." He wiggled a finger at Sergeant Foster. "Let me have that box."

Foster handed him the box.

Wolfe looked at Philip Tingley: "When you stole this from the safe you had no key for it. So you had to pry it open?"

"No," Philip denied, "I didn't pry it open."

"The metal is gouged and twisted—"

"I can't help that. I didn't do it. I suppose Judd did. I took it to a locksmith and told him I had lost my key, and had him make one that would open it."

"Then it was locked yesterday afternoon?"

"Yes."

"Good." Wolfe looked pleased with himself. "That settles it, I think. Let's see." Whereupon he grasped the box firmly in both hands and shook it violently from side to side. His attitude suggested that he was listening for something, but the banging of the shoes against the metal sides of the box was all there was to hear. He nodded with satisfaction. "That's fine," he declared.

"Nuts," Cramer said.

"By no means. Some day, Mr. Cramer—but no, I suppose never. I would like a few words with you and Archie. If your men will take these gentlemen to the front room?"

When they were shut off by the sound-proofed door Cramer advanced on Wolfe with his jaw leading the way. "Look here—"

"No," Wolfe said decisively. "I tolerate your presence here and that's all. Take a guest from my house with a warrant, will you? I want to know what has been removed from Mr. Tingley's office."

"But if Judd—"

"No. Take them if you want to, get them out of here, and I'll proceed alone."

"Do you know who killed Tingley?"

"Certainly. I know all about it. But I need something. What has been removed from that office?"

Cramer heaved a sigh. "Damn you, anyway. The corpse. Two bloody towels. The knife and the weight. Five small jars with some stuff in them which we found in a drawer of Tingley's desk. We had the stuff analyzed and it contained no quinine. We were told they were routine samples."

"That's all?"

"Yes."

"No other sample jars were found?"

"No."

"Then it's still there. It ought to be. It must be. . . . Archie, go and get it. Find it and bring it here. Mr. Cramer will telephone his men there to help you."

"Huh," Cramer grunted. "I will?"

"Certainly you will."

"As for me," I put in, "I'm a wonder at finding things, but I get better results when I know what I'm looking for."

"Pfui! What was it I spit out yesterday at lunch?"

"Oh, is that it? Okay." I beat it, then.

It was only a three-minute ride to Tingley's, and I figured it might take longer than that for Wolfe to get Cramer to make the phone call, so I took a taxi to East 29th Street and picked up the roadster and drove it on from there. The entrance door at the top of the stone steps was locked, but just as I was lifting my fist to beat a tattoo I heard the chatter of feet inside, and in a moment the door opened and a towering specimen looked down at me.

"You Goodwin?" he demanded.

"I am Mr. Goodwin. Old Lady Cramer—"

"Yeah. You sound like what I've heard of you. Enter."

I did so, and preceded him up the stairs. In Tingley's office an affair with a thin little mouth in a big face was awaiting us, seated at a table littered with newspapers.

"You fellows are to help me," I stated.

"Okay," the one at the table said superciliously.

"We'd just as soon have the exercise. But Bowen did this room. If you think you can find a button after Bowen—"

"That will do, my man," I said graciously. "Bowen's all right as far as he goes, but he lacks subtlety. He's too scientific. He uses rules and calipers, whereas I use my brain. For instance, since he did that desk, it's a hundred to one that there's not an inch of it unaccounted for, but what if he neglected to look in that hat?" I pointed to Tingley's hat still there on the hook. "He might have, because there's nothing scientific about searching a hat; you just take it down and look at it."

"That's wonderful." Thin Mouth said. "Explain some more."

"Sure; glad to." I walked across. "Do you ask why Tingley would put an object in his hat? It was the logical place for it. He wanted to take it home with him, and meanwhile he wanted to keep it hidden from someone who might have gone snooping around his desk and other obvious places. He was not an obvious man. Neither am I." I reached up and took the hat from the hook.

And it was in the hat!

That made up for all the bad breaks that had come my way over a period of years. Nothing like that will ever happen again. It was so utterly unexpected that I nearly dropped it when it rolled out of the hat, but I grabbed and caught it and had it—a midget-sized jar, the kind they used for samples in the factory. It was about two thirds full with a label on it marked in pencil, "11–14–Y."

"You see," I said, trying my damnedest not to let my voice tremble with excitement, "it's a question of brains."

They were gawking at me, absolutely speechless. I

got out my penknife and, with a tip of a blade, dug out a bit of the stuff in the jar and conveyed it to my mouth. My God, it tasted sweet—I mean bitter!

I spat it out. "I'm going to promote you boys," I said indulgently. "And raise your pay. And give you a month's vacation."

I departed. I hadn't even taken off my coat and hat. . . .

It was too bad dinner had to be delayed the first day that Fritz was back on the job after his grippe, but it couldn't be helped. While we were waiting for Carrie Murphy to come, I went to the kitchen and had a glass of milk and tried to cheer Fritz up by telling him that grippe often leaves people so that they can't taste anything.

At half past seven Wolfe was at his desk and I was at mine with my notebook. Seated near me, with a dick behind his chair, was Philip Tingley. Beyond him were Carrie Murphy, Miss Yates, and another dick. Inspector Cramer was at the other end of Wolfe's desk, next to Guthrie Judd. None of them looked very happy, Carrie in particular. It was her Wolfe started on, after Cramer had turned the meeting over to him.

"There shouldn't be much in this," Wolfe said bluntly. What he meant was he hoped there wouldn't be, that close to dinnertime. "Miss Murphy, did you go to Miss Yates's apartment yesterday evening to discuss something with her?"

Carrie nodded.

"Did she make a telephone call?"

"Yes."

"Whom did she call and at what time?"

"Mr. Arthur Tingley. It was eight o'clock."

"At his home or his office?"

"His office." She stopped to swallow. "She tried

his home first, but he wasn't there, so she called the office and got him."

"She talked with him?"

"Yes."

"Did you?"

"No."

Wolfe's eyes moved: "Miss Yates. Is Miss Murphy's statement correct?"

"It is," said Gwendolyn firmly.

"You recognized Tingley's voice?"

"Certainly. I've been hearing it all my life—"

"Of course you have. Thanks." Wolfe shifted again. "Mr. Philip Tingley. Yesterday afternoon your father—your father—your brother asked you to be at his office at seven-thirty in the evening. Is that right?"

"Yes!" Philip said aggressively.

"Did you go?"

"Yes, but not at seven-thirty. I was ten minutes late."

"Did you see him?"

"I saw him dead. On the floor behind the screen. I saw Amy Duncan there, too, unconscious, and I felt her pulse and—"

"Naturally. Being human, you displayed humanity." Wolfe made a face. "Are you sure Arthur Tingley was dead?"

Philip grunted. "If you had seen him—"

"His throat had been cut?"

"Yes, and the blood had spread—"

"Thank you," Wolfe said curtly. "Mr. Guthrie Judd."

The two pairs of eyes met in midair.

Wolfe wiggled a finger at him. "Well, sir, it looks as if you'll have to referee this. Miss Yates says Tingley was alive at eight o'clock and Philip says he was dead at seven-forty. We'd like to hear from you what shape he was in at seven-thirty. Will you tell us?"

"No."

"If you don't you're an ass. The screws are all loose now. There is still a chance this business will be censored for the press if I feel like being discreet. But I'm not bound, as law officers are, to protect the embarrassing secrets of prominent people from the public curiosity. I'm doing a job and you can help me out a little. If you don't—" Wolfe shrugged.

Judd breathed through his nose.

"Well?" Wolfe asked impatiently.

"Tingley was dead." Judd bit it off.

"Then you did enter that building and go to that office? At half past seven?"

"Yes. That was the time of the appointment. Tingley was on the floor with his throat cut. Near him was a young woman I had never seen, unconscious. I was in the room less than a minute."

Wolfe nodded. "I'm not a policeman, and I'm certainly not the district attorney, but I think it is quite likely that you will never be under the necessity of telling this story in a courtroom. They won't want to inconvenience you. However, in the event that a subpoena takes you to the witness stand, are you prepared to swear to the truth of what you have just said?"

"I am."

"Good." Wolfe's gaze swept to Miss Yates. "Are you still positive it was Tingley you talked to, Miss Yates?"

She met his eyes squarely. "I am." Her voice was perfectly controlled. "I don't say they're lying. I don't know. I only know if it was someone imitating Arthur Tingley's voice, I've never heard anything to equal it."

"You still think it was he?"

"I do."

"Why did you tell me this morning that when you got home yesterday you stood your umbrella in the bathtub to drain?"

"Because I—"

She stopped, and it was easy to tell from her face what had happened. An alarm had sounded inside her. Something had yelled at her, "Look out!"

"Why," she asked, her voice a shade thinner than it had been, but quite composed, "did I say that? I don't remember it."

"I do," Wolfe declared. "The reason I bring it up, you also told me you went home at a quarter past six. It didn't start raining until seven, so why did your umbrella need draining at six-fifteen?"

Miss Yates snorted. "What you remember," she said sarcastically. "What you say I said, that I didn't say—"

"Very well. We won't argue it. There are two possible explanations. One, that your umbrella got wet without any rain. Two, that you went home, not at six-fifteen, as you said you did, but considerably later. I like the second one best because it fits so well into the only satisfactory theory of the murder of Arthur Tingley. If you had gone home at six-fifteen, as you said, you wouldn't very well have been at the office to knock Miss Duncan on the head when she arrived at ten minutes past seven. Of course, you could have gone and returned to the office, but that wouldn't change things any."

Miss Yates smiled. That was a mistake, because the muscles around her mouth weren't under control, so they twitched. The result was that instead of looking confident and contemptuous she merely looked sick.

"The theory starts back a few weeks," Wolfe resumed. "As you remarked this morning, that business and that place were everything to you; you had no life except there. When the Provisions & Beverages Corporation made an offer to buy the business, you became alarmed, and upon reflection you were convinced that sooner or later Tingley would sell. That old factory would of course be abandoned, and probably you with it. That was intolerable to you. You considered ways of preventing it, and what you hit on was adulterating the product, damaging its reputation sufficiently so that the Provisions & Beverages Corporation wouldn't want it. You chose what seemed to you the lesser of two evils. Doubtless you thought that the reputation could be gradually re-established."

Carrie was staring at her boss in amazement.

"It seemed probable," Wolfe conceded, "that it would work. The only trouble was, you were overconfident. You were, in your own mind, so completely identified with the success and very existence of that place and what went on there, that you never dreamed that Tingley would arrange to check on you secretly. Yesterday afternoon you learned about it when you caught Miss Murphy with a sample of a mix you had made. And you had no time to consider the situation, to do anything about it, for a sample had already reached Tingley. He kept you waiting in the factory until after Philip had gone and he phoned his niece—for obviously you didn't know he had done that—and then called you into his office and accused you."

"It's a lie," Miss Yates said harshly. "It's a lie! He didn't accuse me! He didn't—!"

"Pfui! He not only accused you, he told you that he had proof. A jar that Miss Murphy had previously delivered to him that afternoon, from a mix you had made. I suppose he fired you. He may have told you he intended to prosecute. And I suppose you implored him, pleaded with him, and were still pleading with him, from behind, while he was stooping over the washbasin. He didn't know you had got the paperweight from his desk, and never did know it. It knocked him out. You went and got a knife and finished the job, there where he lay on the floor, and you were searching the room, looking for the sample jar which he had got from Miss Murphy, when you heard footsteps."

A choking noise came from her throat.

"Naturally, that alarmed you," Wolfe continued. "But the steps were of only one person, and that a woman. So you stood behind the screen with the weight in your hand, hoping that, whoever it was, she would come straight to that room and enter it, and she did. As she passed the edge of the screen, you struck. Then you got an idea upon which you immediately acted by pressing her fingers around the knife handle, from which, of course, your own prints had been wiped—"

A stifled gasp of horror from Carrie Murphy interrupted him. He answered it without moving his eyes from Miss Yates: "I doubt if you had a notion of incriminating Miss Duncan. You probably calculated— and for an impromptu and rapid calculation under stress is was a good one—that when it was found that the weight had been wiped and the knife handle had not, the inference would be, not that Miss Duncan had killed Tingley, but that the murderer had clumsily tried to pin it on her. That would tend to divert suspicions from you, for you had been on friendly terms with her and bore her no grudge. It was a very pretty finesse for a hasty one. Hasty, because you were now in a panic and had not found the jar. I suppose you had previously found that the safe door was open and had looked in there, but now you tried it again. No jar was visible, but a locked metal box was there on the shelf. You picked it up and shook it, and it sounded as if the jar were in it."

Cramer growled, "I'll be damned."

"Or," Wolfe went on, "it sounded enough like it to satisfy you. The box was locked. To go to the factory again and get something to pry it open with—no. Enough. Besides, the jar was in no other likely place, so that must be it. You fled. You took the box and went, leaving by a rear exit, for there might be someone in front—a car, waiting for Miss Duncan. You hurried home through the rain, for it was certainly raining then, and had just got your umbrella stood in the tub and your things off when Miss Murphy arrived."

"No!" Carrie Murphy blurted.

Wolfe frowned at her. "Why not?"

"Because she—she was—"

"Dry and composed and herself? I suppose so. An exceptionally cool and competent head has for thirty years been content to busy itself with tidbits." Wolfe's gaze was still on Miss Yates. "While you were talking with Miss Murphy you had an idea. You would lead the conversation to a point where a phone call to Tingley would be appropriate, and you did so; and you called his home first and then his office, and faked conversation with him. The idea itself was fairly clever, but your follow-up was brilliant. You didn't mention it to the police and advised Miss Murphy not to, realizing it would backfire if someone entered the office or Miss Duncan regained consciousness before eight o'clock. If it turned out that someone had, and Miss Murphy blabbed about the phone call, you could say that you had been deceived by someone imitating Tingley's voice, or even that you had faked the phone call for its effect on Miss Murphy; if it turned out that someone hadn't, the phone call would stick, with Miss Murphy to corroborate it."

A grunt of impatience came from Cramer.

"Not much more," Wolfe said. "But you couldn't open the box with Miss Murphy there. And then the police came. That must have been a bad time for you. As soon as you got a chance you forced the lid open, and I can imagine your disappointment and dismay when you saw no jar. Only a pair of child's shoes and an envelope! You were in a hole, and in your desperation you did something extremely stupid. Of course, you didn't want the box in your flat, you wanted to get rid of it, but why the devil did you mail it to Mr. Cramer? Why didn't you put something heavy in it and throw it in the river? I suppose you examined the contents of the envelope, and figured that if the police got hold of it their attention would be directed to Guthrie Judd and Philip. You must have been out of your mind. Instead of directing suspicions against Philip or Judd, the result was just the opposite, for it was obvious that neither of them would have mailed the box to the police, and therefore some other person had somehow got it."

Gwendolyn Yates was sitting straight and stiff. She was getting a hold on herself, and doing a fairly good job of it. There were no more inarticulate noises from her throat, and she wasn't shouting about lies and wasn't going to. She was a tough baby and she was tightening up.

"But you're not out of your mind now," Wolfe said, with a note of admiration in his tone. "You're adding it up, aren't you? You are realizing that I can prove little or nothing of what I've said. I can't prove what Tingley said to you yesterday, or what time you left there, or that you got the box from the safe and took it with you, or that it was you who mailed it to Mr. Cramer. I can't even prove that there wasn't someone there at eight o'clock who imitated Tingley's voice over the telephone. I can't prove anything."

"Except this." He shoved his chair back, opened a drawer of his desk, and got something, arose, walked around the end of the desk, and displayed the object in front of Carrie Murphy's eyes.

"Please look at this carefully, Miss Murphy. As you see, it is a small jar two-thirds full of something. Pasted on it is a plain white label bearing the notation in pencil, 'Eleven dash fourteen dash Y.' Does that mean anything to you? Does that 'Y' stand for Yates? Look at it—"

But Carrie had no chance to give it a thorough inspection, let alone pronounce a verdict. The figure of Miss Yates, from eight feet away, came hurtling through the air. She uttered no sound, but flung herself with such unexpected speed and force that the fingers of her outstretched hand, missing what they were after, nearly poked Wolfe's eye out. He grabbed for her wrist but missed it, and then the dick was out of his chair and had her. He got her from behind by her upper arms and had her locked.

She stood, not trying to struggle, looked at Wolfe, who had backed away, and squeaked at him, "Where was it?"

He told her. . . .

We were sitting down to a dinner that was worthy of the name when the doorbell rang. I went to answer it.

The pair that entered certainly needed a tonic. Leonard Cliff looked like something peeking out at you from a dark cave. Amy Duncan was pale and puffy, with bloodshot eyes.

"We've got to see Mr. Wolfe," Cliff stated. "We've just been talking with a lawyer, and he says—"

"Not interested," I said brusquely. "Wolfe's out of the case. Through. Done."

Amy gasped. Cliff grabbed my arm. "He can't be! He can't! Where is he?"

"Eating dinner. And, by the way. I've been trying to get you folks on the phone. Some news for you. Miss Yates is under arrest: they just took her away from here. Mr. Wolfe would like to have her prosecuted for feeding him quinine, but the cops prefer to try her for murder. She's guilty of both."

"What!"

"What!"

"Yep." I waved airily. "I got the evidence. It's all over. You won't get your pictures in the paper anymore."

"You mean—she—they—it—we—"

"That's one way of putting it. I mean, the operation has been brought to a successful conclusion. You're just ordinary citizens again."

They stared at me, and then at each other, and then went into a clinch. The condition they were both in, it certainly couldn't have been merely physical attraction. I stood and regarded them patiently. Pretty soon I cleared my throat. They didn't pay any attention.

"When you get tired standing up," I said, "there's a chair in the office that will hold two. We'll join you after dinner."

I returned to help Wolfe with the snipe fired with brandy.

FRAME-UP
FOR MURDER

I

I was tailing a man mamed Jonas Putz. You can forget
Putz. I mention him only to explain how I happened to
be standing, at five o'clock that Monday afternoon, in a
doorway on the uptown side of 38th Street around the
corner from Lexington Avenue. After spending an hour
or so at the Tulip Bar of the Churchill, with an eye on
Putz at a proper distance, I had followed him out to the
street and then downtown, on foot; and after a few
blocks I got the notion that someone else was also
interested in his movements. When he stopped a couple of times to look at shop windows, I stopped, too,
naturally, and so did someone else, about twenty paces
back of me. I had first noticed her in the lobby of the
Churchill, because she rated a glance as a matter of
principle—the principle that a man owes it to his eyes
to let them rest on attractive objects when there are
any around.

She was still tagging along when I turned the corner at 38th Street, and I was wondering whether her interest in Putz had any connection with the simple little problem Nero Wolfe had been hired to solve; and, if so, what. When Putz crossed Madison Avenue and went on to the entrance of the building he lived in, and entered, I was through with him for the day, since he hadn't gone to a certain address, and it was only out of curiosity, to see what the female stalker would do, that I kept going and posted myself in a doorway across the street from Putz's entrance. My curiosity was soon satisfied.

She came right along straight to my post, stopped, faced me at arm's length, and spoke. "You are Archie Goodwin."

I raised my brows. "Prove it."

She smiled a little. "Oh, I have seen you once, at the Flamingo, and I have seen your picture in the paper. Are you detecting somebody?"

She looked about as foreign as she sounded—enough to suggest a different flavor, which can broaden a man, but not enough to make it seem too complicated. Her chin was slightly more pointed than I would have specified if I had had her made to order, but everybody makes mistakes. Her floppy-brimmed hat and the shoulder spread of her mink stole made her face look smaller than it probably was.

She wasn't an operative, that was sure. Her interest in Putz must be personal, but still it might be connected with our client's problem.

I smiled back at her. "Apparently we both are. Unless you're Putz's bodyguard?"

"Putz? Who is that?"

"Now, really. You spoke first. Jonas Putz. You ought to know his name, since you tailed him all the way here from the Churchill."

She shook her head. "Not him. I was after you. This is a pickup. I am picking you up." She didn't say "picking," but neither did she say "peecking." It was in between.

"I am honored," I assured her. "I am flattered. I like the way you do it. Usually girls who pick me up beat around the bush. Look; if you'll tell me why you're interested in Putz, I'll tell you why I am, and then we'll see. We might—"

"But I'm not! I never heard of him. Truly!" She started a hand out to touch my arm, but decided not to. "It is you I am interested in! When I saw you at the Churchill I wanted to speak, but you were going, and I followed, and all the way I was bringing up my courage. To pick you up." That time it was "peeck."

"O.K." I decided to table Putz temporarily. "Now that you've picked me up, what are you going to do with me?"

She smiled. "Oh, no. You are the man. What we do, that is for you to say."

If she had been something commonplace like a glamorous movie star I would have shown her what I thought of her passing the buck like that by marching off. If I had been busy I might have asked her for her phone number. As it was, I merely cocked my head at her.

"Typical," I said. "Invade a man's privacy and then put the burden on him. Let's see. Surely we can kill time together somehow. Are you any good at pool?"

"*Poule?* The chicken?"

"No, the game. Balls on a table and you poke them with a stick."

"Oh, the billiards. No."

"How about shoplifting? There's a shop nearby and I need some socks. There's room for a dozen pairs in that pocketbook, and I'll cover the clerk."

She didn't bat an eye. "Wool or cotton?"

"Cotton. No synthetics."

"What colors?"

"Mauve. Pinkish mauve." If I have given the impression that her chin was pointed enough to be objectionable, I exaggerated. "But we ought to plan it properly. For instance, if I have to shoot the clerk, we should separate, you can pick me up later. Let's go around the corner to Martucci's and discuss it."

She approved of that. Walking beside her, I noted that the top of the floppy-brimmed hat was at my ear level. With it off, her hair would have grazed my chin if she had been close enough. At Martucci's the crowd wouldn't be showing for another quarter of an hour, and there was an empty table in a rear corner. She asked for vermouth frappé, which was wholesome, but not very appropriate for a shoplifting moll. I told her so.

"Also," I added, "since I don't know your name, we'll have to give you one. Slickeroo Sal? Too hissy, maybe. Fanny the Finger? That has character."

"Or it could be Flora the Finger," she suggested. "That would be better because my name is Flora. Flora Gallant. Miss Flora Gallant."

"The 'Miss' is fine," I assured her. "I don't mind shooting a clerk, but I would hate to have to shoot a husband. I've heard of someone named Gallant—has a place somewhere in the Fifties. Any relation?"

"Yes," she said, "I'm his sister."

That changed things some. It had been obvious that she was no doxy. Now that she was placed, some of the tang was gone. One of the main drawbacks of marriage is that a man knows exactly who his wife is; there's not a chance that she is going to turn out to be a runaway from a sultan's harem or the Queen of the Fairies. A female friend of mine had told me things about Alec Gallant. He was a dress designer who was crowding two others for top ranking in the world of high fashion. He thumbed his nose at Paris and sneered at Rome and Ireland, and was getting away with it. He had refused to finish three dresses for the Duchess of Harwynd because she postponed flying over from London for fittings. He declined to make anything whatever for a certain famous movie actress because he didn't like the way she handled her hips when she walked. He had been known to charge as little as $800 for an afternoon frock, but it had been for a favorite customer, so he practically gave it away.

I looked at his sister over the rim of my glass as I took a sip, not vermouth, and lowered the glass. "You must come clean with me, Finger. You are Alec Gallant's sister?"

"But yes! I wouldn't try lying to Archie Goodwin. You are too smart."

"Thank you. It's too bad your brother doesn't sell socks; we could pinch them at his place instead of imposing on a stranger. Or maybe he does. Does he sell socks?"

"Good heavens, no!"

"Then that's out. As a matter of fact, I'm getting cold feet. If you're a shopkeeper's sister, you probably have a resistance to shoplifting somewhere in your subconscious, and it might pop up at a vital moment. We'll try something else. Go back to the beginning. Why did you pick me up?"

She fluttered a little hand. "Because I wanted to meet you."

"Why did you want to meet me?"

"Because I wanted you to like me."

"All right, I like you. That's accomplished. Now what?"

She frowned. "You are so blunt. You are angry with me. Did I say something?"

"Not a thing. I still like you, so far. But if you are Miss Flora Gallant you must have followed me all the way from the Churchill for one of two reasons. One would be that the sight of me was too much for you, that you were so enchanted that you lost all control. I reject that because I'm wearing a brown suit, and I get that effect only when I'm wearing a gray one. The other would be that you want something, and I ask you bluntly what it is, so we can dispose of that and then maybe go on from there. Let's have it, Finger."

"You are smart," she said. "You do like me?"

"So far, I do. I could tell better if that hat didn't shade your eyes so much."

She removed the hat, no fussing with it, and put it on a chair, and actually didn't pat around at her hair. "There," she said, "then I'll be blunt too. I want you to help me. I want to see Mr. Nero Wolfe."

I nodded. "I suspected that was it. I don't want to be rude, I am enjoying meeting you, but why didn't you just phone for an appointment?"

"Because I didn't dare. Anyway, I didn't really decide to until I saw you at the Churchill and I thought there was my chance. You see, there are three things. The first thing is that I know he charges very big fees, and I am not so rich. The second thing is that he doesn't like women, so there would be that against me. The third thing is that when people want to hire him, you always look them up and find out all you can about them, and I was afraid my brother would find out that I had gone to him, and my brother mustn't know about it. So the only way was to get you to help me, because you can make Mr. Wolfe do anything you want him to. Of course, now I've spoiled it."

"Spoiled it how?"

"By letting you pull it out of me. I was going to get friendly with you first. I know you like to dance, and I am not too bad at dancing. I would be all right with you—I know, because I saw you at the Flamingo. I thought I would have one advantage: being French I would be different from all your American girls; I know you have thousands of them. I thought in a week or two you might like me well enough so I could ask you to help me. Now I have spoiled it." She picked up her glass and drank.

I waited until she had put her glass down. "A couple of corrections. I haven't got thousands of American girls, only three or four hundred. I can't make Mr. Wolfe do anything I want him to; it all depends. And a couple of questions? What you want him to do—does it involve any marital problems? Your brother's wife or someone else's wife that he's friendly with?"

"No. My brother isn't married."

"Good. For Mr. Wolfe that would be out. You say you're not so rich. Could you pay anything at all? Could you scrape up a few hundred without hocking that stole?"

"Yes. Oh, yes. I am not a *pauvre*—pardon—a pauper. But Mr. Wolfe would sneer at a few hundred."

"That would be his impulse, but impulses can be sidetracked, with luck. I suggest that you proceed with your plan as outlined." I looked at my wrist. "It's going on six o'clock. For the Flamingo we would have to go home and dress, and that's too much trouble, but there's nothing wrong with the band at Colonna's in the Village. We can stick here for an hour or so and get acquainted, and you can give me some idea of what your problem is, and you can go right ahead with your program, getting me to like you enough to want to help you. Then we can to to Colonna's and eat and dance. Well?"

"That's all right," she conceded, "but I ought to go home and change. I would look better and dance better."

I objected. "That can come later. We'll start at the bottom and work up. If you dress, I'll have to, too, and I'd rather not. As you probably know, I live in Mr. Wolfe's house, and he might want to discuss something with me. He often does. I would rather phone and tell him I have a personal matter to attend to and won't be home for dinner. You passed the buck. You said I'm the man and it's for me to say."

"Well, I would have to phone too."

"We can afford it." I got a dime from a pocket and proffered it.

At ten-thirty the next morning, Tuesday, I was in the office on the first floor of the old brownstone on West 35th Street which is owned and dominated by Nero Wolfe, when I remembered something I had forgotten to do. Closing the file drawer I was working on, I went to the hall, turned left, and entered the kitchen, where Fritz Brenner, chef and housekeeper, was stirring something in a bowl.

I spoke. "I meant to ask, Fritz: What did Mr. Wolfe have for breakfast?"

His pink, good-natured face turned to me, but he didn't stop stirring. "Why? Something wrong?"

"Of course not. Nothing is ever wrong. I'm going to jostle him and it will help to know what mood he's in."

"A good one. He was very cheerful when I went up for the tray, which was empty. He had melon, eggs à la Suisse with oatmeal cakes and croissants with blackberry jam. He didn't put cream in his coffee, which is always a good sign. Do you have to jostle him?"

I said it was for his own good—that is, Wolfe's—

and headed for the stairs. There is an elevator, but I seldom bother to use it. One flight up was Wolfe's room, and a spare, used mostly for storage. Two flights up was my room, and one for guests, not used much. Mounting the third flight, I passed through the vestibule to the door to the plant rooms, opened it and entered.

By then, after the years, you might think those ten thousand orchids would no longer impress me, but they did. In the tropical room I took the side aisle for a look at the pink Vanda that Wolfe had been offered six grand for, and in the intermediate room I slowed down as I passed a bench of my favorites, Miltonia hybrids. Then on through to the potting room.

The little guy with a pug nose, opening a bale of osmundine over by the wall, was Theodore Horstmann, orchid nurse. The one standing at the big bench, inspecting a seed pod, was my employer.

"Good morning," I said brightly. "Fred phoned in at ten-fourteen. Putz is at his office, probably reading the morning mail. I told Fred to stay on him."

"Well?"

I'll translate it. What that "well" meant was, "You know better than to interrupt me here for that, so what is it?"

Having translated it, I replied to it, "I was straightening up a file when I suddenly realized that I hadn't told you that there's an appointment for eleven o'clock. A prospective client, someone I ran across yesterday. It might be quite interesting."

"Who is it?"

"I admit it's a woman. Her name is Flora Gallant; she's the sister of a man named Alec Gallant, who makes dresses for duchesses that dukes pay a thousand bucks for. She could get things for your wife wholesale if you had a wife."

He put the seed pod down. "Archie."

"Yes, sir."

"You are being transparent deliberately. You did not suddenly realize that you hadn't told me. You willfully delayed telling me until it is too late to notify her not to come. How old is she?"

"Oh, middle twenties."

"Of course. Ill-favored? Ill-shaped? Ungainly?"

"No, not exactly."

"She wouldn't be if you ran across her. What does she want?"

"It's a little vague. I'd rather she told you."

He snorted. "One of your functions is to learn what people want. You are trying to dragoon me. I won't see her. I'll come down later. Let me know when she has gone."

"Yes, sir." I was apologetic, "You're absolutely right. You'd probably be wasting your time. But when I was dancing with her last evening I must have got sentimental, because I told her I would help her with her problem. So I'm stuck. I'll have to tackle it myself. I'll have to take a leave of absence without pay, starting now. Say a couple of weeks, that should do it. We have nothing important on, and of course Fred can attend to Putz, and if you—"

"Archie, this is beyond tolerance. This is egregious."

"I know it is, but I'm stuck. If I were you I'd fire me. It may take—"

The house phone buzzed. He didn't move, so I went and got it. After listening to Fritz, I told him to hold on, and turned: "She's at the door. If she comes in, it will disrupt your schedule, so I'd better go down and take her somewhere. I'll—"

"Confound you," he growled. "I'll be down shortly."

I told Fritz to put her in the office and I would be right down, hung up and went. On my way through the intermediate room I cut off a raceme of Miltonia and took it along. Orchids are good for girls, whether they have problems or not. At the bottom of the stairs, Fritz was posted on guard, awaiting me. He is by no means a woman hater, but he suspects every female who enters the house of having designs on his kitchen and therefore needing to be watched. I told him O.K., I'd see to her, and crossed to the office.

She was in the red leather chair facing the end of Wolfe's desk. I told her good morning, went and got a pin from my desk tray and returned to her.

"Here," I said, handing her the raceme and pin. "I see why you asked me what his favorite color is. He'll like that dress if he's not too grouchy to notice it."

"Then he'll see me?"

"Yeah, he'll see you, any minute now. I had to back him into a corner and stick a spear in him. I doubt if I like you that much, but my honor was at stake, and I—well, if you insist—"

She was on her feet, putting her palms on my cheeks and giving me an emphatic kiss.

Since it was in the office and during hours, I merely accepted it.

"You should have another one," she said, sitting again, "for the orchids. They're lovely."

I told her to save it for a better occasion. "And," I added, "don't try it on Mr. Wolfe. He might bite you." The sound of the elevator, creaking under his seventh of a ton, came from the hall. "Here he comes. Don't offer him a hand. He doesn't like to shake hands even with men, let alone women."

There was the sound of the elevator door opening, and footsteps, and he entered. He thinks he believes in civility, so he stopped in front of her, told her good morning, and then proceeded to the over-sized, custom-made chair behind his desk.

"Your name is Flora Gallant?" he growled. The growl implied that he strongly doubted it and wouldn't be surprised if she had no name at all.

She smiled at him. I should have warned her to go slow on smiles. "Yes, Mr. Wolfe. I suppose Mr. Goodwin has told you who I am. I know I'm being nervy to expect you to take any time for my troubles—a man as busy and important as you are—but, you see, it's not for myself. I'm not anybody, but you know who my brother is? My brother Alec?"

"Yes. Mr. Goodwin has informed me. An illustrious dressmaker."

"He is not merely a dressmaker. He is an artist—a great artist." She wasn't arguing, just stating a fact. "The trouble is about him, and that's why I must be careful with it. That's why I came to you—not only that you are a great detective—the very greatest, of course; everybody knows that—but also that you are a gentleman. So I know you are worthy of confidence."

She stopped, apparently for acknowledgment. Wolfe obliged her: "Umph." I was thinking that I might also have warned her not to spread the butter too thick.

She resumed, "So it is understood I am trusting you?"

"You may," he growled.

She hesitated, seeming to consider if that point was properly covered, and decided that it was. "Then I'll tell you. I must explain that in France, where my brother and I were born and brought up, our name was not 'Gallant.' What it was doesn't matter. I have been in this country only four years. Alec came here in 1946, more than a year after the war ended. He had changed his name to Gallant and entered legally under that name. Within five years he had made a reputation as a designer, and then—I don't suppose you remember his fall collection in 1953?"

Wolfe merely grunted.

She fluttered a little hand. "But of course you are not married, and feeling as you do about women—" She let that hang. "Anyway, that collection showed everybody what my brother was—a creator, a true creator. He got financial backing, more than he needed, and opened his place on Fifty-fourth Street. That was when he sent for me to come to America, and I was glad to. From 1953 on, it has been all a triumph—many triumphs. Of course I have not had any hand in them, but I have been with him and have tried to help in my little way. The glory of great success has been my brother's, but then, he can't do everything in an affair so big as that. You understand?"

"No one can do everything," Wolfe conceded.

She nodded. "Even you, you have Mr. Goodwin. My brother has Carl Drew, and Anita Prince, and Emmy Thorne—and me, if I count. But now trouble has come. The trouble is a woman—a woman named Bianca Voss."

Wolfe made a face. She saw it and responded to it. "No, not an *affaire d'amour*, I'm sure of that. Though my brother has never married, I am certain this Bianca Voss has not attracted him that way. She first came there a little more than a year ago. My brother had told us to expect her, but we don't know where he had met her or where she came from. He designed a dress and a suit for her, and they were made there in the shop, but no bill was ever sent her. Then he gave her one of the rooms, the offices, on the third floor, and she started to come every day, and soon the trouble began. My brother never told us she had any authority, but she took it and he allowed her to. Sometimes she interferes directly, and sometimes through him. She pokes her nose into everything. She got my brother to discharge a fitter, a very capable woman, who had been with him for years. She has a private telephone line in her office upstairs, but no one else has. About two months ago some of the others persuaded me to try to find out about her, what her standing is, and I asked my brother, but he wouldn't tell me. I begged him to, but he wouldn't."

"It sounds," Wolfe said, "as if she owns the business. Perhaps she bought it."

Flora shook her head. "No, she hasn't. I'm sure she hasn't. She wasn't one of the financial backers in 1953, and since then there have been good profits, and anyway, my brother has control. But now she's going to cheapen it and spoil it, and he's going to let her, we don't know why. She wants him to design a factory line to be promoted by a chain of department stores using his name. She wants him to sponsor a line of Alec Gallant cosmetics on a royalty basis. And other things. We're against all of them, and my brother is, too, really, but we think he's going to give in to her, and that will ruin it."

She stopped to swallow. "Mr. Wolfe, I want you to ruin her."

He grunted. "By wiggling a finger?"

"No, but you can. I'm sure you can. I'm sure she has some hold on him, but I don't know what. I don't know who she is or where she came from. I don't know if Bianca Voss is her real name. She speaks with an accent, and it may be French, but if it is, it's from some part of France I don't know; I'm not sure what it is. I don't know when she came to America; she may be here illegally. She may have known my brother in France during the war; I was young then. You can find out. If she has a hold on my brother, you can find out what it is. If she is blackmailing him, isn't that against the law? Wouldn't that ruin her?"

"It might. It might ruin him too."

"Not unless you betrayed him." She gave a little gasp and added hastily, "I don't mean that, I only mean I am trusting you, you said I could, and you could make her stop, and that's all you would have to do. Couldn't you do just that?"

"Conceivably." Wolfe wasn't enthusiastic. "I fear, madam, that you're biting off more than you can chew. The procedure you suggest would be prolonged, laborious, and extremely expensive. It would probably require elaborate investigation abroad. Aside from my fee, which would not be modest, the outlay would be considerable and the outcome highly uncertain. Are you in a position to undertake it?"

"I am not rich myself, Mr. Wolfe. I have some savings. But my brother—if you get her away, if you release him from her—he is truly *généreux*—pardon—he is a generous man. He is not stingy."

"But he isn't hiring me, and your assumption that she is coercing him may be groundless." Wolfe shook his head. "No. Not a reasonable venture. Unless, of course, your brother himself consults me. If you care to bring him? Or send him?"

"Oh, I couldn't!" She waved it away. "You must see that isn't possible! When I asked him about her, I told you, he wouldn't tell me anything. He was annoyed. He is never abrupt with me, but he was then. I assure you, Mr. Wolfe, she is a villain. You are *sagace*—pardon—you are an acute man. You would know it if you saw her, spoke with her."

"Perhaps," Wolfe was losing patience. "Even so, my perception of her villainy wouldn't avail. No, madam."

"But you would know I am right." She opened her bag, fingered in it with both hands, came out with something, left her chair to step to Wolfe's desk, and put the something on the desk pad in front of him.

"There," she said, "that is three hundred dollars. For you that is nothing, but it shows how I am in earnest." She returned to the chair. "I know you never leave your home on business, you wouldn't go there, and I can't ask her to come here so you can speak with her, she would merely laugh at me, but you can. You can tell her you have been asked in confidence to discuss a matter with her and ask her to come to see you. You will not tell her what it is. She will come—she will be afraid not to—and that alone will show you she has a secret, perhaps many secrets. Then, when she comes, you will ask her whatever occurs to you. For that you do not need my suggestions. You are *sagace*."

"Pfui," Wolfe shook his head. "Everybody has secrets; not necessarily guilty ones."

"Yes," she agreed, "but not secrets that would make them afraid not to come to see Nero Wolfe. When she comes and you have spoken with her, we shall see. That may be all or it may not. We shall see."

I do not say that the three hundred bucks there on his desk was no factor. Even though income tax would take two thirds of it, there would be enough left for three weeks' supply of beer or for two days' salary for me. Another factor was plain curiosity: would Bianca Voss come or wouldn't she? Another was the chance that it might develop into a decent fee. Still another was her saying "We shall see" instead of "We'll see" or "We will see." He will always stretch a point, within reason, for people who use words as he thinks they should be used. But all of those together might not have swung him if he hadn't known that if he turned her down, and she went, I was pigheaded enough to go with her on leave of absence.

So he muttered at her, "Where is she?"

"At my brother's place. She always is."

"Give Mr. Goodwin the phone number."

"I'll get it. She may be downstairs." She got up and started for the phone on Wolfe's desk, but I told her to use mine and left my chair, and she came and sat, lifted the receiver, and dialed. In a moment she spoke. "Doris? Flora. Is Miss Voss around? . . . Oh. I thought she might have come down. . . . No, don't bother; I'll ring her private line."

She pushed the button down, told us, "She's up in her office," waited a moment, released the button, and dialed again. When she spoke, it was with another voice, as she barely moved her lips and brought it out through her nose, "Miss Bianca Voss? Hold the line, please. Mr. Nero Wolfe wishes to speak with you. . . . Nero Wolfe, the private detective."

She looked at Wolfe and he got at his phone. Having my own share of curiosity, I extended a hand for my receiver, and she let me take it and left my chair. As I got it to my ear Wolfe was speaking.

"This is Nero Wolfe. Is this Miss Bianca Voss?"

"Yes." It was more like "Yiss." "What do you want?" The "wh" and the "w" were way off.

"If my name is unknown to you, I should explain—"

"I know your name. What do you want?"

"I wish to invite you to call on me at my office. I have been asked to discuss certain matters with you, and—"

"Who asked you?"

"I am not at liberty to say. I shall—"

"What kind of matters?" The *"wh"* was more off.

"If you will let me finish. The matters are personal and confidential and concern you closely. That's all I can say on the telephone. I assure you that you would be ill-advised—"

A snort stopped him—a snort that might be spelled "Tzchaahh!" Followed by: "I know your name, yes! You are scum, I know, in your stinking sewer! Your slimy little ego in your big gob of fat! And you dare to—owul-gghh!"

That's the best I can do at reporting it. It was part scream, part groan, and part just noise. It was followed immediately by another noise, a mixture of crash and clatter, then others, faint rustlings, and then nothing.

I spoke to my transmitter: "Hello, hello, hello. Hello! Hello?"

I cradled it, and so did Wolfe. Flora Gallant was asking. "What is it? She hung up?" We ignored her. Wolfe said, "Archie? You heard."

"Yes, sir. So did you. If you want a guess, something hit her and she dragged the phone along as she went down and it struck the floor. The other noises, not even a guess, except that at the end she put the receiver back on and cut the connection or someone else did. It could be—"

Flora had grabbed my sleeve with both hands and was demanding. "What is it? What happened?"

I put a hand on her shoulder and made it emphatic: "I don't know what happened. There was a collection of sounds. You heard what I told Mr. Wolfe. Apparently something fell on her and then hung up the phone."

"But it couldn't! It is not possible!"

"That's what it sounded like. What's the number? The one downstairs."

She just gawked at me. I looked at Wolfe and he gave me a nod, and I jerked my arm loose, sat at my desk, got the Manhattan book, flipped to the G's and got the number, PL2–0330, and dialed it.

A refined female voice came, "Alec Gallant, Incorporated."

"This is a friend of Miss Voss," I told her. "I was just speaking to her on the phone, on her private line, and from the sounds I got, I think something may have happened to her. Will you send someone up to see? Right away. I'll hold the wire."

"Who is this speaking, please?"

"Never mind that. Step on it. She may be hurt."

I heard her calling to someone: then apparently she covered the transmitter. I sat and waited. Wolfe sat and scowled at me. Flora stood for some minutes at my elbow, staring down at me, then turned and went to the red leather chair and lowered herself onto its edge. I looked at my wristwatch: 11:40. It had said 11:31 when the connection with Bianca Voss had been cut.

More waiting, and then a male voice came: "Hello?"

"This is Carl Drew. What is your name please?"

"My name is Watson—John H. Watson. Is Miss Voss all right?"

"May I have your address, Mr. Watson?"

"Miss Voss knows my address. Is she all right?"

"I must have your address, Mr. Watson. I must insist. You will understand the necessity when I tell you that Miss Voss is dead. She was assaulted in her office and is dead. Apparently, from what you said, the assault came while she was on the phone with you, and I want your address. I must insist."

"Who assaulted her?"

"I don't know. Damn it, how do I know? I must—"

I hung up, gently not to be rude, swiveled and asked Flora, "Who is Carl Drew?"

"My brother's business manager. What happened?"

I looked at Wolfe. "My guess was close. Miss Voss is dead. In her office. He said she was assaulted, but he didn't say with what or by whom."

He glowered at me, then turned to let her have it. She was coming up from the chair, slow and stiff. When she was erect, she said, "No. No! It isn't possible!"

"I'm only quoting Carl Drew," I told her.

"But it's crazy! He said she is dead? Bianca Voss?"

"Distinctly." She looked as if she might be needing a prop, and I stood up.

"But how—" She let it hang. She repeated, "But how—" stopped again, turned, and was going.

When Wolfe called to her, "Here, Miss Gallant, your money!" she paid no attention, but kept on, and he poked it at me, and I took it and headed for the hall.

I caught up with her halfway to the front door, but when I offered it, she just kept going so I blocked her off, took her bag, opened it, dropped the bills in, closed it and handed it back.

I spoke. "Easy does it, Finger. Take a breath. Going without your stole?"

"Oh." She swallowed. "Where is it?" I got it for her.

"In my opinion," I said, "you need a little chivalry. I'll come and get you in a taxi."

She shook her head. "I'm all right."

"You are not. You'll get run over."

"No, I won't. Don't come. Just let me . . . please."

She meant it, so I stepped to the door and pulled it open, and she crossed the sill. I stood there and watched, thinking she might stumble going down the steps of the stoop, but she made it to the sidewalk and turned west toward Tenth Avenue. Evidently she wasn't completely paralyzed, since Tenth was one-way uptown.

There are alternative explanations for the fact that I did not choose to return immediately to the office. One would be that I was afraid to face the music—not the way to put it, since the sounds that come from Wolfe when he is good and sore are not musical. The other would be that purely out of consideration for him I decided he would rather be alone for a while. I prefer the latter. Anyway, I made for the stairs, but I was only halfway up the first flight when his bellow came, "Archie! Come here!"

I about-faced, descended, crossed the hall and stood on the threshold. "Yes, sir? I was going up to my room to see if I left the faucet dripping."

"Let it drip. Sit down."

I went to my chair and sat down. "Too bad," I said regretfully. "Three hundred dollars may be hay, but—"

"Shut up."

I lifted my shoulders half an inch and dropped them. He leaned back comfortably and eyed me.

"I must compliment you," he said, "on the ingenuity of your stratagem. Getting me with you on the phone, so that I could corroborate your claim that both you and Miss Gallant were here in my office at the moment the murder was committed was well conceived and admirably executed. But I fear it was more impetuous than prudent. You are probably in mortal jeopardy, and I confess I shall be seriously inconvenienced if I lose your services, even though you get only a long term in prison. So I would like to help, if I can. It will be obvious, even to a slower wit than Mr. Cramer's, that you and Miss Gallant arranged for the attack to occur on schedule, precisely at the moment that Miss Voss was speaking to me on the phone; and therefore, patently, that you were in collusion with the attacker. So our problem is not how to fend suspicion from you, but whether you can wriggle out of it, and if so how. No doubt you have considered it?"

"Yeah. Sure."

"And?"

"I think it's hopeless. I'm in for it. Not a prison term; I'll get six thousand volts. I know it will inconvenience you, but it will inconvenience me too. I regret it very much because it has been a rare experience working for you." I uncrossed my legs. "Look. Naturally,

you are boiling. I let her come here, yes. I—uh—
persuaded you to see her, yes. If you're in a tantrum,
O.K., go ahead and tantrum and get it over with."

"I am not in a tantrum and 'tantrum' is not a verb."

"Then I take it back. Apparently it's worse than a
tantrum, since instead of ragging me, you burlesque it.
Can't you just tell me what you think of me?"

"No. It's not in my vocabulary. You realize what
we are in for?"

"Certainly. If it was murder, and evidently it was,
Flora Gallant will tell them where she was and what
happened. Then we will have visitors, and not only
that, but if and when someone is nominated for it and
put on trial, we will be star witnesses because we heard
it happen. Not eyewitnesses, earwitnesses. We can time
it right to the minute. You will sit for hours on a hard
wooden bench in a courtroom, with no client and no fee
in sight. I know how you feel and I don't blame you. Go
ahead and tell me what you think of me."

"You admit you are answerable?"

"No. I was unlucky."

"That doesn't absolve you. A man is as responsible
for his luck as for his judgment. How long have you
known that woman?"

"Nineteen hours. She picked me up on Thirty-
eighth Street at five o'clock yesterday afternoon."

"Picked you up?"

"Yes. I thought she was tailing Putz, but she said
she was after me. That gave me a sense of well-being
and stimulated my manhood. I took her to a bar and
bought her a drink—she took vermouth—and it came
out that it was you she was really after. Thinking there
might be a fee in it, I took her to a place and fed her
and danced with her. If it had led to a fee, that would
have gone on my expense account, but now I don't
suppose—"

"No."

"Very well. She didn't tell me the whole story, but enough so it seemed possible it was worth half an hour of your time, and I told her to come at eleven this morning."

"How long were you out?"

"Until midnight. Altogether, seven hours."

"Did you take her home?"

"No. She was against it. I put her in a taxi."

"Did she phone you this morning before she came?"

"No."

"How did she come? In a cab?"

"I don't know. Fritz may know; he let her in."

"She probably did." His lips tightened. He released them. "Cabs and cars have thousands of accidents every day. Why couldn't hers have been one of them?" He came forward in the chair and rang for beer. "Confound it. It will save time and harassment if we have a report ready. You will type one. Your meeting with her yesterday, your conversation with her, and what occurred here today, including everything that was said. We will both sign it."

"Not everything that was said last evening."

"No, I suppose not. You said you got sentimental. What I sign I read, and I certainly wouldn't read that."

I swiveled and pulled the typewriter around and got out paper and carbons. Reports, especially when they are to be signed statements, have to be in triplicate.

That kept me busy the rest of the day, with an hour out for lunch and various interruptions, mostly phone calls, including one from Lon Cohen, of the *Gazette*, to ask for the low-down on the murder of Bianca Voss. I wondered why the cops had been so free and fast about Flora Gallant's call on Nero Wolfe, but that wasn't it: one of the *Gazette*'s journalists had seen me at Colonna's with her, and Lon is one of a slew of people who have the idea that whenever I am seen anywhere near anybody who is anyhow connected with a death by violence, Nero Wolfe is looming. I told him our only interest in the Voss murder was not to get involved in it, which was no lie.

Over the years I have reported hundreds of long conversations to Wolfe, verbatim, some after a week or more had passed, and that typing job was no strain on my memory, but I took my time because I had to be darned sure of it, since he was going to sign it. Also he was going to read it, and in his present mood he would be delighted to tell me that he had not said "prolonged, difficult, and extremely expensive." He had said "prolonged, laborious, and extremely expensive." And I would have to retype a whole page.

So I took my time, and was on the last paragraph when he came down to the office from his afternoon session in the plant rooms, which is from four to six. When he had got settled at his desk I gave him the first five pages and he started reading. Back at the typewriter, I shot a glance at him now and then, and saw that his frown was merely normal. Finished, I took him the remainder, returned to my desk to arrange the carbons, and then got up to shake down my pants legs and stretch.

He is a fast reader. When he got to the end he cleared his throat. "One thing. Did I say 'not necessarily guilty ones'? Didn't I say 'not always guilty ones'?"

"No, sir. As you know, you like the word 'necessarily.' You like the way you say it. You may remember—"

The doorbell rang. I went to the hall, flipped the switch of the stoop light, and took a look through the one-way glass panel of the front door. It wasn't necessary to go closer to recognize Inspector Cramer, of Homicide.

II

I stepped into the office and told Wolfe, "Him." He compressed his lips and took in air through his nose.

"I see you've signed the statement," I said. "Shall I open the door a crack and slip it through to him and tell him that covers it and give him your regards?"

"No. A crack is open both ways. If he has a warrant for you, he could slip that through to you. Let him in."

I wheeled, walked to the front door, swung it wide, and made it hearty, "Just the man we wanted to see, Inspector Cramer! Do come in."

He was already in. By the time I had shut the door and turned around he had shed his hat and coat and dropped them on a chair, and by the time I had put the hat on the shelf where he knew darned well it belonged, and the coat on a hanger, and got to the office, he was already in the red leather chair and talking.

". . . and don't tell me you didn't know a crime had been committed or any of that tripe, and you had firsthand knowledge of it, both you and Goodwin, and do you come forward with it? No. You sit here at your desk and to hell with the law and the city of New York and your obligations as a citizen and a licensed private detective, and you—"

Wolfe had his eyes closed. I, back at my desk, had mine open. I always enjoy seeing Inspector Cramer worked up. He is big and brawny to start with, and then he seems to be expanding all over, and his round red face gets gradually redder, bringing out its contrast with his gray hair.

When he stopped for breath, Wolfe opened his eyes. "I assure you, Mr. Cramer, this is uncalled for. Mr. Goodwin has indeed been sitting here, but not idly. He has been fulfilling our obligations, his and mine, as citizens and licensed private detectives." He lifted sheets of paper. "This is a statement, signed by both of us. After you have read it, we'll answer questions if they're relevant."

Cramer didn't move, and Wolfe wouldn't, so I arose and got the statement and took it to Cramer. He snatched it from me, no thanks, glared at Wolfe, glanced at the heading on the first page, glared at me as I sat, and started to read. First he skimmed through it, and then went back and really read it. Wolfe was leaning back with his eyes closed. I passed the time taking in the changes of expression on Cramer's face. When he reached the end he turned back to one of the earlier pages for another look, and then aimed his sharp gray eyes at Wolfe.

"So you had it ready," he said, not with gratitude.

Wolfe opened his eyes and nodded. "I thought it would save time and trouble."

"Yeah. You're always thoughtful. I admit it agrees pretty well with Flora Gallant's story, but why shouldn't it? Is she your client?"

"Pfui. That statement makes it quite clear that I have no client."

"It does if it's all here. Did you leave anything out?"

"Yes. Much of Mr. Goodwin's conversation with Miss Gallant last evening. Nothing pertinent."

"Well, we'll want to study it. Of course some details are vitally important—for instance, that it was exactly eleven-thirty-one when you heard the blow."

Wolfe objected. "We heard no blow, identifiably. The statement does not say that we heard a blow."

Cramer found the place on page 9 and consulted it. "O.K. You heard a groan and a crash and rustles. But there was a blow. She was hit in the back of the head with a chunk of marble, a paperweight, and then a scarf was tied around her throat to stop her breathing. You say here at eleven-thirty-one."

I corrected him. "Not when we heard the groan. After that there were the other noises, then the connection went, and I said hello a few times, which was human but dumb. It was when I hung up that I looked at my watch and saw eleven-thirty-one. The groan had been maybe a minute earlier, say eleven-thirty. If a minute is important."

"It isn't. But you didn't hear the blow?"

"Not to recognize it as a blow, no."

He went back to the statement, frowning at it, reading parts of some pages and just glancing at others. He looked up at Wolfe. "I know how good you are at arranging words. This implies that Flora Gallant was a complete stranger to you, that you had never had anything to do with her or her brother or any of the people at that place, but it doesn't say so in so many words. I'd like to know."

"The implication is valid," Wolfe told him. "Except as related in that statement, I have never had any association with Miss Gallant or her brother or, to my knowledge, with any of their colleagues. Nor has Mr. Goodwin. . . . Archie?"

"Right," I agreed.

"I'll accept that for now." Cramer folded the statement and put it in his pocket. "Then you had never heard Bianca Voss' voice before and you couldn't recognize it on the phone?"

"Of course not."

"And you can't hear it now, since she's dead. So you can't swear it was her talking to you."

"Obviously."

"And that raises a point. If it was her talking to you, she was killed at exactly half past eleven. Now there are four important people in the organization who had it in for Bianca Voss. They have admitted it. Besides Flora Gallant, there is Anita Prince, fitter and designer, been with Gallant eight years; Emmy Thorne in charge of contacts and promotion, been with him four years; and Carl Drew, business manager, been with him five years. None of them killed Bianca Voss at half past eleven. From eleven-fifteen on, until the call came from Goodwin calling himself John H. Watson, Carl Drew was down on the main floor, constantly in view of four people, two of them customers. From eleven o'clock on, Anita Prince was on the top floor, the workshop, with Alec Gallant and two models and a dozen employees. At eleven-twenty Emmy Thorne called on a man by appointment at his office on Forty-sixth Street, and was with him and two other men until a quarter to twelve. And Flora Gallant was here with you. All airtight."

"Very neat," Wolfe agreed.

"Too damn neat. Of course there may be others who wanted Bianca Voss out of the way, but as it stands now, those four are out in front. And they're all—"

"Why not five? Alec Gallant himself?"

"All right, make it five. They're all in the clear, including him, if she was killed at eleven-thirty. So suppose she wasn't. Suppose she was killed earlier—half an hour or so earlier. Suppose when Flora Gallant phoned her from here and put you on to talk with her, it wasn't her at all, it was someone else imitating her voice, and she pulled that stunt, the groan and the other noises, to make you think you had heard the murder at that time."

Wolfe's brows were up. "With the corpse there on the floor?"

"Certainly."

"Then you're not much better off. Who did the impersonation? Their alibis still hold for eleven-thirty."

"I realize that. But there were nineteen women around there altogether, and a woman who wouldn't commit a murder might be willing to help cover up after someone else had committed it. You know that."

Wolfe wasn't impressed. "It's very tricky, Mr. Cramer. If you are supposing Flora Gallant killed her, it was elaborately planned. It wasn't until late last evening that Miss Gallant persuaded Mr. Goodwin to make an appointment for her here for eleven this morning. Did she kill Miss Voss, station someone there beside the corpse to answer the phone, rush down here and maneuver me into ringing Miss Voss' number? It seems a little farfetched."

"I didn't say it was Flora Gallant." Cramer hung on. "It could have been any of them. He or she didn't have to know she was going to come to see you and get you to ring that number. His plan might have been to ring it himself, before witnesses, to establish the time of the murder, and when your call came, whoever it was there by the phone got rattled and went ahead with the act. There are a dozen different ways it could have happened. Hell, I know it's tricky. I'm not asking you to work your brain on it. You must know why I brought it up."

Wolfe nodded. "Yes, I think I do. You want me to consider what I heard—and Mr. Goodwin. You want to know if we are satisfied that those sounds were authentic. You want to know if we will concede that they might have been bogus."

"That's it. Exactly."

Wolfe rubbed his nose with a knuckle, closing his eyes. In a moment he opened them. "I'm afraid I can't help you, Mr. Cramer. If they were bogus, they were well executed. At the time, hearing them, I had no suspicion that it was flummery. Naturally, as soon as I learned that they served to fix the precise moment of a murder, I knew they would be open to question, but I can't challenge them intrinsically. . . . . Archie?"

I shook my head. "I pass." To Cramer: "You've read the statement, so you know that right after I heard it my guess was that something hit her and she dragged the phone along as she went down and it struck the floor. I'm not going to go back on my guess now. As for our not hearing the blow, read the statement. It says that it started out as if it was going to be a scream, but then it was a groan. She might have seen the blow coming and was going to scream, but it landed and turned the scream into a groan, and in that case we wouldn't hear the blow. A chunk of marble hitting a skull wouldn't make much noise. As for supposing she was killed half an hour or so earlier, I phoned within three minutes, or John H. Watson did, and in another six or seven minutes Carl Drew was talking to me, so he must have seen the body, or someone did, not more than five minutes after we heard the groan. Was she twitching?"

"According to Drew, no. You don't twitch long with a scarf as tight as that around your throat."

"What about the medical examiner?"

"He got there at two minutes after twelve. With blood he might have timed it pretty close, but there wasn't any. That's out."

"What about the setup? Someone left that room quick after we heard the sounds. If it was the murderer, he or she had to cradle the phone and tie the scarf, but that wouldn't take long. If it was a fill-in, as you want to suppose, all she had to do was cradle the phone. Whichever it was, wasn't there anyone else around?"

"If there was they're keeping it to themselves. So far. As you know, Bianca Voss wasn't popular around there. Anyway, that place is a mess, with three different elevators—one in the store, one at the back for service and deliveries, and one in an outside hall with a separate entrance so they can go up to the offices without going through the store."

"That makes it nice. Then it's wide open."

"As wide as a barn door." Cramer stood up. To Wolfe: "So that's the best you can do. You thought the sounds were open to question."

"Not intrinsically. Circumstantially, of course."

"You know a lot of long words, don't you? After we study this statement we may have some questions." He was going. After two steps he turned. "I don't like gags about homicide, murder is no joke, but I can mention that if it was Bianca Voss you had on the phone, she had you wrong. Scum. Stinking sewer. That's too strong. That's a little too strong." He headed out.

When I returned to the office from going to hold his coat for him, which he didn't deserve after his parting crack, Wolfe had turned his chair to reading position and was opening a book.

Crossing to my desk to get the carbons of the statement for filing, I remarked, "That would help, if he can prove that what we heard was a phony. You might not have to sit on a hard bench in a courthouse, after all."

"He won't. No such luck." He looked at me. "Archie."

"Yes, sir."

"Am I a dolt?"

"No. That would be a little too strong."

"Then I will not be taken for one."

"That sounds as if you're contemplating something. Can I be of any help?"

"At the moment, no."

"Any instructions for this evening?"

"No."

He went to his book and I went to the cabinet with the carbons.

The next morning, Wednesday, eating breakfast in the kitchen with the paper propped up in front of me—which is routine, of course—I read the account of the Bianca Voss murder. There were various details that were news to me, but nothing startling or even helpful. It included the phone call from John H. Watson, but didn't add that he had been identified as Archie Goodwin, and there was no mention of Nero Wolfe. I admit that the cops and the D.A. have a right to save something for themselves, but it never hurts to have your name in the paper, and I had a notion to phone Lon Cohen at the *Gazette* and give him an exclusive. However, I would have to mention it to Wolfe first, so it would have to wait until eleven o'clock. He eats breakfast in his room from a tray delivered by Fritz, and doesn't come down to the office until after his morning session with the orchids.

As a matter of fact, another item in the paper meant more to me personally. Sarah Yare had committed suicide. Her body had been found Tuesday evening in her little walk-up apartment on East Thirteenth Street. I have never written a fan letter to an actress, but I had been tempted to a couple of years back when I had seen Sarah Yare in *Thumb a Ride*. The first time I saw it I had a companion, but the next three times I was alone. The reason for repeating was that I had the impression I was infatuated and I wanted to wear it down, but when the impression still stuck after three tries, I gave up. Actresses should be seen and heard from no closer than the fifth row, and not touched. At that, I might have given the impression another test in a year or two if there had been an opportunity, but there wasn't. She quit *Thumb a Ride* abruptly some months later, and the talk was that she was an alco and done for.

So I read that item twice. It didn't say that it had been pronounced suicide officially and finally, since she had left no note, but a nearly empty bourbon bottle had been there on a table, and on the floor by the couch she had died on there had been a glass with enough left in it to identify the cyanide. The picture of her was as she had been formerly when I had got my impression that I was infatuated. I asked Fritz if he had ever seen Sarah Yare, and he asked what movies she had been in, and I said none, that she was much too good for a movie.

I didn't get to suggest phoning Lon Cohen to Wolfe because when he came down to the office at eleven o'clock, I wasn't there. As I was finishing my second cup of coffee a phone call came from the district attorney's office inviting me to drop in for a chat, and I went, and spent a couple of hours at Leonard Street with an assistant D.A. named Brill. When we got through, I knew slightly more than I had when we started, but he didn't. He had a copy of our statement on his desk, and what could I add to that? He had a lot of fun, though. He would pop a question at me and then spend nine minutes studying the statement to see if I had tripped.

Getting home a little before noon, I was prepared to find Wolfe having a fresh attack of grump. He likes me to be there when he comes down from the plant rooms to the office, and while he can't very well complain when the D.A. calls me on business that concerns us, this wasn't our affair. We had no client and no case and no fee in prospect. But I got a surprise. Instead of being grumpy, he was busy, with the phone book open before him on his desk. He had actually gone clear around to my desk, stooped to get the book, lifted it and carried it back to his chair. Unheard of.

"Good morning," I said. "What's the emergency?"

"No emergency. I needed to know a number."

"Did you find it?"

"Yes."

I sat. He wants you at his level because it's too much trouble to tilt his head back. "Nothing new," I said, "at the D.A.'s office. Do you want a report?"

"No. I have an errand for you. I have formed a conjecture that I think is worth testing. You will go to Alec Gallant's place on Fifty-fourth Street and speak with Mr. Gallant, his sister, Miss Prince, Miss Thorne, and Mr. Drew. Separately if possible. You will tell each of them— You read the paper this morning as usual?"

"Certainly."

"You will tell each of them that I have engaged to make certain inquiries about Miss Sarah Yare, and that I shall be grateful for any information they may be able and willing to furnish. Specifically, I would like to see any communications they may have received from her, say in the past month. Don't raise one brow like that. You know it disconcerts me."

"I've never seen you disconcerted yet." I let the brow down a little. "What's the conjecture?"

"It may be baseless. You don't need it to perform the errand."

"Now?"

"Yes. Without delay."

"If they ask me who engaged you, what do I say?"

"That you don't know. You are merely following instructions."

"If I ask you who engaged you, what do you say?"

"I tell you the truth. No one. Or more accurately, I have engaged myself. I think I may have been hoodwinked and I intend to find out. You may be fishing where there are no fish. They may all say they have never had any association with Sarah Yare, and they may be telling the truth or they may not. You will have that in mind and form your conclusions regarding it. If any of them acknowledge association with her, pursue it enough to learn the degree of intimacy, but don't labor it. That can wait until we bait a hook. You are only to discover if there are any fish."

I stood up. "It may take a while if the cops and the D.A. are working on them, and they probably are. How urgent is it? Do you want progress reports by phone?"

"Not unless you think it necessary. You must get all five of them."

"Right. Don't wait dinner for me." I went.

On the way uptown in the taxi I was exercising my brain. I will not explain at this point why Wolfe wanted to know if any of the subjects had known Sarah Yare and if so, how well, for two reasons: first, you have certainly spotted it yourself; and second, since I am not so smart as you are, I had not yet come up with the answer. Anyway, that was underneath. On top, what I was using my brain for was the phone book. Unquestionably it was connected with his being hoodwinked, since that was what was biting him, and therefore it probably had some bearing on the call that had been made from his office to Bianca Voss, but what could he accomplish by consulting the phone book? For that I had no decent guess, let alone an answer, by the time I paid the hackie at 54th and Fifth Avenue.

Alec Gallant, Incorporated, on the north side of the street near Madison Avenue, was no palace, outside or in. The front was maybe thirty feet, and five feet of that was taken up by the separate entrance to the side hall. The show window, all dark green, had just one exhibit: a couple of yards of plain black fabric—silk or rayon or nylon or cottonon or linenon—draped on a little rack. Inside, nothing whatever was in sight—that is, nothing to buy. The wall-to-wall carpet was the same dark green as the show window. There were mirrors and screens and tables and ash trays, and a dozen or more chairs, not fancy, more to sit in than to look at. I had taken three steps on the carpet when a woman standing with a man by a table left him to come to meet me. I told her my name and told her I would like to see Mr. Gallant.

The man, approaching, spoke, "Mr. Gallant is not available. What do you want?"

That didn't strike me as a very tactful greeting to a man who, for all he knew, might be set to pay $800 for an afternoon frock, but of course with a murder on the premises, he had had a tough twenty-four hours, so I kept it pleasant.

"I'm not a reporter," I assured him, "or a cop, or a lawyer drumming up trade. I'm a private detective named Archie Goodwin, sent by a private detective named Nero Wolfe to ask Mr. Gallant a couple of harmless questions. Not connected with the death of Bianca Voss."

"Mr. Gallant is not available."

I hadn't heard his voice in person before, only on the phone, but I recognized it. Also he looked like a business manager, with his neat, well-arranged face, his neat well-made dark suit, and his neat shadow-stripe four-in-hand. His cheeks wanted to sag and he was a little puffy around the eyes, but the city and county employees had probably kept him from getting much sleep.

"May I ask," I said, "if you are Mr. Carl Drew?"

"I am, yes."

"Then I'm in luck. I was instructed to see five different people here—Mr. Gallant. Miss Gallant, Miss

Prince, Miss Thorne, and Mr. Carl Drew. Perhaps we could sit down?"

He ignored that. "See us about what?"

The woman had left us, but she was in earshot if her hearing was good, and Wolfe had said to see them separately, if possible. "If you don't mind," I said, "I'd rather see you one at a time because I have to report to Mr. Wolfe and I'm apt to get confused talking with two people at once. So if that lady is Miss Prince or Miss Thorne—"

"She isn't. And I'm busy. What do you want?"

"I want information, if you have any, about a woman who died yesterday. Not Bianca Voss. Miss Sarah Yare."

He blinked. "Sarah Yare? What about her?"

"She is dead. She killed herself. Yesterday."

"I know she did. That was tragic. But I can't give you any information about it. I haven't any."

"I'm not after information about her death. That's up to the police. What I'm after— Someone has engaged Mr. Wolfe to make inquiries about her, and he sent me to ask you people if you had any messages or letters from her in the past month or so, and if so, will you let him see them?"

"Messages or letters?"

"Right."

"But what—who engaged him?"

"I don't know." I was not permitting my face or voice to show that I had caught sight of a fish. "If you have had messages or letters, and would like to know who wants to see them before you produce them, I suppose Mr. Wolfe would tell you. He would have to."

"I have no messages or letters."

I was disappointed. "None at all? I said the past month or so, but before that would help. Any time."

He shook his head. "I have never had any. I doubt if she ever wrote a letter—that is, to anyone here—or any messages, except phone messages. She always did everything by telephone. And for the past month or so—longer than that, more than a year—she hasn't been—uh—she hasn't been around."

"I know." I was sympathetic, and I meant it, though not for him. "Anyway, I don't think Mr. Wolfe would be interested in letters about clothes. I think it's personal letters he wants, and he thought you might have known her well enough personally to have some."

"Well, I haven't. I can't say I didn't know her personally; she was a very fine customer here for two years, and she was a very personal person. But I never had a personal letter from her."

I had to resist temptation. I had him talking, and there was no telling if or when I would get at the others. But Wolfe had said not to labor it, and I disobey instructions only when I have reason to think I know more about it than he does, and at the moment I didn't even know why he had been consulting the phone book. So I didn't press. I thanked him, and said I'd appreciate it if he would tell me when Mr. Gallant would be available.

He said he would find out, and left me, going to the rear and disappearing around the end of a screen, and soon I heard his voice, but too faint to get any words. There was no other voice, so, being a detective, I figured it out that he was on a phone. That accomplished, I decided to detect whether the woman, who was seated at a table going through a portfolio, had been listening. If so, and if my bringing up Sarah Yare had more significance for her than it had for me, she was keeping it to herself.

Drew reappeared, and I met him in the middle of the room. He said that Mr. Gallant was in his office with Miss Prince and could let me have five minutes. Another fish. Certainly Drew had told Gallant what my line was, and why did I rate even five seconds? As Drew led me to an elevator and entered with me, and pushed the button marked 2, I had to remember to look hopeful instead of smug.

The second floor hall was narrow, with bare walls, and not carpeted. As I said, not a palace. Following Drew down six paces and through a door, I found myself in a pinup paradise. All available space on all four walls was covered with women, drawings and prints and photographs, both black and white and color, all sizes, and in one respect they were all alike: none of them had a stitch on. It hadn't occurred to me that a designer of women's clothes should understand female anatomy, but I admit it might help. The effect was so striking that it took me four or five seconds to focus on the man and woman seated at a table. By that time Drew had pronounced my name and gone.

Though the man and the woman were fully clothed, they were striking too. He reminded me of someone, but I didn't remember who until later. Lord Byron. A picture of Lord Byron in a book in my father's library that had impressed me at an early age. It was chiefly Gallant's dark, curly hair backing up a wide, sweeping forehead, but the nose and chin were in it too. The necktie was all wrong; instead of Byron's choker, he was sporting a narrow ribbon tied in a bow with long ends hanging.

The woman didn't go with him. She was strictly modern, small and trim, in a tailored suit that had been cut and fitted by an expert, and while her face was perfectly acceptable, the main thing was her eyes. They were as close to black as eyes ever get, and they ran the show. In spite of Alec Gallant's lordly presence, as I approached the table I found myself aiming at Anita Prince's eyes.

Gallant was speaking. "What's this about Sarah Yare?"

"Just a couple of questions." He had eyes, too, when you looked at them. "It shouldn't take even five minutes. I suppose Mr. Drew told you?"

"He said Nero Wolfe is making an inquiry and sent you. What kind of an inquiry? What about?"

"I don't really know." I was apologetic. "The fact is, Mr. Gallant, on this I'm just an errand boy. My instructions were to ask if you got any messages or letters from her in the past month or so, and if so, will you let Mr. Wolfe see them?"

"My heaven!" He closed his eyes, tilted his head back and shook it—a lion pestered by a fly. He looked at the woman. "This is too much. Too much!" He looked at me. "You must know a woman was assassinated here yesterday. Of course you do!" He pointed at the door. "There!" His hand dropped to the desk like a dead bird. "And after that calamity, now this, the death of my old and valued friend. Miss Yare was not only my friend; in mold and frame she was perfection, in movement she was music, as a mannequin she would have been divine. My delight in her was completely pure. I never had a letter from her." His head jerked to Anita Prince. "Send him away," he muttered.

She put fingers on his arm. "You gave him five minutes, Alec, and he has had only two." Her voice was smooth and sure. The black eyes came to me. "So you don't know the purpose of Mr. Wolfe's inquiry?"

"No, Miss Prince, I don't. He tells me only what he thinks I need to know."

"Nor who hired him to make it?"

So Drew had covered the ground. "Not that either. He'll probably tell you, if you have what he wants, letters from her, and you want to know why he wants to see them."

"I have no letters from her. I never had any. I had no personal relations with Miss Yare." Her voice sharpened a little. "Though I saw her many times, my contact with her was never close. Mr. Gallant preferred to fit her himself. I just looked on. It seems—" She stopped for a word, and found it. "It seems odd that Nero Wolfe should be starting an inquiry immediately after her death. Or did he start it before?"

"I couldn't say. The first I knew, he gave me this errand this morning. This noon."

"You don't know much, do you?"

"No. I just take orders."

"Of course you do know that Miss Yare committed suicide?"

I didn't get an answer in. Gallant, hitting the table with a palm, suddenly shouted at her. "Name of God! Must you? Send him away!"

"I'm sorry, Mr. Gallant," I told him. "I guess my time's up. If you'll tell me where to find your sister and Miss Thorne, that will—"

I stopped because his hand had darted to an ash tray, a big metal one that looked heavy, and since he wasn't smoking, he was presumably going to let fly with it. Anita Prince beat him to it. With her left hand she got his wrist, and with her right she got the ash tray and moved it out of reach. It was very quick and deft.

Then she spoke, to me. "Miss Gallant is not here. Miss Thorne is busy, but you can ask Mr. Drew downstairs. You had better go."

I went. In more favorable circumstances I might have spared another five minutes for a survey of the pinups, but not then, not if I had to dodge ash trays. So I went.

That is, I started. But when I was near enough to the door to start a hand out for the knob, it suddenly swung in at me, and I had to jump back to give it room, and there was Flora Gallant.

Turning to close the door, she saw me and stopped, right against me. She backed up, then whirled to face the table.

Anita Prince spoke. "You know Mr. Goodwin, don't you? Your alibi?"

Flora didn't answer. Gallant had left his chair and was coming around the end of the table to her, and she extended her hands and he took them.

"My dear," he said. "My dear sister. Was it bad?"

"It's all right," she said. "It was so long."

"Who was it? The one that croaks like a frog?"

"No, not him. There were two of them, one named Brill and one named Bowen. It was so long."

It would be, I thought, with the district attorney himself taking a hand.

"More than three hours," she said. "Most of the time it wasn't about me; it was about you and the others. I suppose because I have an alibi." Her head turned. "Yes, Anita, I know Mr. Goodwin—as you say, my alibi. Carl told me he was here asking questions."

Flora turned to me. "Well—hello."

I returned it. "Hello. If you've been answering questions for three hours, I guess you've had enough for a while, so I'll just ask—"

She cut me off. "Not here." She moved. "I don't mind you asking me questions." She was touching my arm. "But tête-à-tête." She turned to her brother. "It wasn't too bad, Alec. I'll tell you later." She stepped into the hall, and I followed, pulling the door shut.

"My room is so small," she said, "that you can't stretch your legs." She touched my arm again. "I know. You ought to see it, anyway. I'm sure you're a better detective than any of them. Come along."

Leading me along the hall toward the front, on past the elevator, nearly to the end, she opened a door, stood aside for me to enter, and followed me in.

"This was her room," she said. "When you're through asking me questions, you can go over it and maybe you can detect something. Maybe you'll find something they missed."

I glanced around. There were coats, suits, dresses, all kinds. They were on dummies scattered around—on hangers strung on a pole along a wall and piled on a big long table. Half of one wall was a mirror from floor to ceiling. At the far side of the room was a desk, with a pad and pen stand and calendar and other objects on its top, including a telephone—the one, presumably, that Wolfe and I had heard hit the floor.

Flora crossed to the desk and sat down on a chair near an end of it. "You sit in her chair," she invited me.

"It's hardly worth taking the trouble to sit," I told her. "However," I turned Bianca Voss' chair around and sat. "Only a question or two—one really. Apparently Carl Drew told you what it is."

"He said you wanted to know if we have any letters from Sarah Yare, and Nero Wolfe wants to see them. I haven't any."

"Then that answers it. It doesn't make much of a tête-à-tête, does it?"

"No."

"I get the impression that everybody around here was pretty fond of Sarah Yare. Were you?"

"Yes."

"I suppose you first met her before she—when she had the world by the tail."

"Yes."

I looked at her. Her face had full light on it from a window, and her chin was more pointed than ever, her eye rims were red, and her lips were too tight. That was nothing remarkable; after all, not only had she just returned from three hours of nagging by Brill and Bowen about a murder—murder of a woman as she occupied the chair I was sitting in—but also someone she had been fond of had just died in a very unpleasant manner. But there was something about her—I guess her eyes—that made me feel that if I went after her I would get something. The trouble was, I would be exceeding instructions, and I still didn't know what Wolfe had been doing with the phone book.

So I merely said, "Well, I guess that covers it."

"Archie," she said.

"Yes, Finger?"

"You kissed me good night when you put me in the taxi."

"So I did. It's nice of you to remember."

"Would you kiss me now?"

It was a little complicated. When Wolfe is investigating a murder case for a client, and I am helping, I do not go around kissing the suspects. But we had no client, and I was working on Sarah Yare, not Bianca Voss. Besides, if I declined, she would think I had decided there was something repellent about her, and I hadn't decided a thing about her or anyone else. So I arose. So did she, which was sensible. One on his feet and one in a chair is no way to kiss.

She drew away. "Then you still like me."

"I think I do. I could tell better after a few more."

"Then I can ask you. I couldn't ask if you were not—if you were my enemy. Now I can. Why are you asking all of us about Sarah Yare?"

"Because Mr. Wolfe told me to."

"Why did he tell you to?"

"I don't know."

"Or course you know. He tells you everything. Why?"

I shook my head. "No good, Finger. Either I don't know or I do know but am not saying. What's the difference? It happens that I really don't know, but it doesn't matter whether you believe that or not."

"I don't. You're lying to me. You are my enemy. You told Carl Drew that someone engaged Mr. Wolfe to make an inquiry. Who engaged him?"

"I don't know."

"Of course you know. Was it Carl Drew?"

"Don't know."

"Was it Emmy Thorne?"

"Don't know."

"Was it Anita Prince?"

"Don't know."

She grabbed my arms. I wouldn't have thought her little hands had so much muscle. Her face was right under mine, tilted up to me. "I have to know, Archie. There's a reason why I must know. What can I do? What can I do to make you tell me?"

Instructions or no instructions, that was too much. I would find out what was biting her. "I can't tell you what I don't know," I said, "but maybe I can help. Sit down and calm down and we'll see. It's quite possible—"

The door opened. I was facing it. Flora let go of my arms and turned. A voice which I had myself frequently heard croak more or less like a frog sounded. "Huh? You?"

It was my old friend and foe, Sergeant Purley Stebbins, of Homicide. In two steps he stopped and was glaring. Behind one of his shoulders appeared the saggy cheeks and puffy eyes of Carl Drew. Behind the other appeared an attractive display of hair about the color of white gold, a nice smooth brow, a pair of blue eyes not at all puffed, and a nose that went with them fine. The rest of her was shielded by Purley Stebbins' broad frame.

Purley took another step, and another. He probably thought a slow and measured advance would be more impressive and menacing, and, as a matter of fact, it was, or would have been if I hadn't seen it before.

"Greetings," I said.

"The scene of a murder," he said, "and you." He came to a stop an arm's length from me.

I grinned at him. "This time," I said, "you're in for a disappointment. I haven't got the answer ready for you because I'm not interested. Sorry, but my mind is elsewhere. Actually I'm just on a fishing trip." My eyes went to Carl Drew, who had approached on the left. "If that's Miss Thorne, would you mind introducing me, Mr. Drew?"

"That's me," she said. "No introduction required. You're Archie Goodwin." Now that all of her was in view, I could see that the mouth and chin were no letdown from the other details.

"Fishing," Purley croaked. "For what?"

"Fish." I put one brow up. He thinks I do that because I know he can't, but my motives are my business. "Listen, sergeant. Don't let's start ring-around-a-rosy and end in a squat. If you demand to know why I'm poking my nose in a murder, you know darned well what you'll get, so what's the use? Even if I told you what I'm here for—and I'm not going to—you wouldn't have the faintest idea if or how it's connected with what you're here for. Neither have I. Anyhow, I'm about finished and I've had no lunch. All I want is a few words in private with Miss Thorne. . . . If you will be so good, Miss Thorne?"

"Certainly," she said. "My room is down the hall."

"Just a minute," Stebbins growled. "Maybe you'd like a ride downtown." To me.

"I've already been downtown. I spent two hours at the D.A.'s office this morning."

"Did you tell them you were coming here?"

"I didn't know I was coming here. I went home, and Mr. Wolfe sent me on an errand."

"And I find you here. And you're obstructing justice and withholding evidence, as usual."

"Nuts. What evidence?"

"I don't know, but I'll find out. I'm not going to waste time horsing around with you." He moved. "Miss Gallant, what has this guy been saying to you?"

That would not do. Wolfe hadn't told me he wanted to keep his conjecture to himself, but I took it for granted that he did, since he hadn't even told me, and he certainly wouldn't want Purley Stebbins sticking his big thumb in, not to mention Cramer and the rest of the Homicide gang. And if Flora didn't spill it, one of the others probably would.

Action was called for. I stepped in front of Purley and told Flora, "Come on, I want to tell your brother something I want you to hear. Come along." She took half a second for a glance at Purley, then left her chair, and I took her arm. As we headed for the door I told Carl Drew and Emmy Thorne, "You too. I want you all to hear. Come along."

They came. Going down the hall they were right behind Flora and me, and on their heels was Stebbins. On past the elevator. At Gallant's room I turned the knob and swung the door wide, and stood on the sill to say my piece.

"Sorry to interrupt you again, Mr. Gallant, but Sergeant Stebbins is trying to exceed his authority, as usual. He wants me to tell him what I came to see you people about, and I won't, and he thinks he's going to squeeze it out of you. Of course you can tell him if you want to, but there's no reason why you should, and if you ask me, I wouldn't. Sometimes the police are entirely too inquisitive. They mean well, but so did the boy who aimed a rock at a rabbit and hit his sister."

Flora slid past me to enter the room. Carl Drew wanted in, too, and I moved aside for him, and Stebbins followed him, glaring at me as he passed. I felt a touch on my elbow and turned.

"That was quite a speech," Emmy Thorne said. "I would have clapped if I had known you were through."

"Glad you liked it. Absolutely unrehearsed. No script."

"Wonderful. If you want some words in private, my room is at the end of the hall. This way."

Conclusion

Her room was about half the size of the two others I had seen, and there was no display of either women or clothes. A table had piles of magazines and portfolios, and there was only one chair besides the one at her desk. I stood until she was seated and then pulled the other chair up.

"Flora says you dance well," she said.

"Good for her. I can chin myself twenty times too."

"I've never tried that." Her left eye had more blue in it than the right one, or maybe it was the light. "What is this nonsense about letters from Sarah Yare?"

"You know," I said, "my tie must be crooked or I've got a grease spot. Mr. Drew resented me, and Mr. Gallant was going to throw an ash tray at me. Now you start in. Why is it nonsense to ask a simple question politely and respectfully?"

"Well," she conceded, "maybe 'nonsense' isn't exactly the word. Maybe 'gall' would be better. What right have you to march in here and ask questions at all? Polite or not."

"None. It's not a right, it's a liberty. And you're at liberty to tell me to go climb a tree if you find the question ticklish. Have you any letters from Sarah Yare?"

She laughed. She had good teeth. Then, abruptly, she cut the laugh off. "Good Lord," she said, "I didn't think I would ever laugh again. This awful business, what happened here yesterday, and then Sarah. No, I have no letters from her." Her blue eyes, straight at me, were cool and keen. "Why should I find the question ticklish?"

"No reason that I know of. You said I had gall to ask it."

"If it hurt your feelings I take it back. What else?"

Again I had to resist temptation. With Drew the temptation had been purely professional; with her it was only partly professional and only partly pure. Cramer had said she was in charge of contacts, and one more might be good for her.

Having resisted, I shook my head. "Nothing else, unless you know of something. For instance, if you know of anyone who might have letters."

"I don't." She regarded me. "Of course I'm curious. I'm wondering what it's about—your coming here. You told Mr. Drew that you don't know, that you don't even know who hired Nero Wolfe to inquire about her."

"That's right. I don't."

"Then you can't tell me. I can't turn on the charm and coax it out of you. Can I?"

"I'm afraid not." I stood up. "Too bad. I would enjoy seeing you try. You're probably pretty good at it."

In the hall, on my way to the elevator, I stopped at Gallant's door and cocked an ear. I heard a rumble (that was Purley); and a soprano murmur (that was Anita

Prince); and a bellicose baritone (that was Gallant). But the door was too thick for me to get the words.

Emerging from the building, I turned left, found a phone booth on Madison Avenue, dialed the number I knew best, got Fritz and asked for Wolfe.

His voice came, "Yes, Archie?"

"It's full of fish. Swarming. Sarah Yare bought her clothes there for two years and they all loved her. Apparently she never wrote letters. They all want to know who hired you and why, especially Flora Gallant. I've had no lunch and I'm half starved, but I stopped to phone because there may be some urgency. Stebbins walked in on me, and of course he wanted to know what I was doing there."

"You didn't tell him?"

"Certainly not. When he said he would get it out of them, I got them all together and made a speech—you know, a man's brain is his castle. But one of them might spill it any minute, and I thought you ought to know right away, in case that would mess up your program, if you've really got one."

"It won't. Not if I get on with it. I have further instructions for you. You will go—"

"No, sir. I can kid my stomach along with a sandwich and a glass of milk, but no more errands until I get some idea of where we're headed for. Do you want to tell me on the phone?"

"No. But very well. It is not exigent, and Fritz is keeping your lunch warm. Come home."

"Right. Fifteen minutes."

I hung up and went out and flagged a taxi.

Ordinarily Wolfe and I lunch in the dining room, but when I'm eating solo I prefer the kitchen, so I headed for it. When I was ready for coffee, I took it to the office with me.

"I feel better," I told Wolfe. "I wish Purley were here now. How do you want it, from start to finish?"

"No." He put his book down. "You've told me all I need to know."

"You don't want any of it? Not even the speech I made?"

"You can type it for the files, for posterity. As I told you, I have instructions."

"Yeah." I sipped coffee. "But first what are we doing and why?"

"Very well." He leaned back. "As I told you this morning, I thought I might have been hoodwinked and I intended to find out. It was quite possible that that performance here yesterday—getting us on the phone just in time to hear a murder committed—was flummery. Indeed, it was more than possible. Must I expound that?"

"No. Even Cramer suspected it."

"So he did. But his theory that Bianca Voss had been killed earlier and that another woman, not the murderer, was there beside the corpse, waiting for a phone call, was patently ridiculous. Must I expound that?"

"No, unless it was a lunatic. Anyone who would do that, even the murderer, with the chance that someone might come in any second, would be batty."

"Of course. But if she wasn't killed at the time we heard those sounds, she must have been killed earlier, since you phoned almost immediately and sent someone to that room. Therefore the sounds didn't come from there. Miss Gallant did not dial that number. She dialed the number of some other person whom she had persuaded to perform that hocus-pocus."

He turned a hand over. "I had come to that conclusion, or call it conjecture, before I went to bed last night, and I had found it intolerable. I will not be mistaken for a jackass. Reading the paper at breakfast this morning, I came upon the item about the death of Sarah Yare, and my attention was caught by the fact that she had been an actress. An actress can act a part. Also she had been in distress. Also she had died. If she had been persuaded to act that part, it would have been extremely convenient—for the one who persuaded her—for her to die before she learned that a murder had been committed and that she had been an accessory after the fact. Certainly that was mere speculation, but it was not idle, and when I came down to the office I looked in the phone book to see if Sarah Yare was listed, found that she was, and dialed her number. Algonquin nine, one-eight-four-seven."

"What for? She was dead."

"I didn't lift the receiver. I merely dialed it, to hear it. Before doing so I strained my memory. I had to recall a phenomenon that was filed somewhere in my brain, having reached it through my ears. As you know, I am trained to attend, to observe and to register. So are you. That same phenomenon is filed in your brain. Close your eyes and find it. Stand up. Take your ears back to yesterday, when you were standing there, having surrendered your chair to Miss Gallant, and she was at the phone, dialing. Not the first number she dialed; you dialed that one yourself later. Concentrate on the second one, when, according to her, she was dialing the number of the direct line to Bianca Voss' office."

I did so. I got up and stood where I had stood while she was dialing, shut my eyes and brought it back. In ten seconds I said, "O.K. Shoot."

The sound came of his dialing. I held my breath till the end, then opened my eyes and said positively, "No. Wrong. The first and third and fourth were wrong. I'm not sure about the second, but those three—"

"Close your eyes and try it again. This will be another number."

The dialing sound came, the seven units. I opened my eyes. "That's more like it. I would say that was it; anyway the first four. Beyond that, I'm a little lost. But in that case—"

"Satisfactory." He pushed the phone away and sat back. "The first four were enough. The first number, which you rejected, as I did this morning, was Plaza two, nine-oh-two-two, the number of Bianca Voss' direct line according to the phone book—the number which Miss Gallant pretended to be dialing. The second, which you accepted, was Sarah Yare's number, Algonquin nine, one-eight-four-seven."

"I see." I sat down and took a gulp of coffee, which had cooled enough for gulping. "Quite a performance."

He didn't acknowledge the applause. "So it was still a plausible conjecture, somewhat strengthened, but no more than that. If those people, especially Miss Gallant, could not be shown to have had some association with Sarah Yare, it would be untenable. So I sent you to inquire, and what you found promoted the conjecture to an assumption, and surely a weighty one. What time is it?"

He would have had to twist his neck a whole quarter turn to look at the wall clock. I obliged. "Five to four."

"Then instructions for your errand must be brief, and they can be." He mustn't be late for his afternoon session in the plant rooms. "You will go to Sarah Yare's address on Thirteenth Street and look at her apartment. Her phone might have been discontinued since that book was issued. I need to know that the instrument is still there and operable before I proceed. If I intend to see that whoever tried to make a fool of me regrets it, I must take care not to make a fool of myself." He pushed his chair back, gripped the arms and hoisted his bulk. "Have I satisfied you?"

I drank the last of the coffee, now cold, then went to the hall for my coat and hat, and departed.

It was not my day. At the address of the late Sarah Yare on East 13th Street I stubbed my toe again. I was dead wrong about the janitor of that old walk-up. He looked as if anything would go, so I merely told him to let me into Sarah Yare's apartment to check the telephone, and the bum insisted on seeing my credentials. So I misjudged him again. I offered him a sawbuck and told him I only wanted two minutes for a look at the phone with him at my elbow, and he turned me down. The upshot was that I went back home for an assortment of keys, returned, posted myself across the street, waited a full hour to be sure the enemy was not peeking, and broke and entered, technically.

I won't describe it; it was too painful. It was an awful dump for a Sarah Yare—even for a down-and-outer who had once been Sarah Yare. But the telephone was there, and it was working. I dialed to make sure, and got Fritz, and told him I just wanted to say hello and would be home in fifteen minutes, and he said that would please Mr. Wolfe because Inspector Cramer was there.

"Is Stebbins with him?"

"No, he's alone."

"When did he come?"

"Ten minutes ago. At six o'clock. Mr. Wolfe said to admit him and is with him in the office. Their voices are very loud. Hurry home, Archie."

I did so. Ascending the stoop and letting myself in, not banging the door, I tiptoed down the hall and stopped short of the office door, thinking to get a sniff of the atmosphere before entering.

Wolfe's voice came: ". . . and I didn't say I have never known you to be right, Mr. Cramer. I said I have never known you to be more wrong. That is putting it charitably, under provocation. You have accused me of duplicity. Pfui!"

"Nuts." Cramer had worked up to his grittiest rasp. "I have accused you of nothing. I have merely stated facts. The time of the murder was supposed to be established by you and Goodwin hearing it on the phone. Is that a fact? Those five people all have alibis for that time. One of them was here with you. Is that a fact? When I put it to you yesterday that that phone business might have been faked, that she might have been killed earlier, all I got was a run-around. You could challenge it circumstantially, but not intrinsically—whatever that means. Is that a fact? So that if you and Goodwin got to the witness stand you might both swear that you were absolutely satisfied that you had heard her get it at exactly half past eleven. Is that a fact? Giving me to understand that you weren't interested, you weren't concerned, you had no—"

"No," Wolfe objected. "That was broached."

"You said you had never had any association with any of those people besides what was in your statement, so how could you be concerned, with Bianca Voss dead? Tell me this: did any of them approach you, directly or indirectly, between seven o'clock yesterday and noon today?"

"No."

"But—" He bore down on the "but." "But you sent Goodwin there today. And when Stebbins ran into him and asked him what he was there for, he said he was on a fishing trip. And they all refuse to tell what Goodwin said to them or what they said to him. That is a fact. They say it was a private matter and had no connection with the murder of Bianca Voss. And when I come and ask you what you sent Goodwin there for, you say you will probably be ready to tell me within twenty-four hours. And what I said was absolutely justified. I did not accuse you of duplicity. You know what I said."

"I do indeed, Mr. Cramer." I couldn't see Wolfe, but I knew he had upturned a palm. "This is childish and futile. If a connection is established between your murder investigation and the topic of Mr. Goodwin's talks with those people today it will be only because I formed a conjecture and acted on it. I hope to establish it within twenty-four hours, and meanwhile it will do no harm to give you a hint. Have you any information on the death of a woman named Sarah Yare?"

A pause. Cramer was certainly interrupting his glare to blink. "Why?" he demanded.

"I merely put the question."

"All right, I'll answer it. I have some—yes. Presumed a suicide, but it's being checked. I have two men on it. What about it?"

"I suggest that you assign more men to it, good ones, and explore it thoroughly. I think we shall both find it helpful. I may soon have a more concrete suggestion, but for the present that should serve. You know quite well—"

The doorbell rang. I wheeled and looked through the one-way glass pane of the front door. It wasn't a visitor on the stoop, it was a mob. All of them were there: Gallant. Flora. Anita Prince, Emmy Thorne and Carl Drew. Fritz appeared from the kitchen, saw me and stopped. I got my notebook and pen from pockets and wrote:

That phone works.
The five subjects are at the door.

I told Fritz to stand by, tore out the sheet, entered the office and crossed to Wolfe's desk, and handed it to him.

Wolfe read it, frowned at it for three seconds, turned his head and called "Fritz!"

He appeared at the door. "Yes, sir?"

"Put the chain bolt on and tell those people they will be admitted shortly. Stay there."

"Yes, sir." He went.

Wolfe looked at Cramer. "Mr. Gallant, his sister. Miss Prince, Miss Thorne and Mr. Drew have arrived, uninvited and unexpected. You'll have to leave without being seen. In the front room until they have entered. I'll communicate with you later."

"Like hell I'll leave." Cramer was on his feet. "Like hell they're unexpected." He was moving toward the hall, his intention plain—taking over as receptionist.

"Mr. Cramer!" It snapped at his back, turning him. "Would I lie so clumsily if they had been expected, would I have let you in? Would I have sat here bickering with you? Either you leave or I do. If you admit them, you'll have them to yourself, and I wish you luck."

Cramer's jaw was clamped. "You think I'm going to sneak out and sit on your stoop until you whistle?"

"That would be unseemly," Wolfe conceded. "Very well." He pointed at a picture on the wall to his left behind him—a pretty waterfall. "You know about that. You may take that station, but only if you engage not to disclose yourself unless you are invited. Unequivocally."

The waterfall covered a hole in the wall. On the other side, in a wing of the hall across from the kitchen, the hole was covered by nothing, and you could not only see through but also hear through. Cramer had used it once before, a couple of years ago.

He stood, considering, his jaw clamped again. Wolfe demanded, "Well? They're waiting. For you or for me?"

Cramer said, "O.K., I'll try it your way," turned and marched to the hall, and turned left.

"All right, Archie. Bring them in."

* * *

"While I was in the hall, admitting the guests and helping with coats, Fritz was in the office moving chairs, and when we entered, there was a row of them lined up facing Wolfe's desk. And then, when I had pronounced their names and Wolfe had acknowledged each one by inclining his head an eighth of an inch, Flora wouldn't accept my idea of the proper seating arrangement. I thought it would be desirable to have her handy, in the chair nearest me—for professional reasons, not personal ones—but she didn't agree. She took the one at the other end of the row, farthest from me, presumably because it was near her brother in the red leather chair beyond the end of Wolfe's desk. Next to her was Carl Drew, then Anita Prince, then Emmy Thorne at my end.

When they were all seated, including me, Wolfe turned to Gallant. "I presume, sir, you are the spokesman?"

"I speak for us, yes, but it is enough that I speak for myself. I want to know why you sent a man to ask me questions about Sarah Yare."

Wolfe nodded. "Of course. Naturally your curiosity was aroused. But evidently you have been provoked to more than curiosity; you have been impelled to call on me in a body; so I want to know something too. Why were Mr. Goodwin's questions so provocative?"

"Pah!" Gallant hit a chair arm with a fist. "I answered his question; you can answer mine! I have asked it!"

Anita Prince put in, "We came because we think it is important, but we don't know why. The police insist on knowing why Mr. Goodwin was there, what he wanted."

"And you refused to say. Only because Mr. Goodwin advised you to?"

"No," Emmy Thorne declared. "Because it was none of their business. And we have a right to know why you sent him, whether his questions were provocative or not." That girl was strong on rights.

Wolfe's eyes went from right to left and back again. "There's no point in dragging this out. I sent Mr. Goodwin to see you because I suspected I had been gulled and wanted to find out; and further, because I had guessed that there was a connection between Sarah Yare and her death, and the murder of Bianca Voss. By coming here *en masse*, you have made that guess a conviction, if any doubt had remained."

"I knew it," Flora mumbled. She looked at her brother. "I knew it! That was why—"

"*Tais toi*," Gallant commanded her. He jerked back to Wolfe: "I'll tell you why we came here. We came for an explanation. We came—"

Carl Drew put in, "For an understanding," he declared. "We're in trouble, all of us, you know that, and we need your help, and we're ready to pay for it. First we have to know what the connection is between Sarah Yare and what happened to Bianca Voss."

Wolfe shook his head. "You don't mean that. You mean you have to know whether I have established the connection, and if so, how. I'm prepared to tell you, but before I do so I must clarify matters. There must be no misunderstanding. For instance, I understand that all of you thought yourselves gravely endangered by Miss Voss' presence. You, Miss Prince; you, Miss Thorne; and you, Mr. Drew—your dearest ambitions were threatened. Your future was committed to the success and glory of that enterprise, and you were convinced that Miss Voss was going to cheapen it, and perhaps destroy it. Do you challenge that?"

"Of course not." Emmy Thorne was scornful. "Everybody knew it."

"Then that's understood. . . . That applied equally to you, Miss Gallant, but with special emphasis. You also had a more intimate concern, for your brother. You told me so. . . . As for you. Mr. Gallant, you are manifestly not a man to truckle, yet you let that woman meddle in your affairs. Presumably you were under severe constraint. Were you?"

Gallant opened his mouth and closed it. He looked at his sister, returned to Wolfe, and again opened his mouth and closed it. He was under constraint now, no doubt about that.

He forced it out, "Yes. I was under her heel." He set his jaw. He unset it. "The police know. They found out enough, and I have told them the rest. She was a bad woman, though I didn't know it until too late. I met her in France during the war. We were in the *Résistance* together when I married her. Only afterwards I learned that she was *perfide*. She had been a traitor to France; I couldn't prove it, but I knew it. I left her and changed my name and came to America—and then last year she found me and made demands. I was under her heel."

Wolfe grunted. "That won't do, Mr. Gallant. I doubt if it has satisfied the police, and it certainly doesn't satisfy me. In this situation you might have killed her, but surely you wouldn't have let her take charge of your business and your life. What else was there?"

"Nothing. Nothing!"

"Pfui. Of course there was. And if the investigation is prolonged, the police will discover it. I advise you to disclose it and let me get on and settle this affair. Didn't her death remove her heel?"

"Yes. Thank God, it did. And I am not blind; I can see that that points at me." Gallant hit the arms of the chair with his palms. "But she is gone and I can tell you. With her gone, there is no evidence to fear. She had two brothers, and they, like her, were traitors, and I killed them. I would have killed her, too, but she escaped me. During the war it would have been merely an episode, but it was later, much later, when I found out about them, and by then it was a crime. With her evidence I was an assassin, and I was doomed. Now she is gone, thank God, but I did not kill her. You know I did not. At half past eleven yesterday morning I was in my workshop with Miss Prince and many others, and you can swear that she was killed at that moment. That is why we came to see you, to arrange to pay—"

"You are in error, Mr. Gallant. I cannot swear that Bianca Voss was killed 'at that moment.' On the contrary, I'm sure she wasn't, for a variety of reasons. There are such minor ones as the extraordinary billingsgate she spat at me on the phone, quite gratuitous; and her calling me a gob of fat. A woman who still spoke the language with so marked an accent would not have the word 'gob' so ready, and probably wouldn't have it at all."

He waved "gob" away. "But the major reasons are more cogent. In the first place, it was too pat. Since the complexities of nature permit a myriad of coincidences, we cannot reject one offhand, but we can discriminate. That one—that the attack had come just at the moment when Miss Gallant had got Mr. Goodwin and me on the phone with Miss Voss—that was highly suspect. Besides, it was indiscreet of the murderer to strike exactly then. Indeed, foolhardy. Why not wait until she had hung up? Whoever was talking with her would certainly hear the sounds and take alarm. As I told Mr. Cramer, it was open to challenge circumstantially, though not instrinsically. However, there was another challenge, on surer ground. In fact, conclusive. Miss Gallant did not dial Plaza two, nine-oh-two-two, Miss Voss' number, as she pretended. She dialed Algonquin nine, one-eight-four-seven, Sarah Yare's number."

A noise, a sort of low growl, came from the waterfall. I was farthest away, and I heard it distinctly, so it must have reached their ears, too, but Wolfe's last words had so riveted their attention that it didn't register.

It did with Wolfe, and he added hastily, "I didn't know that yesterday. I became certain of it only after you rang my doorbell, when Mr. Goodwin handed me this note." He tapped it there on his desk. "It's first words are, 'That phone works.' I had sent him to learn if Sarah Yare's phone was in operation. Obviously, Miss Gallant had arranged with miss Yare to impersonate Bianca Voss, and it is a reasonable—"

"Wait a minute," Gallant had come forward in the red leather chair. "You can't prove that."

"Directly, no. Inferentially, yes.

"And how do your know she dialed Sarah Yare's number? You weren't where you could see the dial, and neither was Goodwin."

Wolfe nodded. "Evidently you have discussed it with her. You're quite right, Mr. Gallant; we couldn't see the dial. Nevertheless, we can supply evidence, and we think it will be persuasive. I am not—"

"What kind of evidence?"

"That's no good, Alec." It was Emmy Thorne, the contact girl. "You can't push Nero Wolfe. He has his teeth in it, you can see that. You know what we decided."

"I'm not sure," Anita Prince objected, "that we decided right."

"I am. Carl?"

"Yes." Drew was chewing his lip. "I think so. Yes."

"Flora? It's up to you."

135

"I guess so." Flora's voice didn't want to work, and she tried again. "I guess so." A little better.

Emmy nodded. "Go ahead, Alec. You can't push him."

Gallant looked at his sister and back at Wolfe. "All right. We will pay you to help us. I will pay you. My sister is innocent and she must not suffer. It would be an offense against nature, against God Himself. She has told me all about it, and she was stupid, but she is innocent. She did arrange with Sarah Yare, as you said, but only to move you. She had read much about you and had a great opinion of your abilities. She was desperate about Bianca Voss. She knew you demanded high fees, much beyond her resources, so she conceived a plan. She would persuade you to talk with Bianca Voss on the phone, and she would get Sarah instead, and Sarah would abuse you with such violence that you would be offended and resent it, and you would be moved to move against Bianca Voss. It was stupid—yes, very stupid—but it was not criminal."

Wolfe's eyes, on him, were half closed. "And you want to pay me to help her."

"Yes. When she learned that your man was there asking about Sarah Yare, and after she had talked with him, I saw that she was frightened and asked her why, and she told me what she had done. I consulted the others, and it was apparent that you suspected what had happened, and that was dangerous. We decided to come and ask you to help. My sister must not suffer."

Wolfe's eyes moved. "Miss Gallant, you heard your brother. Do you corroborate it?"

"Yes!" That time it was too loud.

"You did those things? As he related them?"

"Yes!"

"When did you arrange with Sarah Yare to impersonate Bianca Voss? Yesterday morning before you came here?"

"No. Monday night. Late. After Mr. Goodwin put me in a taxi. After he left me."

Wolfe returned to Gallant. "Again, sir, I am being mistaken for a ninny. I agree with you that your sister was stupid, but you are not the one to proclaim it. You say that she arranged with Sarah Yare to abuse me on the phone, but Miss Yare didn't stop at that. She ended by making noises indicating that she had been violently attacked, and jerked the phone off onto the floor, and made other noises, and then hung up the phone and cut the connection. Was that on her own initiative? Her own idea? Your sister's stupidity can bow to yours if you expected me to overlook that point—or worse, if you missed it yourself."

"I am not stupid, Mr. Wolfe."

"Then you are devious beyond my experience."

"Devious?"

"*Rusé. Subtil.*"

"No. I am not." Gallant took a deep breath, and then another. "*Bien.* We are at the point. Suppose—only to suppose—she arranged that, too, that comedy. Suppose even that she killed Bianca Voss. Was that a crime? No. It was justice. It was the hand of God. Bianca Voss was an evil woman. She was *vilaine.* Are you so filled with virtue that you must condemn my sister? Are you a paragon? For she is in your hands, at your mercy. You know about Sarah Yare, but the police do not. You know she dialed that number, but the police do not, and they will not unless you tell them. By your word it can be that my sister was here with you at the time that Bianca Voss was killed. As I have said, I will pay you. Pay you well. It will be a great service from you, and it deserves payment. I will pay you now."

Wolfe grunted. "That was an admirable speech."

"It was not a speech. I do not make speeches. It was an appeal to your charity. From my heart."

"And to my cupidity." Wolfe shook his head. "No. I am not a paragon. I am not even a steward of the law. But you have ignored two important factors. One, my self-esteem. Even if Bianca Voss deserved to die, I will not permit myself to be taken for a simpleton. Two, another woman died too. Was Sarah Yare also evil? Was she *vilaine?*"

Gallant gawked. I don't suppose Lord Byron ever gawked, but Gallant did. "But she—Sarah killed herself!"

"No. I don't believe it. That's another coincidence I reject. Granted that she may have been wretched enough for that extreme, why did she choose that particular moment? Again too pat. According to the published account, the medical examiner says she died between ten o'clock yesterday morning and two in the afternoon, but now that is narrowed a little. Since she spoke with Mr. Goodwin and me on the phone at eleven-thirty, she died between that hour and two o'clock. I believe that the person who killed Bianca Voss at some time prior to eleven-thirty, having arranged with Sarah Yare to enact that comedy, as you call it, went to Sarah Yare's apartment later and killed her. Indeed, prudence demanded it. So you ask too much of my charity. If only Bianca Voss had died—"

"No!" Gallant exploded. "Impossible! Totally impossible! My sister loved Sarah! She killed her? Insane!"

"But you believe she killed Bianca Voss. You came here believing that. All but one of you did. That was stupid too. She didn't."

Gallant's jaw dropped and he froze with his mouth open. The others made noises. Flora gasped and sat stiffly in her chair.

Carl Drew demanded, "Didn't? You say she didn't?"

"What is this, Mr. Wolfe? A game?" Emmy Thorne asked, coming to her feet.

"No, madam, not a game. Nor a comedy—Mr. Gallant's word. As a man I know said yesterday, murder is no joke." Wolfe's eyes went to Flora. "There was much against you, Miss Gallant, especially the fact that you dialed that other number before you dialed Sarah Yare's, and asked someone you called Doris if Miss Voss was around. Are you too rattled to remember that?"

"No." She was still rigid in her chair. "I'm not rattled, I'm just—" She let it hang. "I remember."

"Of course, the reason for it was obvious, if you had killed Bianca Voss before you came here; you had to know that the body had not been found before you proceeded with your stratagem. But since you had not killed Bianca Voss, why did you make that call?"

"I wanted to make sure that she hadn't gone out. That she was there in her office. You might call her again after I left and find out she hadn't been there. I didn't care if you called her and she denied she had talked to you like that. I thought you would think she was lying. I suppose that was stupid too." Her mouth worked. "How did you know I didn't kill her?"

"You told me. You showed me. . . . If you had killed Bianca Voss and devised that elaborate humbug, certainly you would have decided how to act at the moment of crisis. You would have decided to be surprised, and shocked, and even perhaps a little dazed. But it wasn't like that. You were utterly stunned with bewilderment. When Mr. Goodwin told us what Mr. Drew had said, you exclaimed, "He said she is dead?" Then you said, 'But how?' And repeated it, 'But how?' If you had killed Bianca Voss you would have had to be a master dramatist to write such lines, and an actress of genius to deliver them as you did, and you are neither."

Wolfe waved it away. "But that was for me. For others, for a judge and jury. I must do better, and I think I can. The fact remains that Bianca Voss was murdered. If you are innocent, someone else is guilty. Someone else learned of the arrangement you had made with Sarah Yare, either from you or from her, and persuaded her to add a dramatic climax on some pre-text. Someone else killed Bianca Voss and then estab-lished an invulnerable alibi for the crucial period. Someone else had secured the required amount of cyanide—it doesn't take much. Someone else, having established the alibi, went to Sarah Yare's apartment and poisoned her glass of whisky. That was done before two o'clock, and that should make it simple. Indeed, it has made it simple. Shortly before you came I learned from Mr. Cramer of the police that you arrived at your brother's place yesterday a few minutes after noon. Since you left here at a quarter of twelve, you hadn't time to go first to Thirteenth Street and dispose of Sarah Yare; and you were continuously under the eyes of policemen the remainder of the afternoon. That is correct?"

"Yes," Flora said. "When I left here I wanted to go and see what happened to Sarah, but I was afraid. I didn't know—"

"It's a good thing you didn't, madam. . . . I also learned from Mr. Cramer that you, Mr. Gallant; you, Mr. Drew; and you, Miss Prince, were also constantly under surveillance, for hours, from the time the police arrived. That accounts for four of you and leaves only one."

His eyes narrowed at Emmy Thorne. "It leaves you, Miss Thorne. You were with three men in an office on Forty-sixth Street from eleven-twenty until a quarter to twelve. You arrived at Mr. Gallant's place, and found the police there, shortly before three o'clock.

You may be able to account for the interim satisfactorily. Do you want to try?"

"I don't have to try." Her eyes were narrowed, too, and she kept them straight at Wolfe. "So it is a game."

"Not one you'll enjoy, I fear. Nor will I; I'm out of it now. To disclose your acquisition of the cyanide you would need for Sarah Yare; to show that you entered Bianca Voss' room yesterday morning, or could have, before you left for your business appointment; to find evidence of your visit to Thirteenth Street after your business appointment; to decide which homicide you will be put on trial for—all that is for others. You must see now that it was a mistake. . . . Archie!"

I was up, but halted. Gallant, out of his chair and moving, wasn't going to touch her. His fists were doubled, but not to swing; they were pressed against his chest.

He stopped squarely in front of her and commanded, "Look at me, Emmy."

To do so she would have had to move her head, tilt it back, and she moved nothing.

"I have loved you," he said. "Did you kill Sarah?"

Her lips moved, but no sound came.

His fists opened for his fingers to spread on his chest. "So you heard us that day, and you knew I couldn't marry you because I was married to Bianca, and you killed her. That I can understand, for I loved you. But that you killed Sarah, no. No! And even that is not the worst! Today, when I told you and the others what Flora had told me, you accepted it, you allowed us to accept it, that Flora had killed Bianca, though she denied it. You would have let her suffer for it. Look at me! You would have let my sister—"

Flora was there, tugging at his sleeve, sputtering at him. "You love her, Alec! Don't hurt her now! Don't—"

"Miss Gallant!" Wolfe's voice was a whip cracking. "It's too late for compassion. And I doubt if this is any surprise to you. You told Miss Thorne of your appointment with me and your arrangement with Sarah Yare. Didn't you? Answer me."

"I can't—" She swallowed it.

I thought she needed help. "Come on, Finger," I told her. "It only takes one word. Yes or no?"

"Yes," she told me, not Wolfe. "Yes, I did."

"When? Monday night?"

"Yes. I phoned her."

"Did you tell anyone else?"

"No."

She was still holding Gallant's sleeve. He jerked loose, backed up, folded his arms and breathed; and Emmy Thorne moved. She came up out of her chair, stood rigid long enough to give Gallant a straight hard look, shook her head, spun away from him, and headed for the door, brushing against Flora. Her route took her past Anita Prince, who tilted her head back to look up at her, and on past Carl Drew.

I didn't budge, thinking I wouldn't be needed. The understanding had been that Cramer wouldn't butt in unless he was invited, but circumstances alter understandings. As she made the hall and turned toward the front there were heavy footsteps and a hand gripped her arm—a hand that had had plenty of practice gripping arms.

"Take it easy, Miss Thorne," Cramer said. "We'll have to have a talk."

"*Grand Dieu!*" Gallant groaned, and covered his face with his hands.

ASSAULT ON
A BROWNSTONE

I

My rule is, never be rude to anyone unless you mean it. But when I looked through the one-way glass panel of the front door and saw her out on the stoop, my basic feelings about the opposite sex were hurt. Granting that women can't stay young and beautiful forever, that the years are bound to show, at least they don't have to let their gray hair straggle over their ears or wear a coat with a button missing or forget to wash their face, and this specimen was guilty on all three counts. So, as she put a finger to the button and the bell rang, I opened the door and told her, "I don't want any, thanks. Try next door." I admit it was rude.

"You would have once, Buster," she said. "Thirty years ago I was a real treat."

That didn't help matters any. I have conceded that the years are bound to show.

"I want to see Nero Wolfe," she said. "Do I walk right through you?"

"There are difficulties," I told her. "One, I'm bigger than you are. Two, Mr. Wolfe can be seen only by appointment. Three, he won't be available until eleven o'clock, more than an hour from now."

"All right, I'll come in and wait. I'm half froze. Are you nailed down?"

A notion struck me. Wolfe believes, or claims he does, that any time I talk him into seeing a female would-be client he knows exactly what to expect if and when he sees her, and this would show him how wrong he was.

"Your name, please?" I asked her.

"My name's Annis. Hattie Annis."

"What do you want to see Mr. Wolfe about?"

"I'll tell him when I see him. If my tongue's not froze."

"You'll have to tell me, Mrs. Annis. My name—"

"*Miss* Annis."

"Okay. My name is Archie Goodwin."

"I know it is. If you're thinking I don't look like I can pay Nero Wolfe, there'll be a reward and I'll split it with him. If I took it to the cops they'd do the splitting. I wouldn't trust a cop if he was naked as a baby."

"What will the reward be for?"

"For what I've got here." She patted her black leather handbag, the worse for wear, with a hand in a woolen glove.

"What is it?"

"I'll tell Nero Wolfe. Look, Buster, I'm no Eskimo. Let the lady in."

That wasn't feasible. I had been in the hall with my hat and overcoat and gloves on, on my way for a morning walk crosstown to the bank to deposit a check for $7,417.65 in Wolfe's account, when I had seen her through the one-way glass panel aiming her finger at the bell button. Letting her in and leaving her in the office while I took my walk was out of the question. The other inhabitants of that old brownstone on West 35th Street, the property of Nero Wolfe except for the furniture and other items in my bedroom, were around but they were busy. Fritz Brenner, the chef and housekeeper, was in the kitchen making chestnut soup. Wolfe was up in the plant rooms on the roof for his two-hour morning session with the orchids, and of course Theodore Horstmann was with him.

I wasn't rude about it. I told her there were several places nearby where she could spend the hour and thaw out—Sam's Diner at the corner of Tenth Avenue, or the drug store at the corner of Ninth, or Tony's tailor shop where she could have a button sewed on her coat and charge it to me. She didn't push. I said if she came back at a quarter past eleven I might have persuaded Wolfe to see her, and she turned to go, and then turned back, opened the black leather handbag, and took out a package wrapped in brown paper with a string around it.

"Keep this for me, Buster," she said. "Some nosy cop might take it on himself. Come on, it won't bite. And don't open it. Can I trust you not to open it?"

I took it because I liked her. She had fine instincts and no sense at all. She had refused to tell me what was in it, and was leaving it with me and telling me not to open it—my idea of a true woman if only she would comb her hair and wash her face and sew a button on. So I took it, and told her I would expect her at a quarter past eleven, and she went. When I had seen her descend the seven steps to the sidewalk and turn left, toward Tenth Avenue, I shut the door from the inside and took a look at the package. It was rectangular, some six inches long and three wide, and a couple of inches thick. I put it to my ear and held my breath, and heard nothing. But you never know what science will do next, and there were at least three dozen people in the metropolitan area who had it in for Wolfe, not to mention a few who didn't care much for me, so instead of taking it to the office, to my desk or the safe, I went to the front room and stashed it under the couch. If you ask if I untied the string and unwrapped the paper for a look, your instincts are not as fine as they should be. Anyhow, I had gloves on.

Also there had been nothing doing for more than a week, since we had cleaned up the Brigham forgery case, and my mind needed exercise as much as my legs and lungs, so walking crosstown and back I figured out what was in the package. After discarding a dozen guesses that didn't appeal to me I decided it was the Hope diamond. The one that had been sent to Washington was a phony. I was still working on various details, such as Hattie Annis' real name and station and how she had got hold of it, on the last stretch approaching the old brownstone, and therefore got nearly to the stoop before I saw that it was occupied. Perched on the top step was exactly the kind of female Wolfe expects to see when I talk him into seeing one. The right age, the right face, the right legs—what showed of them below the edge of her fur coat. The coat was not mink or sable. As I started to mount she got up.

"Well," she said. "A grand idea, this outdoor waiting room, but there ought to be magazines."

I reached her level. The top of her fuzzy little turban was even with my nose. "I suppose you rang?" I asked.

"I did. And was told through a crack that Mr. Wolfe was engaged and Mr. Goodwin was out. Mr. Goodwin, I presume?"

146

"Right." I had my key ring out. "I'll bring some magazines. Which ones do you like?"

"Let's go in and look them over."

Wolfe wouldn't be down for more than half an hour, and it would be interesting to know what she was selling, so I used the key on the door and swung it open. When I had disposed of my hat and coat on the hall rack I ushered her to the office, moved one of the yellow chairs up for her, and went to my desk and sat.

"We have no vacancies at the moment," I said, "but you can leave your number. Don't call us, we'll call—"

"That's pretty corny," she said. She had thrown her coat open to drape it over the back of the chair, revealing other personal details that went fine with the face and legs.

"Okay," I conceded. "It's your turn."

"My name is Tammy Baxter. Short for Tamiris. I haven't decided yet which one to use on a theatre program when the time comes. What do you think, Tammy or Tamiris?"

"It would depend on the part. If it's the lead in a musical, Tammy. If it packs some weight, O'Neill for instance, Tamiris."

"It's more apt to be a girl at one of the tables in the night club scene. The one who jumps up and says, 'Come on, Bill, let's get out of here.' That's her big line." She fluttered a gloved hand. "Oh, well. What do you care? Why don't you ask me what I want?"

"I'm putting it off because I may not have it."

"That's nice. I like that. That's a good line, only you threw it away. There should be a pause after 'off.' 'I'm putting it off . . . because I may not have it.' Try it again."

"Nuts. I said it the way I felt it. You actresses are all

alike. I was getting a sociable feeling about you and look what you've done to it. What do you want?"

She laughed a little ripple. "I'm not an actress, I'm only going to be. I don't want anything much, just to ask about my landlady, Miss Annis—Hattie Annis. Has she been here?"

I raised a brow. "Here? When?"

"This morning."

"I'll ask." I turned my head and sang out, "Fritz!" and when he appeared, in the doorway to the hall, I inquired, "Did anyone besides this lady come while I was out?"

"No, sir." He always sirs me when there is company and I can't make him stop.

"Any phone calls?"

"No, sir."

"Okay. Thank you, sir." He went, and I told Tammy or Tamiris, "Apparently not. You say your landlady?"

She nodded. "That's funny."

"Why, did you tell her to come?"

"No, she told me. She said she was going to take something—she was going to see Nero Wolfe about something. She wouldn't say what, and after she left I began to worry about her. She never got here?"

"You heard what Fritz said. Why should you worry?"

"You would too if you knew her. She almost never leaves the house, and she never goes more than a block away. She's not a loony really, but she's not quite all there, and I should have come with her. We all feel responsible for her. Her house is an awful dump, but anybody in show business, or even trying to be, can have a room for five dollars a week, and it doesn't have to be every week. So we feel responsible. I certainly hope . . ." She stood up, letting it hang. "If she comes will you phone me?"

"Sure." She gave me the number and I jotted it

down, and then went to hold her coat. My feelings were mixed. It would have been a pleasure to relieve her mind, but of what? What if her real worry was about the Hope diamond, which she had had under her mattress, and she knew or suspected that Hattie Annis had snitched it? I would have liked to put her in the front room, supplied with magazines, to wait until her landlady arrived, but you can't afford to be sentimental when the fate of a million-dollar diamond is at stake, so I let her go. Another consideration was that it would be enough of a job to sell Wolfe on seeing Hattie Annis without also accounting for the presence of another female in the front room. He can stand having one woman under his roof temporarily if he has to, but not two at once.

At eleven o'clock on the nose the sound of the elevator came, then its usual clang as it jolted to a stop at the bottom, and he entered, told me good morning, went to his desk, got his seventh of a ton deposited in the oversized custom-built chair, fingered through the mail, glanced at his desk calendar, and spoke.

"No check from Brigham?"

"Yes, sir, it came." I swiveled to face him. "Without comment. I took it to the bank. Also my weakness has cropped up again, but with a new slant."

He grunted. "Which weakness?"

"Women. One came, a stranger, and I told her to come back at eleven-fifteen. The trouble is, she's a type that never appealed to me before. I hope to goodness my taste hasn't shifted. I want your opinion."

"Pfui. Flummery."

"No, sir. It's a real problem. Wait till you see her."

"I'm not going to see her."

"Then I'm stuck. She has a strange fascination. Nobody believes in witches casting spells anymore, I certainly don't, but I don't know. As for what she wants to see you about, that's simple. She has got something that she thinks is good for a reward, and she's coming to you instead of the police because she hates cops. I don't know what it is or where she got it. That part's easy, you can deal with that in two minutes, but what about me? Why did I tell her I would try to persuade you to see her? Should I see a psychiatrist?"

"Yes."

He picked up the top item from the little pile of mail, an airmail letter from an orchid hunter in Venezuela, and started to read it. I swung my chair around and started sharpening pencils that didn't need it. The noise of the sharpener irritates him. I was on the sixth pencil when his voice came.

"What's her name?" he demanded.

"Miss Hattie Annis. That's another aspect of it. I don't like the name Hattie."

"Who is she?"

"She didn't say, and I didn't even ask her. That's still another aspect."

"Is she coming or phoning?"

"Coming."

"I'll give her two minutes."

You can appreciate what I had accomplished only if you know how allergic he is to strangers, especially women, and how much he hates to work, especially when a respectable check has just been deposited. Besides that satisfaction I had something to look forward to, seeing his expression when I escorted Hattie Annis in. I thought I might as well go and retrieve the package from under the couch and put it in my desk drawer, but vetoed it. It could wait till she came.

But she didn't come. 11:20. 11:25. At 11:30 Wolfe looked over the top of the book he was reading to say that he had some letters to give me but didn't like to be interrupted, and I said neither did I. At 11:45 he got up and went to the kitchen, probably to sample the chestnut soup, in which he and Fritz had decided to include tarragon for the first time. At noon I went to the hall and mounted two flights to my room, and from there dialed the number Tammy Baxter had given me. After four buzzes I got a male voice:

"Who is this?"

It would be a pleasure to kick anyone who answers a phone like that. "My name," I said, "is Buster. I want to speak to Miss Annis."

"She's not here. Buster what?"

"Then I'll speak to Miss Baxter, please."

"She's not here either. Who is this?"

I hung up.

She never came. When I returned to the office Wolfe was back at his desk, and until lunch time I was busy with the notebook and typewriter. The chestnut soup was fine as usual, but I couldn't taste the tarragon. After lunch Theodore brought files down from the plant rooms and we worked on propagation records while Wolfe read his book and drank beer, and at four o'clock they left for the afternoon session with the orchids, which is from four to six no matter what. As soon as they were gone I dialed the *Gazette* number and got Lon Cohen.

"Just a little personal favor," I told him. "Nothing for publication. Have you had anything, maybe an accident, anything at all, about a woman named Hattie Annis?"

"Hell, I don't know. I never know anything. Spell it."

I spelled it. He said he would call back, and I went and stood at a window and watched a couple of dozen flakes of snow that were darting around pretending they were a blizzard. When the phone rang it was Lon himself, which was a compliment, since he was near the top at the *Gazette*.

"You timed it fine," he said. "Was your Hattie Annis a character that owned a house on 47th Street between Eighth and Ninth?"

"Was? Is."

"Not anymore. A hit-and-run driver got her on Tenth Avenue at Thirty-seventh Street at 11:05 this morning. Three blocks from your place. We just got the identification verified ten minutes ago. They found the car at two o'clock double-parked on West Fortieth Street. It was hot. It had been taken from where the owner had parked it on Thirty-sixth Street. Now give. If Wolfe's interested it wasn't just some hooligan. Who's your client?"

"No client. He's not interested. Have you—"

"Come off it! Give!"

"Not a crumb. You know damn well I've given you plenty of breaks, and I'll hand you another one if and when. If you run a paragraph that Nero Wolfe is asking about Hattie Annis I'll chew your ear personally. Have you got a description of the driver?"

"No. But now that you've called we'll sure try to get one."

"Man or woman?"

"Not even that. Look, Archie, just a helpful hint. I'll put horseradish on my ear."

I told him I didn't like horseradish, which wasn't true, hung up, stood a minute, and stepped to the window. The snowflakes were getting reinforcements. I was deciding how to take it. I had liked her even before I had learned from Tammy Baxter that she was a screwball, and we could use more screwballs. Not that I was blaming myself. It was true that if I had postponed my trip to the bank and kept her there she might still be alive, but what the hell, you can't base your actions on the theory that anyone you don't keep your eye on is apt to get killed. That wasn't it. But I admit my feelings were personal. Even at the minimum, I was sore because I had gone out of my way to maneuver Wolfe into seeing her, and at five minutes past eleven, exactly when I was picking the right words and tone to get him, some skunk was smashing her just three blocks away.

Having settled for that as a minimum, I got rubber gloves from a drawer of my desk, put them on, went to the front room, knelt to reach under the couch for the package, took it to the office, to my desk, untied the string, and, without touching more than I had to, removed the wrapping paper. No Hope diamond. It was a stack of new twenty-dollar bills. I picked it up and flipped the corners, the whole stack. All twenties. I got a ruler from a drawer and measured its thickness—one and seven-eighths inches. New bills run 250 to the inch. Nine thousand dollars.

It was a comedown. Nine grand is not hay, but it is less than one percent of a million; and besides, nothing is more uninteresting than a stack of currency when it's not yours and not going to be. I picked off the top one and gave it a look. B67380945B. Of course they would be more interesting if. . . . I went and got a new twenty from the safe and put them side by side for inspection, first just with my eyes, which are good, and then with a glass Wolfe keeps in his desk. Three minutes with the glass settled it, and I took the bill from the bottom of the stack and one from the middle, and used the glass on them, with the same result. They were phonies.

I returned the three bills to the stack, rewrapped it as before, tied it with the string, also as before, went upstairs to my room, put it in the back of my shirt drawer, went back down to the office, took off the rubber gloves and put them away, sat, and considered matters.

There were a lot of aspects. For instance, the essential thing about counterfeit money is to keep it out of circulation. I was doing so. As for having it in my possession, nobody could prove I didn't still think it was the Hope diamond or the secret Pentagon war plans or used typewriter ribbons.

Take the Wolfe aspect. Consulting him was out. Since there was no prospect of a client and a fee, he would merely instruct me to call the Treasury Department and tell them to come and get it.

Or the conflict-of-interest aspect. The T-men would rather see the skunk get five years for passing phonies than the chair for murder, naturally. Homicide, specifically Inspector Cramer and Sergeant Stebbins, the reverse, also naturally. Not that they are not on speaking terms, but they jostle. I had heard the inside dope on how the Lorber case had been messed up a couple of years ago. I was for Homicide, but if I took the package to West 20th Street and reported my chats with Hattie Annis and Tammy Baxter they would have to call the Treasury within an hour after they opened the package, and the jostling would start.

Or the personal aspect. She had entrusted the package to me. Any reward coming to her now would be in a different jurisdiction, but she had hated cops, and as her trustee it was my duty to see that they didn't horn in on her estate. If there actually was a reward, which was doubtful, I could turn it over to the Actors' Fund. As for my position, no one but Wolfe knew she had come, and even he didn't know she had left a package with me.

Or the logical aspect. Since she had rarely left her house and never went more than a block away, it was a fair assumption that she had found the bills there and that one of her tenants had put them there, probably in his or her room. That was enough to start; going on to assume that he had followed her downtown could wait.

Those were the main aspects. After looking them over, along with a few minor ones, I got the address by finding Annis, Hattie, in the phone book, buzzed the plant rooms on the house phone to tell Wolfe I was going out on an errand, went to the hall for my coat and hat, and left. With the snow coming down thicker and the wind swirling it around there would be no such thing as an empty taxi at that time of day, so I walked, twelve short blocks uptown and one long one across.

It was a dump all right, like hundreds of others in that part of town. I stood across the street for a survey through the snow, blinking it from my lashes. I didn't care to bump into Sergeant Purley Stebbins or any of the others, but of course it wasn't likely that Homicide was around, since it was probably being handled as a routine hit-and-run. There was no police car in sight, and I crossed over and entered the vestibule. It had never been converted for multiple tenancy—only one mailbox, and one button, on the jamb. I pressed it and waited for a click, but none came. Instead, after half a minute, the door opened and a tall thin guy with a marvelous mane of wavy white hair was there, boring a hole through me with deep-set blue-gray eyes.

"You a reporter?" he boomed. It almost blew me back out of the vestibule.

"Not guilty," I told him. "I would like to see Miss Baxter. My name's Goodwin."

"Do you recognize me?" he demanded.

"No. I have a feeling that I would in a better light, but no."

"Raymond Dell."

"Sure. Of course. Certainly."

He turned on his heel and strode down the dim and dingy hall. I entered and shut the door. He kept going, to a door at the end of the hall and on through, and, since he hadn't told me to wait, I followed. As I crossed the sill he was saying, "For you, Tammy. A Philistine. Goodman."

It was the kitchen. Tammy Baxter and another girl, and two men, were seated at a big table with a linoleum top, dining or maybe teaing—sandwiches on paper plates and coffee in big white heavy cups. There was a fifth chair and the white-maned Raymond Dell was taking it and picking up what remained of a sandwich.

"Hi," Tammy said. "Not Goodman, Ray. Goodwin. Archie Goodwin. I met him somewhere. A Philistine but not a barbarian. Martha Kirk, Mr. Goodwin. Raymond Dell. Noel Ferris. Paul Hannah. I don't ask what you want . . . because I may not have it. I hope it's not a sandwich?"

It was neat. She had used only four words, "I met him somewhere," to tell me that she didn't want them to know of her call at Wolfe's office. I humored her. "No, thanks," I said. "It's not urgent. I'll wait somewhere till you finish if you'll tell me where."

"You phoned," Noel Ferris said.

He was looking at me. I met his lazy brown eyes. "I phoned?"

He nodded, a lazy nod. "Around noon." His voice changed: " 'My name is Buster. I want to speak to Miss Annis. Then I'll speak to Miss Baxter, please.' " His voice changed back. "Will that pass?"

It would indeed. On a tape recording my voice doesn't sound like me at all, but he had it to a T, and he had only heard me once on the phone. "Perfect," I said. "I wish I could do it. It's a gift."

"That's nothing." He was bored. He was younger than me, but probably he had been born bored. "But your name's Archie Goodwin. I seem to have heard it. Are you in the theatre?" He waved it away with a lazy hand. "It doesn't matter. Don't bother."

I opened my mouth to bother, but closed it when Tammy Baxter pushed her chair back and got up. As she headed for the door I moved, but stopped when she said, "I'm just going for my lipstick. I'll be back." Paul Hannah was telling Noel Ferris, "Of course you've heard it." Hannah was still younger than Ferris. For a juvenile lead he would have to do something about his chubby cheeks. He was regarding me. "Aren't you the Archie Goodwin that works with Nero Wolfe?"

"For him," I said.

"A detective."

"Right."

"A snoop," Raymond Dell rumbled. "Worse than a Philistine. A monster."

"That's not very polite," Martha Kirk said. She was an ornamental little number, not long out of high school, with a dimple in her chin. I no longer had any illusions about dimples. The most attractive and best-placed ones I had ever seen were on the cheeks of a woman who had fed arsenic to three husbands in a row.

"If Ray knew how to be polite," Noel Ferris drawled, "he would have had his name at the top of a marquee long ago." His eyes moved lazily to me. "Since you're a detective, maybe you can help us. As a service to the arts. We've having a conference, but it's a farce. Just a guessing match. We want to know what's going to happen to this castle of culture now that our Lady Bountiful has been slain."

"By a fiend," Raymond Dell declared. "Worse than a monster!"

"People who steal cars," Paul Hannah said, "and run them over people ought to have their hands and feet cut off."

"How horrible," Martha Kirk said. She had a full rich contralto, enough for one twice her size. "That's brutal, Paul."

"It's not polite," Noel Ferris drawled. "But you might agree if you had seen her, Martha darling. It was my luck to be here when they came to get someone to identify her. *That* was horrible. I would be for one hand and one foot, at least."

Raymond Dell boomed at me, "Is that what you're snooping about?"

"No," I said, "it's after hours. I only snoop from eight to four. I know about Miss Annis because it happened only three blocks from Nero Wolfe's place and the cop on the beat told me, but that's a police matter. I'm just a Philistine trying to rub up against culture."

"So Tammy is culture," Noel Ferris said. "I don't deny that she—but here she is. Tammy, you're culture."

"Sit down," Dell commanded me. "I'll explain why it's hopeless. Utterly hopeless."

"Later, Ray." Tammy Baxter was in the doorway. "Maybe Rodgers and Hammerstein sent him to beg me to take a lead. If I like it I'll buy the house and have the plumbing fixed. Come on, Mr. Goodwin."

She started down the hall and I followed. Toward the front she opened a door on the left, entered and flipped a light switch, and, when I was in, closed the door. It was the parlor, at least it had been the parlor fifty years back, and it was the same furniture. Dark red plush or velvet or whatever it was. An upright piano. The window blinds were down. I dropped my coat and hat on a sofa. She took hold of a chair to move it and found it was heavy, and I helped, and we sat. She didn't sit like an actress. Actresses sit with their knees together and to one side a little, and their feet drawn in, but she kept hers straight front and at a right angle, with her feet flat.

She cocked her head. "I've been trying to guess what brought you. It would be flattering to think it's a social call, but no such luck. When you phoned you asked for Miss Annis first."

"That Noel Ferris is a wonderful mimic," I said. "When I was a boy I could croak like a bullfrog, but I've lost it. I'm more than willing to make it social. If you can stand a drink on top of a sandwich Sardi's is only a six-minute walk."

She shook her head. "I think not. You did ask for Miss Annis?"

"Yes. The fact is, I'm under suspicion. I suspect myself of wanting to see you again, I have no idea why. I suspect my asking for Miss Annis was a trick. After I had spoken with her I would have an excuse to ask for you, and you wouldn't suspect what I was really after. Not a bad idea."

"A grand idea. And now?"

"Now I admit there's another element. You heard me say how I happened to hear about Miss Annis, from the cop on the beat—no, you weren't there."

"No. From the cop on the beat?"

I nodded. "Right in the neighborhood, only three blocks away. And she had told you she was going to see Nero Wolfe. Have you told the police that?"

"I haven't told them anything. They haven't asked me. I was out and wasn't here until nearly four o'clock. They had talked with Noel Ferris and Raymond Dell, and Noel had gone and identified the body. There's nothing I can tell them. It was just a moron or a maniac, or both, with a stolen car. Wasn't it?"

"Evidently." I was looking relieved. "But there's still a chance they may check with everyone here, sometimes they're pretty thorough, and that's the other element. If the police learn that she had said she was going to see Nero Wolfe they'll pester him. It won't make any sense since she didn't see him, but they'll grab at the excuse to pester him, and anyhow they may think she did see him. He has been known to reserve facts. Since, as you say, it was just a moron or maniac with a stolen car, it won't help any for them to know she had said she was going to see Nero Wolfe, so there's no point in your mentioning it. Of course it's not vital, he's been pestered before, but I thought it wouldn't hurt to suggest it. And I still suspect myself. There's the possibility that I've merely cooked up an excuse to see you again."

I admit it wasn't a very good line, but it was the best I had been able to come up with, and anyhow all I had wanted was an approach. It had already got me a look at the inmates. Also it would be interesting to get her reaction. I have mentioned the possibility that she had had the Hope diamond under her mattress, and while a stack of phoney lettuce isn't the same thing as the Hope diamond, far from it, it was still possible. How would she take it?

I soon found out. "I would love to think," she said, "that you bothered to cook up an excuse. I wish I could, but I can't. Why don't you want the police to know that Miss Annis saw Nero Wolfe? What did she say that he doesn't want to tell?"

My brows lifted. "You're mixing us up. I'm the detective. Trick questions like that are no good if you can't back them up. You know darned well she didn't see him."

"But she did. What did she say? Was it before I was there or after?"

I grinned at her. "Come on now, Miss Baxter. I was looking forward to calling you Tammy. Don't spoil it."

"I wouldn't dream of spoiling it. I *can* back it up. You told Noel Ferris on the phone that your name was Buster. Hattie always called men Buster. Even Ray Dell. She had been there and she had called you Buster. It was in your mind and you said that to Noel without thinking. Had you ever before told anyone that your name was Buster?"

At that point, naturally, my mind was occupied. If it hadn't been I might have heard the doorbell ring, and noticed it, and also heard and noticed steps in the hall. I might even have recognized a voice from out in the vestibule. But my mind was too busy.

"You're doing it wrong," I said. "You should have sneaked up on me. You should have asked me casually why I told Ferris my name was Buster, and then it would have depended on how I answered. You might have got me in a hole. I doubt it, but you might. Now it's no good because I've seen your hand. I say I've often told people my name is Buster because that's what my grandmother called me, and what do you say?"

"I say I want to know why you told me this morning she hadn't been there."

"Right. Then I say that if I lied to you this morning, which I am not conceding, I must have had a reason, and the reason must still hold or I wouldn't be dodging like this. Your turn."

"What kind of a reason?" Her eyes, straight at me, weren't sociable at all.

"Oh, nothing fancy. She had told me you were a Russian spy would do. Or that one of her roomers was stealing eggs and I thought it might be you."

"I'd like to wring your neck!"

"Wear gloves. They're working on a method to lift fingerprints from bare skin." I leaned toward her. "Look, Miss Baxter, I really meant it when I asked you to keep

161

it to yourself that Miss Annis told you she was going to see Nero Wolfe. He hates to be pestered. But the way you're riding me, it looks to me as if something's biting you, and if so, maybe I can help and I'd be glad to. I've had a lot of experience with bites. Did Miss Annis tell you why she was going to Mr. Wolfe? Was it something that—"

The door flew open and I turned my head and saw an object that didn't appeal to me at all. He stopped short and glared at me. "You? You again?"

I stood up. "The same for me," I said. "You again. When the door of a room is closed you're supposed to knock. Miss Baxter, this is Sergeant Purley Stebbins of Homicide. Miss Tammy Baxter. There should be a class on manners at the—"

"What are you doing here?"

"Have a heart. What is a man usually doing when he's sitting in a parlor with a pretty girl? Pardon the expression, Miss Baxter, of course you're not merely a pretty girl, but I put it at the sergeant's level."

"Are you telling me or not?"

"Not. Not even if you say please. Shinny on your own side.'

"We'll see." His eyes moved. "Your name is Baxter?"

"Yes. Tammy or Tamiris."

"You live here?"

"Yes."

"How long have you lived here?"

"Three weeks."

"I'm an officer of the law and I'm here to ask some questions. Come with me, please. Goodwin, you wait here."

Of course that was absurd. Since he was taking the pretty girl it would have been silly for me to stay there and twiddle my thumbs, and besides, I was twiddling my brain. Why was he there? What had sicced Homicide on it? So when she got up and went and he followed I tagged along, to the kitchen. The others were still at the table, except Paul Hannah, who was bringing the coffee pot from the range. Tammy joined them. There were more chairs at one side, and Stebbins got one and took it to the table. As I went and sat on one he barked at me, "I told you to wait in there!"

"Yeah. I thought you might want to ask me something. If I'm in the way I can go home."

"I'll deal with you later." He sat and got out his notebook and pencil, and ran his eyes over the audience. "This is just some routine questions," he told them. "As you know, the owner of this house, Hattie Annis, was hit by a car and killed at five minutes past eleven this morning. One of you identified the body."

"I did," Noel Ferris said.

"Okay. We've got the car. It had been stolen. We haven't got the driver yet, and we're making a routine check. I'll start with you, Miss—your name, please?"

"Martha Kirk."

He wrote. "K-I-R-K?"

"Yes."

"Occupation?"

"Dancer."

"Employed at present?"

"No."

"How long have you lived here?"

"Nearly a year."

"Where were you at eleven o'clock this morning?"

"Wait a minute," Raymond Dell rumbled. "This is invasion of privacy. It's monstrous. Are we in Moscow? Look at that child, that coryphée in the bud! Do you dare to imply that she is a murderous fiend?"

"I'm not implying anything. I said this is routine. I'm doing you folks a favor, coming here instead of sending for you. Miss Kirk?"

"I was here. In my room, in bed."

"At eleven o'clock?"

"Yes."

"Was anybody with you?"

Paul Hannah let out a whoop. Noel Ferris drawled, "Now really." Stebbins blushed. "Routine," he said stiffly.

"No, I was alone," Martha Kirk said. "I got up about eleven, a little after, and dressed and went out. I think this is exciting. I never gave an alibi before. I guess I'm not giving one now, because nobody was around."

Stebbins was getting it down. He looked up. "Miss Baxter?"

"You have my name," she said, "and that I've lived here three weeks. I'm going to be an actress if I can make it. Not employed at present. This morning I left here around ten o'clock to go shopping, and between then and noon I was in four or five different stores."

I had her in profile and couldn't tell how well she handled her face when she was lying, but her tone was perfect. Purely matter-of-fact. That's not so easy when someone is present, disposition unknown, who can call you.

Stebbins went to Ferris. "You, sir?"

"Noel Ferris." He spelled it. "Actor out of work because if it's either television or starve, I'll starve. Lived here a year and a half. For two hours this morning, from ten-thirty on, I was calling at casting agencies."

"How many?"

"Four, I think, altogether."

"Can you get corroboration for eleven o'clock?"

"I doubt it. I doubt if I would try. This is so idiotic."

"Maybe so." Stebbins turned a page of his notebook. "And you, sir?"

"Paul Hannah. Hannah with an *h*." He was standing back of Tammy's chair, with a cup of coffee. Standing up he looked even younger than sitting down. "I'm rehearsing in *Do As Thou Wilt*. It goes on at the Mushroom Theatre next month. That is, we hope it does."

"How long have you lived here?"

"Since September. Four Months."

"Where were you at eleven o'clock this morning?"

"I was walking."

"Where?"

"From here to Bowie Street. To the Mushroom Theatre."

"That's three miles. Quite a walk."

"I often walk it. It's good exercise and it saves bus fare."

"Anyone with you?"

"No."

Purley's head turned. "And you, sir?"

Raymond Dell passed a hand over his white mane and cleared his throat. "I answer under protest," he declared. "You deliberately left me to the last. I submit only to hasten your departure. My name is Raymond Dell. It is not entirely unknown. I have lived here four years. I am not engaged at present."

"You're an actor, Mr. Dell?"

His deepest blue-gray eyes darted right and left. "Am I an actor?" he demanded.

They nodded. Ferris said, "You certainly are."

"Where were you at eleven o'clock this morning?"

"I was eating an orange."

"Where?"

"In my room, which is above our heads. I never leave the house before noon. I was reading Sophocles' *Oedipus Rex*. I always read Sophocles in January."

"Were you alone?"

"Certainly!"

Stebbins' head turned right and then left. "Five of you. Are there any others? Any other tenants?"

Tammy Baxter said no.

"Have there been any others recently? In the last two weeks?"

Another no.

"Do any of you know of any enemies Hattie Annis had? Anyone who might—where you going?"

That was for me. I was up and moving. I turned to tell him, "To the parlor for something, whistle if you want me," and proceeded. I did stop in the parlor, for my coat and hat. Opening the front door, and closing it after me, I made no unnecessary noise, not wanting to disturb a police officer in the performance of his duties.

The snow was coming down thicker and the street was white. I was not actually deserting the field of action; it was merely that I had looked at my watch and seen ten minutes past six. Wolfe would be down from the plant rooms, and he would enjoy his beer more if I rang him to say I was being delayed on my errand. Ninth Avenue was closer than Eighth, so I went that way, found a booth in a bar and grill, contributed a dime, and dialed. And got a surprise. Ordinarily Fritz answers the phone when I'm not there, but it was Wolfe's voice.

"Nero Wolfe's residence."

"Me. I'm stuck with—"

"Where are you?"

"Forty-seventh Street. I'll be—"

"How long will it take you to get here?"

"Seventeen minutes. Why?"

"There's a man in the front room. Fritz let him in out of the snow. Come at once."

It wasn't quite as childish as it sounds. An experience a couple of years back had shown that it was just as well for me to be present when Wolfe talked with a stranger. But I ventured to ask, "What's his name?"

"Leach. He showed Fritz his credentials. From the Secret Service Division of the Treasury Department."

"Well. What do you know. I'm on my way." I hung up, having certainly got my dime's worth. A T-man.

III

Headed downtown on the crawling bus, I reflected that there was one nice thing, though only one: I hadn't left the package under the couch in the front room. If what I had heard of T-men was only half true, he would have smelled it. Except for that it was a very foggy prospect. Guessing wouldn't help any, but there was nothing else to do in the bus, so I considered a dozen guesses and didn't like any of them. Dismounting at 34th Street and walking the block and a half to the brownstone, I let myself in, put my coat and hat on the rack, and went to the office. Wolfe was standing over by the big globe, studying it, probably picking out a spot for me to be exiled to. He darted a glance at me, grunted, and went back to the globe.

I spoke. "Did he ask for you or me?"

"Both. See what he wants."

Instead of using the connecting door I went around by the hall and entered from there. He got up from a chair by the window as I appeared—a medium-sized round-shouldered guy who had started going bald. "I'm Archie Goodwin," I said. "Keep your seat." I went to the couch and sat. "Sorry you had to wait."

He took a leather fold from his pocket, flipped it open, and came and held it out for inspection. I gave it a look. His first name was Albert. I nodded. "Right. What can I do for my country?"

"I want to speak with you and Wolfe," he said. "Both of you."

"You can start with me. Mr. Wolfe is busy."

"I'll wait till he's free." He went to the chair and sat.

"It could be an hour. Meanwhile, here we are, and we might as well chat."

"No. I'll wait. You can tell Wolfe that I am acquainted with his methods and I don't approve of them."

He was the final type. He talked final, looked final, and acted final. If I had told him that Wolfe wouldn't be free until tomorrow afternoon he would have said, "I'll wait." So I said, "Then he'll have to change them. You should have let him know before. I'll go tell him." I went around by the hall again, found Wolfe still studying the globe, and announced, "He's a mule. Only both of us will do. There are just three alternatives: bounce him, bring him in, or lock him in until he gets hungry enough to leave by a window. He doesn't approve of your methods."

"What does he want?"

"Nothing doing. He's not very big. Bouncing him would be easy."

"Confound it. Bring him in."

I went and opened the connecting door and called to him, "You win, Leach. This way." He came, passing through, stopped in the center of the room to look right and left, went to the red leather chair near the end of Wolfe's desk, and sat. Wolfe, in no hurry, gave the globe another glance and then moved, detouring around the guest to get to his chair. As I was going to mine Leach spoke:

"If you're busy, Wolfe, it will save time to tell you that the Secret Service Division of the Treasury Department is not the same as the New York Police Department. I know your record and your reputation. We don't like fancy tricks and it doesn't pay to play games with us. I want to make that clear."

A corner of Wolfe's mouth twitched. "Your notebook, Archie. Get that down. If you will please repeat it, sir?"

It didn't faze him. "It was fair and proper to say it," he stated. "I was referring to your well-known habit of withholding information from the police which they are legally entitled to have. Their reasons for not calling you to account may be sound; I'm not criticizing them. But we will not tolerate any such defiance of your obligations under Federal law."

"Archie?"

"Yes, sir." I had my notebook and pen. "I'm getting it."

"Is this gratuitous, Mr. Leach? Or have you a point?"

"I have a point. I have reason to believe that you are in possession of information regarding a counterfeiting operation—counterfeiting of United States currency. You got the information from a Miss Hattie Annis this morning. I want to know what she told you—everything she told you. I also ask if she showed you any counterfeit money. I also ask if she left any counterfeit money with you, and if so, where is it? I also ask why you have not notified the authorities during the seven hours that have passed since she was here."

The corner of Wolfe's mouth twitched again. "I'm afraid your homily and warning were wasted, Mr. Leach. I have never seen a Miss Hattie Annis. Mr. Goodwin told me this morning that a woman of that name was to call to see me at eleven-fifteen o'clock, but she didn't come. Archie?"

"She came at a quarter to ten," I told the mule,

"just as I was leaving on an errand. She didn't enter the house. She told me her name and said she wanted to see Nero Wolfe, that she had something in her handbag for which there would be a reward and she would split it with him. She wouldn't tell me what it was. She said if she took it to the cops they would do the splitting. I told her to come back at a quarter past eleven and I would try to persuade Mr. Wolfe to see her. She said nothing about counterfeiting and she showed me no counterfeit money. She left, and I went on my errand, depositing a check, not counterfeit, at the bank. When Mr. Wolfe came to the office I told him about her and he said he would see her, but she never came. However, that was not the last I heard of her. I learned this afternoon that a woman of that name had been killed by a hit-and-run driver around the corner from here, on Tenth Avenue."

"How did you learn it?"

There was no telling how many sources the Secret Service had around town, so I abandoned the cop on the beat. "From a friend of mine on a newspaper. When she didn't show I wondered if something had happened to her, and I phoned him."

"She's dead," he said. "We can't ask her what she told you."

"That's right. I could be lying to Yonkers and back, but I'm not. I only lie to cops and women. I wouldn't dream of lying to you."

"I wouldn't advise you to. You just came in. Were you out on another errand?"

"Yes."

"What?"

The natural thing would have been to say it was none of his business. But apparently they had tailed Hattie Annis to Wolfe's place, and if so, they might have tailed me to 47th Street, and I was being frank and open. So I said, "Looking into possibilities. Hattie Annis had said she had something that was good for a reward. It could have been something really worth while; you never know. And she had been killed. It wouldn't hurt to poke around a little, and I went up to her house on Forty-seventh Street to see if I could stir up something. I had barely got started when a Homicide sergeant came and took over. I beat it and came home—and found you."

"You admit that she said she was in possession of something that was good for a reward."

"I state it."

"But you deny that she told you it was counterfeit money?"

"I do."

"Do you deny that from what she said you inferred it was counterfeit money?"

"I do. On my way from the bank I decided it was the Hope diamond."

"Why?"

"Because I knew you'd be asking and I thought that would be an interesting twist. You would be thinking she had counterfeits, but the point was that she had the real thing. The counterfeit was in the Smithsonian Institution."

I don't expect you to believe it, but he actually said, "So you admit that you knew we would be asking?"

"By gum," I said, "I guess you've got me. I wonder how I knew?"

Wolfe grunted. "Archie. If you must chaff him, take him somewhere else."

Leach got up. "I'll do the taking. If you're telling the truth, both of you, all right. If not, you'll regret it." He turned and went. I arose and stepped to the hall and offered to hold his coat, but he preferred to do it himself.

171

As I reentered the office Wolfe demanded, "Was that where you were? That woman's house?"

"Yes, sir." I went to my desk and set. "I wouldn't lie to a T-man. Too risky."

"And a policeman came?"

"Yes, sir. Stebbins."

"You have a remarkable talent for getting involved to no purpose. You know quite well how Mr. Cramer will react when he learns that Mr. Stebbins, investigating a death by violence, found you there ahead of him."

"Yeah. That's the least of my worries. I've got a problem. I'll have to take a week off—of course without pay—while I work it out. Beginning now."

"Pfui." His eyes narrowed. "What are you trying to badger me into?"

"No, sir. It's *my* problem. You wouldn't be interested."

"What is it?"

"Well." I considered. "Since I got it on your premises while in your employ I suppose you have a right to know. I have to figure out what to do with nine thousand dollars in counterfeit money that's upstairs in my room."

He snorted. "The Hope diamond, too, of course."

"No, this is straight. Everything I told Leach was true, but I didn't mention that Hattie Annis gave me a package to keep until she returned. She told me not to open it and I didn't, until I learned that she had been killed. Then I took a look. About nine thousand bucks in phony twenty-dollar bills, brand new. They're pretty good; I had to use a glass on them to be sure. I took them up and put them in my shirt drawer. Then I went up to her house to see if I could spot a counterfeiter, and got interrupted by Stebbins."

"Why didn't you mention it to that donkey? And give him the package?"

I eyed him. "Do you really want me to answer that?"

He pulled at the tip of his ear. "No."

"I should hope not. That specimen? If I had given him the package and told him I didn't know what was in it he wouldn't have believed me. He would have taken both of us on a charge of possession. It's a good guess that they had a tail on her, or how did he know she came here? If so, it's barely possible the tail saw her hand me the package. and he'll be back with reinforcements and a search warrant. I'm going to get it out of the house, right now, and I'm going to leave the back way."

"Do so. At once. Don't mail it to him or his organization. Mail it to the police."

"No, sir. As I said, I'm taking a week off. I hope a week will do it."

"Nonsense." He glared. "I am instructing you to mail it. Without delay."

"Sorry." I stood up. "It's *my* problem. First I'll take the package somewhere and come back later for some things. I'll let you know where you can reach me." I moved.

"Archie!"

I turned. "Yes, sir?"

"This is not to be borne. If you go, stay."

I stood facing him. "Okay. I'll bang the door when I leave, since I'm fired. But I'd like to describe the situation, not that you give a damn, just for the record. Hattie Annis may have got killed just because she happened to be there when a baboon came along in a stolen car, but she may not. I think not, for fairly good reasons. If it was deliberate, it's a good guess that she got it because she knew where that counterfeit money came from, so it will be essential evidence if and when he is tagged. Not only will it have to be produced; it will have to be shown that she had it. If I ditch it by mailing it to the police or the Secret Service, no matter who, so it can't be traced, it can't be connected with her and he can't be nailed. That's my problem. She left the package with me. If she was murdered on account of it, I don't owe the murderer any favors and I'm not going to do him one."

I turned and marched out, chin up, with my ego patting me on the back, and mounted the stairs to my room. Getting the package from the drawer, touching nothing but the string, I went back down to the hall for my coat and hat, and, after I had my gloves on, stuck the package in my pocket. As I neared the office door on my way to the kitchen Wolfe's voice came:

"Archie!"

I stuck my head in. "Yes, sir?"

"You will dine here?"

"No. Fire me and feed me? Better not. I'll come and get some clothes and things."

"Very well."

I admit that as I passed through the kitchen and saw Fritz at the range basting two tender young pheasants in the roaster I felt a twinge. I also admit that as I let myself out, crossed the little enclosed space where Fritz grew herbs in the season, and unlocked the gate, I felt another twinge of a different kind. It was just possible that the Treasury Department knew of this back way and had it covered, and missing the pheasant would be the least of my troubles if I got nabbed with that package on me. The passage between two buildings was narrow and dark, and eddies of snow were whirling down. Emerging to the sidewalk on 34th Street, I turned left.

Making sure you are unattended is never difficult, and on a snowy blowy night there's nothing to it. Turning three corners was enough, and I leaned into the

wind and forgot the rear. But at the entrance to Grand
Central Station I stood a couple of minutes with my
eyes open before going to the ramp and on down to a
bank of lockers. Five seconds later, minus a dime and
the package and plus a key, I proceeded to the tunnel
to 45th Street, climbed the stairs, and was in the snow
again for six blocks. The clerk at the Churchill wouldn't
admit he had a room, so I went to the manager's office
and asked for a man I don't need to name for whom I
had once done an important favor. He came through,
both with a room and with an envelope. I wrote on the
envelope, "Property of Archie Goodwin, to be delivered only to him in person," put the key in it and
sealed it, and left it with the assistant manager. I then
went down to the Tulip Bar, having in mind a modest
snack in the neighborhood of three bucks, and saw on the
menu "Suprême of Pheasant Berchoux. . . . . . .$9.00."
Of course I had to, though Berchoux was a complete
stranger. It turned out to be okay, but the sauce wasn't
up to Fritz's by a long shot.

If I have given the impression that I not only knew
what I was doing but also what I was going to do, kindly
erase it. Now that my immediate objective, getting the
package properly cached, was accomplished, I could
proceed as I saw fit, but what would fit? No matter
which direction I headed I would find both the T-men
and the cops already there, jostling each other, and
there was no point in getting my toes trampled. By the
time the waiter brought pecan sour cream pie and
coffee I had my program all planned: ring a friend to
suggest a couple of hours' dancing at the Flamingo, go
to 35th Street and pack a suitcase and bring it to the
hotel, keep the dancing date, take the friend home and
discuss with her whatever she felt like discussing, return to the hotel, sleep nine hours, get up and have
breakfast, go for a walk, and drop in on Lon Cohen at the

Gazette and get the latest dope on Hattie Annis. That struck me as a fine combination of initiative, snap, and staying power.

But I didn't get to carry it through. After attending to the first item, ringing a friend and making a dancing date, I left by the main entrance, got a taxi, gave the hackie the 35th Street number, and asked him if an extra buck for a 15-minute wait while I packed a suitcase appealed to him. He said with the meter running and I said sure. Arriving, I mounted the stoop, used my key, entered, and went to the office, intending merely to tell Wolfe where I could be reached.

He wasn't there. Fritz was standing in the middle of the room, looking grimmer than I had ever seen him. His head jerked for a glance at me and then jerked back to watch what he was watching. It was Albert Leach. He was over by the filing cabinets, with one of the drawers open. He snapped at me: "When did you leave here and where have you been?"

Ignoring him, I asked Fritz, "How did he get in?"

"It was another man." Fritz's tone was as grim as his look. "I put the chain bolt on before I opened the door. He pushed a paper through the crack and I brought it to Mr. Wolfe. It was a search warrant, and Mr. Wolfe said he must be admitted. There are five of them. They have finished with the front room and dining room and kitchen and basement. Mr. Wolfe is with one of them in his room. One of them is on the third floor. Two of them are in the plant rooms. Theodore is with them."

I glanced at my watch. 9:20. "When did they come?"

"About an hour ago. I was taking in the salad and cheese."

"When and how did you leave here?" Leach demanded.

So he had had a man out front. "It could be like this," I told him. "I came in and saw you at the files and

176

didn't recognize you, and naturally I went for you. My best is a kidney punch. You'd be back to normal in a few days. Mr. Brenner would be glad to corroborate me. Has he done the safe, Fritz?"

"Yes. Mr. Wolfe was here."

"Too bad I missed it. I'll be right back."

I went outside first to pay the hackie and dismiss him. Returning, I glanced in at the office and then mounted three flights to the plant rooms. The lights were all on. It was a joke. To do a thorough job on those thousands of pots and the beds of coke, looking for something as small as a wad of bills, would have taken six men six days. The two T-men were in the potting room, going through a bale of osmundine. Theodore was perched on a stool, grinning at them.

"They looking for thripe?" he asked me.

"No," I told him. "The Hope diamond. If they leave a mess keep track of your time cleaning it up. We'll want to send a bill. Keep an eye on them."

He said he would, and I left. One flight down I found no one in my room, and no visible sign of disturbance, and proceeded to the south room, which was a spare. One was there, lifting the mattress to put it back on the bed.

"That's wrong side up," I said.

"It's the way it was," he said.

"I know, but we turn it every Monday, and this is Monday. Turn it over, please."

He straightened to look at me. "No wonder. You're Archie Goodwin."

"Yeah. Have you done the other room on this floor? My room?"

"I have."

"Did you find the secret drawer?"

He bent to straighten the mattress, turning his back. Apparently he didn't care to chat, so I left, descended another flight, and turned right. The door at the end was open, and I crossed the sill. Wolfe was in the big chair by a window, his eyes on a man who was at the shelves on the far wall, removing books to look in back of them. I approached.

"I've made the rounds," I said. "Quite a crew. Leach is going through the files. The one on my floor will probably want to help me pack my suitcase. I'll be at the Churchill, but I don't know the room number yet."

He growled, a low growl in his throat. "Bah," he said.

"Yes, sir. I agree."

"How much longer will they be?"

"I couldn't say. Ten minutes or an hour or all night. I can ask Leach."

"No. Ask him nothing and tell him nothing. Your post is in the hall until they go. There are five of them."

"Yeah, I counted."

"Let me know when they have left. I have phoned Mr. Parker. He will learn in the morning their grounds for getting the search warrant. As they leave ask each of them if he has taken anything, in Fritz's presence." He turned his head to glare at the man by the shelves, who had dropped a book.

I would have preferred to roam around, keeping in touch with the various sectors of the operation, making comments as they occurred to me, but in the circumstances it seemed best to humor him, so I went down to the office and used the phone to cancel the dancing date. Then, telling Fritz to stay put and disregarding questions from Leach, not even looking at him, I stepped to the hall for patrol duty.

It was 10:28 when they left—that is, when they were actually out and I had closed the door. The last quarter of an hour had been spent in a conference in the office of the whole quintet and in Leach trying to think of a question I would reply to. Having found that I wouldn't even tell him if it was still snowing, having gone up to Wolfe's room and found the door locked, and having got no response when he knocked, he came back down, collected his gang from the office, and herded them out. I went and buzzed Wolfe's room on the house phone to notify him, and then to the kitchen for a glass of milk. When I returned to the office Wolfe was there, telling Fritz to bring beer. Ordinarily ten o'clock is his beer deadline, but this was an emergency.

He sat and sent his eyes around, to the book shelves, the globe, the safe, the files, and me. "Is there any chance," he asked, "that we can be heard?"

"Very slim if any." I stood with the milk. "Fritz was here all the time. Not unless they invented something new last week."

"You did your errand?"

"Yes. Okay."

"Sit down." Fritz came with the beer, and Wolfe opened the bottle and poured. He likes plenty of foam. "I want a complete report from the beginning. From the time that woman appeared this morning."

"Why? What's the use? It's my problem."

"Not anymore. Now it's mine. My house has been invaded, my privacy has been outraged, and my belongings have been pawed. Sit down."

I moved to get one of the yellow chairs. He snapped, "Don't be flippant! Sit at your desk!"

"It's not mine," I objected.

"Pfui. Confound it, sit down!"

I did so.

IV

When Wolfe says he wants a complete report he means it—all the words, all the actions, and the music if any. At one time it had been a strain, but after all the years of practice I could rattle it off with no trouble at all. I left nothing out, not even the detail that Tammy Baxter didn't arrange her legs like an actress when she sat. When I got to the end I said, "Before you start with questions I have one. I'm just curious. Why did you fire me? I have reported in full. What did I do or say that was out of line? Why fire me?"

"I didn't."

I stared. "What?"

"I merely said, 'If you go, stay.' That was ambiguous. You are never ambiguous when you quit, and neither am I when I discharge you. You were merely headstrong, as usual." He wiggled a finger to flip it away. "That has no pertinence to the problem. I suppose you have made assumptions?"

"Plenty. That Hattie Annis found the counterfeit money in a room in her house and therefore knew who it belonged to. That the Secret Service knew or suspected that someone in that house was passing counterfeits, but they didn't know who, and they were holding off because what they want is the guy that makes it. That the roomer knew or suspected that Hattie Annis had taken the money, and followed her here, and killed her. He might or might not have known that she didn't have it, that she had given me the package: that doesn't matter. With her dead it couldn't be proved that he had had it."

"Don't expound. I'm awake. Just your assumptions."

"This one has an alternative. Either that it couldn't be Tammy Baxter, since Hattie Annis told her she was coming here, or that it is Tammy Baxter and she followed Hattie Annis here and then had the nerve to wait until I came back and fed me a line, to find out how much I had been told. The second has the edge. Since you're awake you caught what she said: 'She said she was going to take something—she was going to see Nero Wolfe about something.' If she was straight, why the dodge?"

"Of course. What else?"

"That a T-man tailed Hattie Annis here and saw her hand me the package. That one limps, because why didn't he stay on her, and if he stayed on her why didn't he see the driver of the car that killed her? Also if both a T-man and the roomer tailed her here why didn't they bump? I haven't bought that one, but I have this: that the Secret Service has passed on something to the cops. I don't know what or how much, but something. Purley Stebbins wouldn't go up to Forty-seventh Street in a snowstorm to tackle that bunch about a hit-and-run unless he had reason to think one of them was involved. Excuse me for expounding."

"Anything else?"

"That'll do for now."

"When it was your problem you were going to deal with it. How?"

"I was going to take a girl to the Flamingo and dance a couple of hours. I always find that stimulating. I hadn't decided how. Now that it's your problem I think you'll find that you need to be stimulated too. There is absolutely no—"

The doorbell rang. I got up, went to the hall, took a look through the one-way glass panel, saw a familiar red round face and a pair of broad shoulders, and turned to tell Wolfe, "Inspector Cramer."

Only then did I realize how hard the raid of the T-men had hit him, when he did something he had never done before. He arose and came to the hall and on to the front door, made sure the chain bolt was on, opened the door the two inches the chain would allow, and growled at the crack, "Yes?"

"Yes," Cramer growled back. "Open up."

"It's bedtime. What do you want?"

"I want in!"

"Have you a warrant?"

"Nuts. I don't need a warrant to ask you a few questions—and Goodwin."

"At this hour of the night you do. We will be available at eleven in the morning if we are not engaged."

"I had nothing to do with that warrant!"

What followed was as unprecedented as Wolfe's answering the doorbell. I had seen and heard those two tangle many times, but it had never gone beyond words and looks and gestures. There and then it was brawn and bulk. Wolfe tried to shut the door and found it was obstructed. He flattened his palms on it and pushed. Nothing doing. I have never asked Cramer whether he had his shoulder or his foot against it, or his toe in the crack. If the latter, he must have regretted it. Wolfe turned and put his back against the frame, set his heels, and heaved, and the door slammed shut.

"Fine," I said. "It's a three-way jostle now—the Secret Service, the New York Police Department, and us. Fine."

He went to the elevator, opened the door, and turned. "Turn off the doorbell and the telephone. Don't leave the house in the morning. Tell Fritz."

"Yes, sir."

"Can you make a package like the one she gave you? In appearance?"

"Approximately. Near enough for the naked eye."

"Do so in the morning. Goodnight."

"What do I put in it?"

"Anything that will serve. Paper."

"What do I do with it?"

"I don't know. We'll see in the morning. Bring it to my room at half past eight."

He entered the elevator, which groaned as usual at the load, and pulled the door to. I went to the office to try the safe door, take a look at the files, and flip the switches, then to the kitchen to tell Fritz we were breaking off relations with the world, and then up to my room for some privacy.

Fritz takes Wolfe's breakfast up to his room on a tray 17 × 26, and I eat mine in the kitchen. Tuesday morning, as I disposed of orange juice, griddle cakes, sausage, eggs poached with a purée of anchovy paste and sherry, and coffee, with the morning paper on the rack, the counterfeit package of counterfeits was at my elbow. Fritz being a paper and string hoarder had made it simple, and for the contents all I had needed was typewriter paper and the office paper cutter. It wasn't identical, but it was close to it, and the ordinary white string was exactly the same.

I had had to hunt for Hattie Annis in the *Times*. They had given her a measly three inches on page 17, and there was no hint that it was anything but an everyday hit-and-run. It said that the driver had been so muffled up that no good description of him or her had been obtained.

At 8:28 I took the last swallow of coffee, picked up the package, arose, told Fritz the eggs had been even better than usual and went up to Wolfe's room. He was at the table by a window, fully dressed, dipping honey from a jar onto a muffin. I displayed the package and he frowned at it.

"Nine thousand dollars?" he demanded.

"Right. The dimensions are perfect. I have a suggestion. Make another one and mail one to Leach and one to Cramer."

"I have a better one."

He described it. Whether it was better than mine would depend on how it worked out, but at least it was worth trying. He is as good at giving instructions as I am at reporting, and I rarely have to ask any questions, but that time there was one. If a situation developed where authority was needed, which should I call, Cramer or Leach? He wouldn't say. He wouldn't concede that any situation could be desperate enough to justify calling either of them, which left it up to me. I went down and got my coat and hat, stuck the package in my coat pocket, and left the house the back way. Either of the enemy forces might have a sentry out front, or even both, and I didn't want to bother with shaking a tail. The snow had stopped during the night and the sun was edging over the top of the buildings across 34th Street. I flagged a taxi and told the driver 47th and Eighth Avenue.

I rather doubted if anyone would be up and around so early at the castle of culture, but evidently recent events had caused some changes in routine. Five seconds after I pushed the button in the vestibule there were steps inside. The door opened and Paul Hannah was there. He blinked. "My eye," he said. "Rubbing against culture at this hour?"

"I'm a fanatic," I told him. I stepped in. "I got interrupted yesterday by that sergeant. I know it's early, but there's something I want to clear up."

A voice came down from above, Tammy Baxter's: "Who is it, Paul?"

I called up, "Archie Goodwin! Good morning! I know I'm a nuisance, but it can't be helped. Is there any chance of having a conference?"

"With me?"

"With all of you. I have a little problem to settle. Do you suppose they can be roused?"

"I'll see. I don't know if Ray . . . I'll see."

Paul Hannah asked if I had had breakfast and I said yes but I could use a cup of coffee if there was any to spare, and he headed for the rear. I followed, but detoured into the parlor to put my coat and hat on the sofa. As I entered the kitchen Hannah was at the range pouring coffee. "I guess," he said, "I'm a misfit as an actor. I have always liked to get up in the morning and I can't break the habit. What's the problem you want to settle?"

I could have told him he would also have to do something about his chubby cheeks, but didn't. "Nothing much," I said. "Probably nothing at all. Pumpkin pie?"

He nodded. "Another habit, pie for breakfast. My favorites are mince and lemon meringue, but they didn't have any yesterday. Have a piece?" I said no, thanks, and he changed the subject. "What do you think of Clement Brod?"

That was a challenge. When anyone asks what you think of somebody you never heard of, the game is to place him without letting on. You can nearly always win if you play it right, and that time it was a cinch. Without a single fumble I had learned that Clement Brod was a well-off young man in his twenties who had had a book of poems published, had written an off-beat play called *Do As Thou Wilt*, had worn a beard for a year but shaved it off, and owned a Jaguar, by the time Hannah had finished his second piece of pie and third cup of coffee; and I would soon have been an authority on Brod if we hadn't been interrupted. The four of them arrived together—Tammy Baxter, Martha Kirk, Noel Ferris, and Raymond Dell. The girls were dressed for anybody and their faces and hair had been attended to. Ferris had combed his hair but was in shirt sleeves and no tie. Dell's marvelous white mane was tousled and his costume was an ancient blue dressing gown with spots on it. As he entered he boomed: "Monstrous! Flagitious!"

"There's plenty of coffee," Hannah said. "Kippers, anyone?"

Noel Ferris stretched, yawned, muttered, "Give me the sun," and came and sat. Martha Kirk went and got cups. Tammy Baxter said, "You have made history, Mr. Goodwin," and pulled up a chair. Dell sank onto one where it was, took an orange from the pocket of his gown, and started peeling it.

"I apologize," I told them. "I don't know what 'flagitious' means, in fact I didn't know it was pronounced like that, but I admit it's monstrous. My excuse is that I wanted to get here before any of you went out."

"More coffee?" Martha Kirk asked me. Looking up at her, from an angle, the dimple seemed a little off-center, but it wasn't.

"I believe I will, thanks." I wanted to be one of them.

"It had better be good," Noel Ferris drawled. His lazy brown eyes were only half open. "Good heavens! I hope you're not going to evict us?"

I would have liked to tell him it would be a pleasure to evict a man who answered the phone by asking who is this. "No," I said, "for that I would need a badge and I'm strictly private." I took a sip of coffee. "I just want to settle a little matter. Why I phoned yesterday and asked for Miss Annis, I had seen her and talked with her. She had come to see Nero Wolfe, but he was busy, and she was coming back at a quarter past eleven. She never came, and I wondered why. When I phoned of course I didn't know she had been killed."

186

"You asked for Miss Baxter," Ferris said.

"Yeah. I knew she lived here. I had met her somewhere. Later, when I learned what had happened to Miss Annis, I thought over what she had told me, and on account of something she had said, something she had told me was confidential, I wanted to take a look at her effects. I wanted to know what to do about what she had told me in confidence. So I came, and was talking with Miss Baxter when we were interrupted. And here I am again. I'm going to glance through Miss Annis' things, her papers mostly. Did she have a desk somewhere?"

"A good idea." Ferris yawned. "Go to it. Second floor front. If you find a will leaving the house to Ray Dell we'll be fixed for life."

"That's brutal," Martha Kirk said. "The poor woman isn't even in her grave yet."

"She left nothing to me," Dell rumbled. "She regarded me as a sloven. All my eloquence couldn't persuade her that orange peel, as it dries in a waste basket, gives a scent pleasant to a discriminating nose."

"She was right," Martha declared. "It smells terrible."

"Is it all right to do that?" Paul Hannah asked me. "Go through her things? Isn't there a law about it?"

"If there is," Ferris said, "he should break it. We all should, in her memory. She hated cops."

"I won't be breaking any law," I assured them, "unless I pinch something, and I'm not going to. Of course the strictly proper thing would be to get permission from the executor of the estate, but who is it? Do any of you know?"

They didn't.

"Has anyone been here officially? Someone claiming to be an heir? Or a lawyer?"

They said no. "Hattie was a relict," Raymond Dell

declared. "The last of her line. It is my belief that she was without kith or kin—unless we are to be considered her kith. That appeals to me." He thumped his chest. "Raymond Dell, of the kith of Hattie Annis. May I have a napkin, Martha?"

Tammy Baxter spoke for the first time since she had told me I had made history. "You may not find what you're looking for, Mr. Goodwin. That police sergeant was in Miss Annis' room for more than an hour last night after he finished with us. He may have taken it."

"Which suggests a question," Ferris said. He put his cup down. "You're a detective, you ought to know everything. Why the inquisition? Why are we beset? Why did that bloodhound tell us not to leave the jurisdiction? What is the jurisdiction? Why did Hattie go to see Nero Wolfe? What did she tell you in confidence? What do you expect to find among her papers?"

"That's seven questions," I protested. "Have a heart."

"They're damn good questions," Paul Hannah said. He was at the range again. "I'd like to ask them myself. I think we all would. Especially the first two. As far as we know, Hattie was crossing the street and got hit by a goon who had stolen a car." His chubby cheeks were flushed. "Why don't they find him and cut off his hands and feet? What have we got to do with it?"

I shook my head. "Search me. That's not my territory. As for what Miss Annis told me in confidence, now that she's dead it may be that I ought to tell it, and that's what I want to find out. Specifically, about the package she left with me—a little package wrapped in brown paper. She didn't tell me what was in it. I don't want to slander the dead, but from something she said I got the notion that it might have belonged to one of you and she had swiped it. Are any of you minus such a package? Or anything that could be put in such a package?"

"That's horrible," Martha Kirk said. "To accuse Hattie of stealing!"

"He's not accusing her, Martha darling," Ferris told her. "He's eliminating. Detectives spend practically all their time eliminating."

"Could it be a book?" Raymond Dell asked. "My *Tamburlaine* is gone."

"It's not the right shape for a book," I said. "Six inches by three and two inches thick."

"Where is it?" Tammy Baxter asked.

"In my overcoat pocket." I sent my eyes around. "Oh, I left it in the parlor."

"Well, for heaven's sake." Martha Kirk turned her hands up—a dancer's hands. "I'm not a detective, but when I want to know what's in a package I open it. Shall I bring it?"

"No, thank you, Miss Kirk. Miss Annis told me not to open it. She's dead, but as far as I'm concerned it's still her property. Unless you want to claim it?"

"Me? Why should I? It's not mine."

"Miss Baxter?"

Tammy shook her head. "No."

"Mr. Dell?"

"I am minus nothing." He had finally finished the orange. "Nothing but my illusions, my ambitions, and my hopes. They could not be contained in the package you describe."

"Mr. Ferris?"

His eyes were still only half open. "How can I claim it unless I know what's in it?"

"Have you missed anything recently?"

"No. Not even an illusion."

"Mr. Hannah?"

He shook his head. "I guess we're all eliminated. Why, did Hattie tell you it belonged to one of us?"

"No, it was just a notion I got. —By the way, Mr. Dell, that remark you made yesterday about snooping. I snoop only within reason. I could have opened the package and tried whatever is in it for fingerprints. If I found some I could have come and got hold of samples from you people—for instance, from the coffee cups. That would have been snooping. Instead, I just came and asked you." I pushed my chair back and stood. "I apologize again for coming before breakfast, and many thanks for the coffee and the cooperation. You said second floor front, Mr. Ferris?"

"Correct. One flight up. If you find a will leaving it to anyone but us or one of us, burn it."

"I'll do that." I went.

I took my time mounting the stair, trying each step for creaks, in case developments called for silent descent. The fifth from the top didn't creak but it croaked unless you stepped on the inside end. The upper hall had three doors, one toward each end and one about the middle. The one at the rear end was standing open—Raymond Dell's, since he had told Stebbins that his room was above the kitchen. The one in the middle was shut; probably a closet. The one at the front was also shut, and I went and opened it and entered. There was a massive walnut bed, a big old rolltop desk, a worn and faded carpet with big flowers, some chairs; and a hundred or so pictures of men and women all over the walls, most of them in costume, and all of them actors from a mile off.

Of course staying there was no good; I might as well have stayed at home. A floor and ceiling were between me and the parlor, and if he or she took the bait quick, on leaving the kitchen, he could be in and out of the parlor without my hearing or seeing a thing.

There was no place to lurk in the lower hall. Only one place would do. I left, closed the door, went to the landing, and listened. Voices came up, dominated by the boom of Raymond Dell. With that for cover I descended, remembering the fifth step, saw that the hall was clear, made the door to the parlor, opened it, entered, and shut the door gently.

There were three possibilities: a closet if there was one, the upright piano at the right wall, and the sofa itself. One of the other two doors was probably a closet, but I wanted a better view than a keyhole, and with the blinds down there wasn't much light. To be covered by the sofa I would have had to shift its angle. The thought struck me that one of them might already have dived in and out again, and I felt the pocket of my coat. Still there. I went and huddled at the end of the piano, squeezing into the corner, and decided it would do. It would have to. If he looked around first it would cramp my style, but anyhow there would be something to discuss. I straightened up, listened to my ears, and kept an eye on two doors, since the one at the far corner might be to a passage to the kitchen. It was so dark that I could barely see the hands of my wrist watch. 9:42.

I might have been able to hear their voices, at least Dell's, if it hadn't been for the street sounds. Morning crosstown traffic in the Forties can be heard even when it can't be seen. So I quit trying. I learned later that the historic gathering I had assembled soon broke up, but the only sign I got was footsteps in the hall a couple of times. They went on by. I was rubbing one eye and beginning to think he wasn't going to bite, that I had wasted a lot of typewriter paper and carefully selected items from Fritz's hoard of paper and string, when the door to the hall started to open, and I squeezed into the corner fast.

V

He certainly wasn't noisy. I have good ears, but the door closing was just a faint whisper, and so was his crossing to the sofa. But when a package is a tight fit in a pocket it isn't easy to get it out with no noise at all, especially if you're in a hurry, and I heard that, which was the main point. I moved and spoke: "Did you want me?"

It wasn't he, it was she, and she was quick. She made a dash for the door and got there before I did, but it opened in, and of course that was hopeless. I was against it before she had the knob turned. "You rat," she said, not too loud.

I stretched an arm to reach for the wall switch and turned on the light. "I admit I'm surprised," I said. "If I had made book on it you would have been at the bottom."

"You lied," she said. "Yesterday. You said she hadn't been there."

"Sure. Because she might have had reasons for not wanting you to know. Apparently she did."

"She did not! She told me she was going!"

"Maybe. Or maybe you followed her. Anyway, the point isn't why I lied, it's why you sneaked in and snitched that package." I put out a hand. "I'll take it."

She backed up a step. "You will not. It's not yours, it's hers. That's why I came and got it. You have no right to it!"

"Have you?"

"As much as you have. More. This is her house. It belongs here."

I shot out a hand, grabbed her wrist, whirled her off balance, and with the other hand got the package.

"Coward," she said. "If I were a man . . ."

"I wish you were. For instance, Noel Ferris. I don't like the way he answers the phone. Look, Miss Baxter. I may be a rat and a coward, but I'm not a goof. If you felt that I had no right to the package because it belongs here, why didn't you say so? The three men could have held me while you came and got it, or at least they could have tried. But you sneaked in when the coast was clear, or you thought it was. Of course you knew I would miss it, so the point was that I wouldn't know who had taken it. Why?"

"I'm a woman," she said.

"Right. No argument. And?"

"I'm a woman, that's all." She put out a hand and was going to touch me but let it drop. "You have a reputation for knowing all about women, Mr. Goodwin."

"And?"

"And I act like one. Calling you a rat and a coward, that was silly. Of course I know you're not, I know you're a very smart man, and you're honorable and anything but a coward." She put her hand out again, and that time touched my arm. "It's just that I think I may know something about what's in the package on account of what Hattie told me yesterday morning. She said she was going to take it to Nero Wolfe. You say she left it with you and told you something in confidence. If you ask me why I sneaked in here and took it, can't I ask you why you set a trap? Why you told us it was here in your pocket and then sneaked in and hid?"

She talked too much. I had caught her in the very act, and she was turning it into a debating match. I decided to give her a test. "We could keep this up all day," I said. "I'll call Purley Stebbins, the police sergeant who was here yesterday, and he'll come or we'll go and see him. Let him decide about the package. Where's the phone?"

That did it, and I should have been tickled but

wasn't. I believe I haven't mentioned that the idea had occurred to me at our first meeting that it might be interesting to know her better, to learn about such details as her table manners and her reactions to dance music, and a girl is not available for that kind of investigation if she is in the coop on a murder charge. Even before she spoke, the expression on her face was a big hint.

She spoke. "I'd rather not," she said. "Hattie hated cops."

"Hattie is dead."

"Yes, but . . ." She touched my arm. "You said yourself it's still her property and she certainly wouldn't want us to give it to the police. She trusted me, didn't she? When she told me she was going to see Nero Wolfe? Can't you trust me, Mr. Goodwin? Don't you think I'm fit to be trusted?"

I skipped that. She was unquestionably a woman. "All right," I said, "there's an alternative. I'm not too fond of cops myself. We'll go and put it up to Nero Wolfe. Get your coat and hat."

She considered it, twisting her mouth, her head tilted, regarding me. "You won't give me the package if I promise to come later?"

"Of course not."

"All right. I'll go. My coat's up in my room."

I opened the door and she passed through and headed for the stairs. Since I would have at least six minutes, the world record minimum for a human female to get a coat and put it on, I thought I might as well take a look at Hattie Annis' desk, so I went up. The door was standing open, and Paul Hannah appeared on the sill as I approached.

"Oh, there you are," he said. "I was thinking about those questions Ferris asked. You didn't answer them."

"I made a stab at it." I entered and crossed to the

desk. The top was rolled up, the pigeonholes were stuffed full, and stacks of papers and magazines and miscellaneous items left no room on the surface. It would have taken an hour for a quick once-over or four hours for a real job, not counting the drawers. I pulled out the contents of a pigeonhole. "Which question especially?" I asked.

"All of them. I don't get any of it."

"I'm not sure I do. That's why I'm snooping. I'll let you know if I find anything that helps."

"I won't be here. I'm leaving for the theatre. Rehearsal."

"Good luck and don't trip on anything. If Clement Brod's around give him my regards."

He said he would, and went. Opening the six drawers of the desk, none of them locked, and finding that they were stuffed too, I went back to the surface and pigeonholes. There were theatre programs, newspaper clippings, pictures cut out of magazines, cancelled checks—something of everything except letters. Not a single letter. My watch told me that the six minutes had stretched to ten, which was surely enough, when Tammy Baxter's voice came: "Mr. Goodwin! Where are you?"

She was below, at the foot of the stairs, in the same fur coat and fuzzy little turban as the day before. I descended and got my coat and hat from the parlor and put the package in the pocket, and we left, heading west. She was a good woman walker, neither trotting nor jiggling. When we had flagged a taxi on Ninth Avenue and I had climbed in after her and given the hackie the address, I asked, "Do you drive a car?"

"Certainly," she said. "Who doesn't?"

So that was no help. You can't steal a car and run it over somebody if you don't know how to drive. If you think I'm piling it on, that I didn't really suspect she might have killed Hattie Annis, you are wrong. If there's a formula for ruling people out as incapable of murder under any provocation I don't know what it is, and there were four marks against her. But that aspect of the situation was soon to be disposed of. As the taxi rolled to the curb in front of the old brownstone a man got out of a parked car just ahead. It was Albert Leach.

I should have caught on immediately. I should have let Tammy Baxter scramble out by herself instead of giving her a hand. I certainly was a sap that it didn't dawn on me when Leach flashed the leather fold with his credentials and said, "I'm arresting you on suspicion of being in possession of counterfeit United States currency."

My brows went up. "No warrant this time?"

"No warrant is needed if the suspicion is based on reasonable grounds."

"You ought to know. I'm not up on Federal law. But since we're outdoors and you have already searched my room, I suppose 'possession' means having it on my person?"

"It does."

"Okay, that's easily settled." I stretched my arms wide. "Go to it."

"Not here." He touched my shoulder. "Come along."

"I respectfully decline. I'm too heavy for you to carry, so you'll have to drag me. People have been known to plant things on people, and here I have witnesses—this lady and the cab driver. If you undress me and I catch cold I hereby agree not to hold the United States responsible." I stretched my arms again.

He turned and called, "Come here, Ziegler!" and a man climbed out of the car and joined us. "Stand by," Leach said, and moved. He didn't pat or feel; he simply stuck his hand in my pocket and pulled out the package. He backed up, squatted, put the package on the sidewalk, untied the string, and opened the wrapping. He stared a second at the neat white stack of paper, then picked it up and flipped through it, first at one end and then the other.

"Don't soil it, please," I said. "That's good bond." I stretched my arms. "Try again. You've barely started."

He stood up. "I warned you yesterday, Goodwin. It doesn't pay to play games with us. You'll regret this. Come on, Ziegler." He turned and headed for the car, with the makings of the package.

"Hey!" I called. "I want that!"

He ignored me, and it wasn't worth an argument, since I could make another one at a cost of under fifteen cents. When they had got in and rolled away, the hackie called to me, "What's he? FBI?"

"Yes," I told him. "Foiled By Intelligence —What's the idea?"

Tammy Baxter was opening the door of the cab. "I'm going," she said. "I might as well. The package is gone."

"But you're not. Nothing doing. There is still something to discuss. We'll go in and discuss it here, or you can discuss it later with Stebbins. Take your pick."

She hesitated, then swung the door shut. "Okay," I told the driver, "your flag's up," and he fed gas and was off. Tammy turned to me: "What was that in the package? Just blank paper?"

I eyed her. "Show me your credentials," I said.

"What? What credentials?"

"Nuts. Maybe you're right. You might as well go. Then I can go in and ring a man I know on the *Gazette* and give him an item he'll appreciate. Human interest. That Archie Goodwin was ambushed on the sidewalk in front of Nero Wolfe's house by two T-men and a T-woman and arrested for possession of counterfeit United States currency, and only his quick wit and presence of mind saved him. I'll bet he doesn't even know there is a T-woman. I didn't. A picture of you would help. A picture of you would decorate any story. The gorgeous glamorous T-woman. Wait here a second while I go in and get my camera."

"What on earth are you talking about? What's a T-woman?"

"Oh, come on down. When you went to get your coat you phoned him. Two of them waiting here in a car? And the way he went about it? If I'm wrong you can sue the newspaper and me both for libel."

"You wouldn't dare!"

"Ha. You double-talking she-weasel. Giving me the dewy eye and purring at me, 'I'm a woman.' Touching my arm and asking me if you weren't fit to be trusted. Come in and purr at Nero Wolfe a while. Are you coming or going?"

"I have nothing to say to Nero Wolfe. If you can set a trap—"

"Shut up! If I go in alone I ring my newspaper friend before I take off my coat and hat. Which do you want me to use, Tammy or Tamiris?"

No reply. I turned and started up the steps. She came. By the time I had my key out she was there, and I swung the door open and let her precede me. T-women first. She stood while I got rid of my hat and coat and then started for the office, but I stopped her. "In here," I told her, opening the door to the front room, and she passed through. "I'm going to report first," I said. "Help yourself to the magazines. Don't bother to strain your ears; the soundproofing is good. I'm locking the door to the hall only so you won't roam around looking for packages; if you get tired waiting you can leave by a window."

She had something to say but I wasn't interested. Leaving by the hall door, which I locked, and proceeding to the office, I found Wolfe at his desk counting bottle caps he had taken from his drawer. Tuesday is the day for checking the week's beer consumption. I went and stood. When he looked up I asked, "Any more invasions?"

"No," he said. "I had a talk with Mr. Cramer on the phone. He wanted to know what that woman told you yesterday and what you were doing at her house. Of course he wasn't satisfied, he never is, and he may call. I'll be through in a moment." He finished putting the caps in groups of ten, figured the total, scowled at them, muttered, "I don't understand it," and brushed them into a heap. "Didn't I hear a woman's voice?"

"You did. She's in the front room. The bait worked fine, as planned, but it hooked the wrong fish. It is now one sweet mess. I'll have to report in full."

"Very well."

I went to my desk and sat, and gave it to him, omitting nothing. He is the best listener I know of, his most violent reaction being with his fingertip, making circles the size of a quarter on the arm of his chair. When I got to the end and said, "If you have no use for her I'll take her to the Empire State Building and push her off," he moved the fingertip to rub the side of his nose.

He cleared his throat. "It could be that your wit was dulled by your discomfiture. How certain are you that she is a colleague of Mr. Leach?"

"Utterly. Totally. Absolutely. She is probably kept under cover and used only for special occasions. I doubt if Tammy Baxter is her real name."

He leaned back and closed his eyes, and his lips moved—out to a pucker and then in again, out and in, out and in. His record for that performance is around forty minutes. That time it was only three or four. He opened his eyes and spoke. "I need your opinion."

199

"Of her?"

"No. Of a stratagem. That one miscarried, but it has prepared the way for another. I'll describe it."

He did so, and I gave it both ears. It was nothing as complicated or fancy as some of the programs he has cooked up, and I had to answer only three questions as my contribution. And at the end a fourth, when he asked, "Well?"

"Yes," I said, "except for one detail. What if you can't keep her here and Leach is waiting for me at the door?"

He grunted. "Am I a clod? Bring her."

I went and opened the connecting door and said, "In here, Miss Baxter."

VI

As she sat in the red leather chair Wolfe frowned at her on principle and I frowned at her in particular. The chair would have held two of her, and in order to have her knees straight in front and her feet flat she had to sit on the edge. Twenty-four hours earlier I would have thought that she went fine with the red leather, but now my mind was closed.

"Do you know what a premise is, madam?" Wolfe demanded.

"Why . . . yes," she said.

"We have one: that you are an agent of the Secret Service of the Treasury Department. If you're going to waste my time denying it you may as well go. If you do, you know what Mr. Goodwin's intentions are and I approve of them. It would be a readable item. He suffered a contretemps, but so did you and your colleagues. Shall I proceed?"

"I'll listen," she said.

"Good. First, I am concerned only with the exposure of a murderer. With you that is secondary; your target is a counterfeiter. The reason for my concern is personal and not material to this discussion. I wish you success in your pursuit, but I won't let it impede mine. You know who killed Hattie Annis."

"I do not!"

"I think you do. At least you have grounds for a strong suspicion. You were assigned to that house because there was evidence that someone there was involved in a counterfeiting operation, and you have lived there three weeks. Surely you aren't so inept that you learned nothing. You may even have known who it was when you went there, and your purpose was to discover his source of supply. I won't list the reasons for the assumption that he killed Hattie Annis; you know them as well as I do. I don't suggest that you will let a murderer escape his doom if it suits your convenience; it is merely that you give priority to your objective, and I do not. But the advantage is with me. I have the package of counterfeit bills."

Her eyes widened. "You have it? You admit it?"

"I state it, here with you, where Mr. Goodwin makes it two to one if you are moved to quote me. Parenthetically, there is a plausible explanation for the package that was just taken from the pocket of Mr. Goodwin's coat. Yesterday Mr. Leach asked if Hattie Annis had left some counterfeit money here. Obviously there was some somewhere, and presumably it had been a factor in Miss Annis' fate, so I told Mr. Goodwin to make a package of appropriate size and shape to use as bait. That's our explanation for the record; for you the truth is better. We have the package."

"Where is it?"

"Out of your reach, I assure you. Another paren-

thesis: the disclosure of your status removes some difficulties. As an instance, we had supposed that Mr. Leach
knew that Miss Annis had come to this house yesterday
because he or one of his men had followed her here.
But if so, as Mr. Goodwin pointed out to me, why
hadn't he followed her when she left, and why hadn't
he seen the driver of the car that killed her? Now those
questions are answered. She was followed here by the
man who was soon to kill her—and you could name
him—but not by Mr. Leach. He knew she had come
here because you told him. I concede that you are not
without gumption. When you learned that Mr. Goodwin had said on the phone that his name was Buster
you inferred that Miss Annis had spoken with him, and
you left the room, ostensibly to get your lipstick, but
actually to make a phone call." His head turned.
"Archie?"

I nodded. "Oh, she's bright. I'm proud of her."

He returned to her. "Other points are clarified by
the disclosure of your status, but they are minor. I have
a proposal to make. Mr. Goodwin and I are in a pickle.
We want the murderer to be exposed, apprehended,
tried, and convicted; but the package of bogus money
will be an essential item of evidence, and we have it
but can't produce it without embarrassment at the least
and substantial penalty at the worst. You, on the other
hand, have much to gain by producing it. It will more
than compensate for your mishap in arranging for Mr.
Leach to stub his toe. It will be a leaf for your garland.
I propose to make the package available to you. Do you
want it?"

"Of course I want it." She didn't sound enthusiastic.
"And of course this is some very fancy trick. What will
be in it this time?"

Wolfe shook his head. "No trick. I am offering to
trade. We will give you the package Miss Annis left

with Mr. Goodwin, intact, in a manner uncompromising for us but satisfactory to you, if you will answer some questions; and you will not be quoted. This is in good faith, madam."

"What are the questions?"

"I repeat, you will not be quoted. I want information for my own use, not testimony for a tribunal. During the three weeks you have lived in that house have you searched the premises?"

She pinched her lips with her teeth. She looked at me. "What is this, Mr. Goodwin? Another trap?"

"No," I said, "this is straight."

"Is it being recorded?"

"No. When Mr. Wolfe says in good faith he means it, and so do I. He's offering a deal and we're not double-dealers."

She looked at Wolfe. "All right. Yes, I have."

"Did you find what you were looking for?"

"No. The first thing was to find out if it was being made there, and it wasn't. Then to find out where he got it."

"Did you?"

"No. I think I would have pretty soon—if this hadn't happened."

"Did you know who he was when you went there?"

"I knew—" She stopped. She decided to finish it. "I knew a certain person who lived there had passed some. That's all I'm going to tell you unless you tell me something. You said you would give me the package in a manner satisfactory to me. You might think it was satisfactory but I wouldn't. You can't just hand it to me and expect me not to tell where I got it."

"No indeed, but indulge me. I'll tell you in a moment. Have you searched that house thoroughly?"

"Well . . . I made sure that there was no equipment anywhere to make counterfeit money. I wasn't looking for just a few bills. There would have been no point in that."

"When you learned that Miss Annis had found something she was going to bring to me, and you suspected what it was, or she told you what it was, did you try to find it? Did you search her room?"

"No. She only told me about it yesterday morning just before she left, and she showed me the package, but she wouldn't say what was in it."

"Did she tell you where she had found it?"

She thought that one over. Finally she said, "Yes."

"Did you ever search her room?"

"I did once, the first week, looking for equipment."

"Very well." Wolfe rested his elbows on the chair arms and laced his fingers. "This will be the procedure. You will stay here with me. You will give your house key to Mr. Goodwin. He will go and get the package, go to the house and to Miss Annis' room, and choose a place to hide the package. He will choose with care, since a policeman was in that room last evening. He will then phone here, you will go to the house and join him, you will search the room together, and you will find the package. That should be satisfactory. You understand, of course, that if you report this conversation or any part of it we'll deny it in toto. You will have been impelled by your animus against Mr. Goodwin because of the humiliation he subjected you to. Two against one."

She was looking doubtful. "I am capable of good faith too, Mr. Wolfe. But for the record, she brought the package and gave it to Mr. Goodwin. How did it get to her room?"

"She didn't give it to Mr. Goodwin. After she spoke with you she decided not to bring it; or after speaking with Mr. Goodwin she decided not to show it to me, merely to tell me about it, went home and left it there, and returned to this neighborhood. There was plenty of time. Neither of those suppositions can be disproved. I will add that this offer is not made under pressure of desperation. If you decline it, no one will ever see that package again. That will make my job more difficult but by no means impossible. If you accept it, and do not report this discussion, you will betray no trust. On·the contrary, your recovery of the package will be a coup. I have more questions to ask, but if you accept the offer, Mr. Goodwin can go now."

"What questions?"

"A few minor ones and one major one. The major one, naturally, is the name of the murderer."

"I don't know it."

"Pfui. That's a quibble. The name of the person living in that house who had passed counterfeit money. What is it?"

She shook her head. "No," she said emphatically. "Not that. No."

Wolfe grunted. "You prefer to preserve him to lead you to your quarry. So does Mr. Leach; he felt bound to give the police a hint, but not the name. I intend to press the point, but Mr. Goodwin might as well go. —Archie?"

I got up and went to her. "The key, please?"

She was and she wasn't. The glamorous she-weasel tilted her adorable, maybe, face up to me, presumably to see if I was fit to be trusted. I made my face the picture of integrity, virtue, and honor. Apparently that did it, for she opened her bag, took out a key fold, removed one of the keys, and handed it to me.

"You'll get it back," I said, "see you later," and went.

There can be any number of reasons for making sure that you're not being tailed or shaking it off if you have one, but on the whole I don't know of a better one than that you prefer not to have company when you are on your way to pick up nine grand in phony lettuce. It took me two blocks to learn that unquestionably I had company, and two more to decide that it was Homicide, not Secret Service. That was cockeyed. I was risking, if not my life, at least my liberty and pursuit of happiness, to give Homicide first call on a murderer, and they were dogging me. It took me an extra ten minutes to make it to the Churchill, since I had to be absolutely certain that I had lost him.

Having got the envelope with the key at the manager's office, I didn't relax en route to Grand Central; and having got the package from the locker, I changed my attitude. Now, if I got a bad break and was spotted, I no longer minded being followed to my destination; I merely didn't want to be stopped. Getting a taxi at the 42nd Street entrance, I told the driver I was in a hurry two dollars' worth, and he made it to 47th and Eighth Avenue in seven minutes. From there I walked and, without bothering to reconnoiter, used the borrowed key and entered. No one was visible or audible. I lost no time mounting a flight, getting into Hattie Annis' room, and shutting the door. I opened the bottom drawer of her desk, took the package from my pocket and shoved it underneath some papers, closed the drawer, and breathed. Of course I would have to do better than that, but at least it wasn't on me. As I was dropping my coat on a chair there was a knock at the door, and I called, "Come in!"

It was Noel Ferris, with a hat on and a coat over his

arm. He came in a couple of steps. "I thought I heard someone," he drawled. "Back again? Who let you in?"

"I just say open sesame."

He nodded. "I asked for that. Naturally, you could open the Gate of Hell with a hairpin, though I can't imagine why you'd want to. So you haven't found what you're looking for?"

"Nope."

"I'd be glad to help if I didn't have an appointment. I doubt—hello, Ray. The bloodhound's at it again."

Raymond Dell appeared on the sill and boomed, "Monstrous! A maggot at a carcass."

"Oh, the carcass is at the morgue. This is only the debris. I'd like to stay and help you keen, but I have to go." He went. Dell entered, crossed to a chair, and sat. "If my memory serves," he rumbled, "your name is Goodman."

"Right. Algernon Goodman. Call me Buster."

"I call no one Buster. In the name of heaven, can you find no better way to pass the time than pawing over the refuse of a departed soul?"

The question was, what would move him, short of picking him up and tossing him out? I wanted to get the package out of the drawer quick, since Purley Stebbins had certainly gone through the desk. Luckily I hit on it. "Well," I said, "I could find a worse way—sitting and watching someone else doing the pawing."

"*Touché!*" He arose. "An excellent line! Good enough for a curtain! Magnificent!" He turned and marched out, and I went and shut the door.

I glanced around. I had considered the problem on the way, and first I went to the door that might be a closet. It was, and to my surprise it wasn't a mess—a row of dresses and suits and skirts on hangers, boxes stacked on a shelf, shoes on a rack. No good. Tammy Baxter, if that was her name, had said that Stebbins had been in here more than an hour, and he could have done that closet in five minutes. I shut the door. The desk and the chest of drawers were even worse. I went to the piano and got up on the stool, lifted the hinged top, and looked in. Plenty of room, but no. It would interfere with the hammers, and what if one of them had come in after Stebbins had left and played a funeral march?

It would have to be the bed. There was no key in the door to the hall, but there was a bolt, and I went and slipped it, and then went to the bed and lifted an end of the mattress. There were two of them. The top one was soft, and the bottom one, stiff as a board, rested on wooden slats. No box spring. I got out my pocket-knife and made a slit on the underside of the top mattress, near the corner. I had never touched the package with my bare hands and this was no time to break the precedent, so before I took it from the drawer I got a glove from my overcoat pocket and put it on. With the package inside the mattress, the bed tidied, and the glove back in the overcoat pocket, I opened the door, descended to the lower hall, went to the telephone in a niche under the stairs, and dialed the number I knew best. Fritz answered, and I said I wanted to speak to Wolfe.

"But Archie! He and the lady are at lunch!"

"That's dandy. I'm not. This is one time to break a rule. Tell him I sound depressed."

In two minutes I had Wolfe's voice: "Yes?"

"Yes. All set. I'll be at the door to let her in. Have you got the name?"

"No. She has supplied further details, but I can't pry the name out of her. She is extremely difficult."

"That is not news. Okay, I'm waiting."

"She'll be there shortly. As you know, a person at

my table, man or woman, is a guest, and a guest must be allowed to finish a meal."

"By all means. Good heavens, yes. I'll go out and get a sandwich."

"You will not." He hung up.

That was at 1:22 P.M. It was 1:57 when she arrived. I know how to wait; I once spent nine rainy hours in a doorway waiting for someone to show at an entrance across the street; but that thirty-five minutes was a little tough. If either Homicide or Secret Service appeared on the scene, no matter for what, and found me there, the program would certainly be disrupted, and it might possibly be ruined. But a guest must be allowed to finish a meal. Of all the crap! There was no glass in the front door, and after the first fifteen minutes I spent most of the time peering through one of the little glass panels at the side, when I wasn't glancing at my watch. When she finally came I had the door open by the time she had one foot in the vestibule.

"Miss Annis' room," I said, and she went to the stairs. I followed her up, and in, and shut the door. You can't allow a guest to handle her own coat, so I took it and put it on a chair. "Did you stop on the way to make a phone call?" I demanded.

"That's not fair," she said. "I'm not a double-dealer either."

"Good. I'm glad you're not double something. I suppose we ought to spend a few minutes looking, for the record, but first there's a little detail. The name of the certain person. Initials will do."

She shook her head. "No. I settled that with Mr. Wolfe. I won't."

"You will if you want the package. You will not be quoted. We just want to know. We'll take it from there."

"No."

"Then no package."

"That's silly." Her brows were up. "Really, Mr. Goodwin. As smart as you are? Knowing that I know it's here in this room? I never said I would tell you the name. What will you do, grab it and run? Besides, I haven't seen the package yet. You wouldn't trick me, of course not, but seeing is believing. When I have it I might possibly . . . where is it?"

"When you have it you'll tell me the name."

"I didn't say that. I don't promise. Where is it?"

"I'd like to wring your neck."

"That makes us even. Where is it?"

There was no point in prolonging it. I quit. "You'd better look around a little," I said. "Your story is going to be that after Leach drove off you went in the house with me, and Mr. Wolfe and I stuck to it that we knew nothing about any counterfeit money, and you thought it was just possible that Miss Annis had left it here or brought it back here. That I said I had an appointment and went, and you stayed and had lunch with Mr. Wolfe, trying to worm something out of him. That when you left you came here to search Miss Annis' room, and found that I was already here with the same idea, and you found the package. With a story it helps to have some of it based on fact so you should look around. Say two minutes."

She shrugged—the kind of shrug that means I might as well humor him, he means well—and went to the desk and opened a drawer. I went and opened the hall door and glanced out, saw no one, and left the door open. "From here on," I told her, "you might follow the script. It will develop your dramatic talents. You might purr with pleasure if and when you find it. I'm supposed to be looking too, so I will."

I went and climbed onto the piano stool and lifted the lid, and the stool turned and nearly dumped me.

When she had finished with the desk drawers she looked at me, but I said, "Try the closet." There was some satisfaction, though not much, in making her work for it. And what do you suppose she did? She went straight to the bed, to the head, grabbed a corner of the mattress, and yanked it up. I stood and watched. She moved to the foot and yanked again, saw the slit, stuck her hand in, and came out with the package.

"By gum," I said, "I'll bet that's it! Was it inside the mattress?"

She went to the sofa and sat and started untying the string. I said, "There might be something else," stepped to the bed, lifted the mattress, and inserted my hand in the slit. You never know what modern science will do next. They might have an electronic smeller that could prove I had handled it, and it was just as well to have an answer. So my hand was in the slit and my back to the hall door when a man's voice came, not loud but mean: "I want that. Hand it over."

I jerked my hand out and whirled, and the voice said, "Stay where you are, Goodwin." It was Paul Hannah. He was standing in front of her with a knife in his hand—a kitchen knife with a shiny blade a foot long. His chubby cheeks were flushed and his eyes were as mean as his voice.

"You damn fool," I said. "Drop it." I moved a foot, but the point of the knife went closer to Tammy's middle, and I stopped. "I thought you were downtown rehearsing," I said. "You'll never get anywhere in show business if you skip rehearsals."

He ignored it. I was a good twelve feet away. The knife went closer to her, nearly touching. "Hand it over," he said. "Quick."

"Give it to him," I said. "What the hell."

She has claimed, since, that she misunderstood me. She has conceded that I might have meant give him the package, but that at the time she thought I was telling her to charge. Nuts. The truth is just the opposite; she would have handed it over if I hadn't told her to. She was simply born contrary, and what she did was an automatic reaction to my telling her to give it to him. She brought her legs up and jerked her body sideways, and of course I jumped—or rather, dived. I went for the arm that held the knife, but missed because her feet had bumped him. By the time I braked and turned he was back on balance and she had tumbled off the sofa onto the floor, hanging on to the package, and damned if he didn't ignore me and go for her, holding the knife high. I sprang and got his wrist and brought it down and over, and heard it crack. He let out a squeal and the knife dropped, and in my enthusiasm I gave his arm another twist, and he crumpled to the floor just as Tammy got back on her feet. And as Raymond Dell appeared in the doorway and boomed: "Who is dog and who is bear?"

"No bear," I said. "Hyena." I picked up the knife. "He was waving this at Miss Baxter. I'll quit disturbing you if you'll go and call Watkins 9–8241, get Sergeant Stebbins, and tell him I have a murderer here for him. Not Goodman, Goodwin. I'll repeat the number: Watkins 9–8241."

"I'll go," Tammy said, and was moving, but I got her arm.

"You will not," I said firmly. "You wouldn't call that number, at least not first. —If you please, Mr. Dell?"

"Monstrous," he said, and turned and went.

I glanced at Paul Hannah, still on the floor, holding his right wrist with his left hand, and let go of Tammy's arm. "I know you didn't promise," I said, "but I may have saved you from a scratch. Just as a personal favor, may I have the name now?"

"Go climb a tree," she said.

VIII

One afternoon a couple of months later, the day after a jury of four women and eight men made it thumbs down for Paul Hannah, I got back to the office from doing an errand and found Wolfe at his desk working on one of those highbrow crossword puzzles in the *London Observer*. As I sat at my desk he looked up.

"A message for you," he said. "Call Byron 7–6232."

"Thanks. It's not urgent."

He grunted. "I recognized the voice."

"Sure."

"I am not inquisitive about your personal affairs, but I like to know when you pursue an acquaintance that began in this office. I didn't know you were cultivating her."

"I didn't either. I'll have to look up 'cultivate.' "

"To seek the society of. To court intimacy with."

I gave it a thought. "I don't like that 'court.' I suppose you could say that when two prizefighters sign up for a bout they are seeking each other's society. You might even say that when one of them aims a jab at the other one's nose he is courting intimacy with him. As you see, it's very complicated."

"It is indeed. You understand that my only concern is with any possible untoward effect on the operation of this office. I trust there will be none."

"So do I," I said.

ABOUT THE AUTHOR

REX STOUT, the creator of Nero Wolfe, was born in Noblesville, Indiana, in 1886, the sixth of nine children of John and Lucetta Todhunter Stout, both Quakers. Shortly after his birth, the family moved to Wakarusa, Kansas. He was educated in a country school, but, by the age of nine, was recognized throughout the state as a prodigy in arithmetic. Mr. Stout briefly attended the University of Kansas, but left to enlist in the Navy, and spent the next two years as a warrant officer on board President Theodore Roosevelt's yacht. When he left the Navy in 1908, Rex Stout began to write free-lance articles, worked as a sightseeing guide and as an itinerant bookkeeper. Later he devised and implemented a school banking system which was installed in four hundred cities and towns throughout the country. In 1927 Mr. Stout retired from the world of finance and, with the proceeds of his banking scheme, left for Paris to write serious fiction. He wrote three novels that received favorable reviews before turning to detective fiction. His first Nero Wolfe novel, *Fer-de-Lance*, appeared in 1934. It was followed by many others, among them, *Too Many Cooks, The Silent Speaker, If Death Ever Slept, The Doorbell Rang* and *Please Pass the Guilt*, which established Nero Wolfe as a leading character on a par with Erle Stanley Gardner's famous protagonist, Perry Mason. During World War II, Rex Stout waged a personal campaign against Nazism as chairman of the War Writers' Board, master of ceremonies of the radio program "Speaking of Liberty" and as a member of several national committees. After the war, he turned his attention to mobilizing public opinion against the wartime use of thermonuclear devices, was an active leader in the Authors' Guild and resumed writing his Nero Wolfe novels. Rex Stout died in 1975 at the age of eighty-eight. A month before his death, he published his seventy-second Nero Wolfe mystery, *A Family Affair*.

Share in a publishing event!
Rex Stout's Nero Wolfe returns in

Murder in E Minor
by Robert Goldsborough.

Here are special advance preview chapters from
MURDER IN E MINOR, which will be available
as a Bantam hardcover on April 1, 1986, at
your local bookseller.

I

November, 1977

Nero Wolfe and I have argued for years about whether the client who makes his first visit to us before or after noon is more likely to provide an interesting—and lucrative—case. Wolfe contends that the average person is incapable of making a rational decision, such as hiring him, until he or she has had a minimum of two substantial meals that day. My own feeling is that the caller with the greater potential is the one who has spent the night agonizing, finally realizes at dawn that Wolfe is the answer, and does something about it fast. I'll leave it to you to decide, based on our past experience, which of us has it better pegged.

I'd have been more smug about the timing of Maria Radovich's call that rainy morning if I'd thought there was even one chance in twenty that Wolfe would see her, let alone go back to work. It had been more than two years since Orrie Cather committed suicide—with Wolfe's blessing and mine. At the time, the realization that one of his longtime standbys had murdered three people didn't seem to unhinge Wolfe, but since then I had come to see that the whole business had rocked him pretty good. He would never admit it, of course, with that ego fit for his seventh of a ton, but he was still stung that someone who for years had sat at his table, drunk his liquor, and followed his orders could be a cool and deliberate killer. And even though the D.A. had reinstated both our licenses shortly after Orrie's death, Wolfe had stuck his head in the sand and still hadn't pulled it out. I tried needling him back to work, a tactic that had been successful in the past, but I got stonewalled, to use a word he hates.

"Archie," he would say, looking up from his book, "as I have told you many times, one of your most commendable attributes through the years has been your ability to badger me into working. That former asset is now a liability. You may goad me if you wish, but it is futile. I will not take the bait. And desist using the word 'retired.' I prefer to say that I have withdrawn from practice." And with that, he would return to his book, which currently was a re-reading of *Emma* by Jane Austen.

It wasn't that we did not have opportunities. One well-fixed Larchmont widow offered twenty grand for starters if Wolfe would find out who poisoned her chauffeur, and I couldn't even get him to see her. The murder was never solved, although I leaned toward the live-in maid, who was losing out in a triangle to the gardener's daughter. Then there was the Wall Street money man—you'd know his name right off—who said Wolfe could set his own price if only we'd investigate his son's death. The police and the coroner had called it a suicide, but the father was convinced it was a narcotics-related murder. Wolfe politely but firmly turned the man down in a ten-minute conversation in the office, and the kid's death went on the books as a suicide.

I couldn't even use the money angle to stir him. On some of our last big cases, Wolfe insisted on having the payments spread over a long period, so that a series of checks—some of them biggies—rolled in every month. That, coupled with a bunch of good investments, gave him a cash flow that was easily sufficient to operate the old brownstone on West Thirty-fifth Street near the Hudson that has been home to me for more than half my life. And operating the brownstone doesn't come cheap, because Nero Wolfe has costly tastes. They include my salary as his confidential assistant, errand boy, and—until two years ago—man of action, as well as those of Theodore Horstmann, nurse to the ten thousand orchids Wolfe grows in the plant rooms up on the roof, and Fritz Brenner, on whom I would bet in a cook-off against any other chef in the universe.

I still had the standard chores, such as maintaining the orchid germination records, paying the bills, figuring the taxes, and handling Wolfe's correspondence. But I had lots of free time now, and Wolfe didn't object to a little free-lancing. I did occasional work for Del Bascomb, a first-rate local operative, and also teamed with Saul Panzer on a couple of jobs, including the Masters kidnapping case, which you may have read about. Wolfe went so far as to compliment me on that one, so at least I knew he still read about crime, although he refused to let me talk about it in his presence anymore.

Other than having put his brain in the deep freeze, Wolfe kept his routine pretty much the same as ever: Breakfast on a tray in his room; four hours a day—9 to 11 a.m. and 4 to 6 p.m.—in the plant rooms with Theodore; long conferences with Fritz on menus and food preparation; and the best meals in Manhattan. The rest of the time, he was in his oversized chair behind his desk in the office reading and drinking beer. And refusing to work.

Maria Radovich's call came at nine-ten on Tuesday morning, which meant Wolfe was up with the plants. Fritz was in the kitchen, working on one of Wolfe's favorite lunches, sweetbreads in bechamel sauce and truffles. I answered at my desk, where I was balancing the checkbook.

"Nero Wolfe's residence. Archie Goodwin speaking."

"I need to see Mr. Wolfe—today. May I make an appointment?" It was the voice of a young woman, shaky, and with an accent that seemed familiar to me.

"I'm sorry, but Mr. Wolfe isn't consulting at the present time," I said, repeating a line I had grown to hate.

"Please, it's important that I see him. I think my—"

"Look, Mr. Wolfe isn't seeing any one, honest. I can suggest some agencies if you're looking for a private investigator."

"No, I want Mr. Nero Wolfe. My uncle has spoken of him, and I am sure he would want to help. My uncle knew Mr. Wolfe many years ago in Montenegro, and—"

"Where?" I barked it out.

"In Montenegro. They grew up there together. And now I am frightened about my uncle . . ."

Ever since it became widely known that Wolfe had retired—make that withdrawn from practice—would-be clients had cooked up some dandy stories to try to get him working again. I was on their side, but I knew Wolfe well enough to realize that almost nothing would bring him back to life. This was the first time, though, that anyone had been ingenious enough to come up with a Montenegro angle, and I admire ingenuity.

"I'm sorry to hear that you're scared," I said, "but Mr. Wolfe is pretty hard-hearted. I've got a reputation as a softie, though. How soon can your uncle be here? I'm Mr. Wolfe's confidential assistant, and I'll be glad to see him, Miss . . ."

"Radovich, Maria Radovich. Yes, I recognized your name. My uncle doesn't know I am calling. He would be angry. But I will come right away, if it's all right."

I assured her it was indeed all right and hung up, staring at the open checkbook. It was a long-shot, no question, but if I had anything to lose by talking to her, I couldn't see it. And just maybe, the Montenegro bit was for real. Montenegro, in case you don't know, is a small piece of Yugoslavia, and it's where Wolfe comes from. He still has relatives there; I send checks to three of them every month. But as for old friends, I doubted any were still alive. His closest friend ever, Marko Vukcic, had been murdered years ago, and the upshot was that Wolfe and I went tramping off to the Montenegrin mountains to avenge his death. And although Wolfe was anything but gabby about his past, I figured I knew just about enough to eliminate the possibility of a close comrade popping up. But there's no law against hoping.

I got a good, leisurely look at her through the one-way panel in the front door as she stood in the drizzle ringing our bell. Dark-haired, dark-eyed, and slender, she had a touch of Mia Farrow in her face. And like Farrow in several of her rolés, she seemed frightened and unsure. But looking through the glass, I was convinced that with Maria Radovich, it was no act.

She jumped when I opened the door. "Oh! Mr. Goodwin?"

"The selfsame," I answered with a slight bow and an earnest smile. "And you are Maria Radovich, I presume? Please come in out of the twenty-percent chance of showers."

I hung her trenchcoat on the hall rack and motioned toward the office. Walking behind her, I could see that her figure, set off by a skirt of fashionable length, was a bit fuller than I remembered Mia Farrow's to be, and that was okay with me.

"Mr. Wolfe doesn't come down to the office for another hour and ten minutes," I said, motioning to the yellow chair nearest my desk. "Which is fine, because he wouldn't see you anyway. At least not right now. He thinks he's retired from the detective business. But I'm not." I flipped open my notebook and swiveled to face her.

"I'm sure if Mr. Wolfe knew about my uncle's trouble, he would want to do something right away," she said, twisting a scarf in her lap and leaning forward tensely.

"You don't know him, Miss Radovich. He can be immovable, irascible, and exasperating when he wants to, which is most of the time. I'm afraid you're stuck with me, at least for now. Maybe we can get Mr. Wolfe interested, later, but to do that, I've got to know everything. Like for starters, who is your uncle and why are you worried about him?"

"He is my great-uncle, really," she answered, still using only the front quarter of the chair cushion. "And he is very well-known. Milan Stevens. I am sure you have heard of him—he is music director, some people say conductor, of the New York Symphony."

Not wanting to look stupid or disappoint her, or both, I nodded. I've been to the symphony four or five times, always with Lily Rowan, and it was always her idea. Milan Stevens may have been the conductor one or more of those times, but I wouldn't take an oath on it. The name was only vaguely familiar.

"Mr. Goodwin, for the last two weeks, my uncle has been getting letters in the mail—awful, vile letters. I think someone may want to kill him, but he just throws the letters away. I am frightened. I am sure that—"

"How many letters have there been, Miss Radovich? Do you have any of them?"

She nodded and reached into the shoulder bag she had set on the floor. "Three so far, all the same." She handed the crumpled sheets over, along with their envelopes, and I spread them on my desk. Each was on six-by-nine-inch notepaper, plain white, the kind from an inexpensive tear-off pad. They were hand-printed, in all caps, with a black felt-tip pen. One read:

MAESTRO
QUIT THE PODIUM NOW! YOU ARE DOING DAMAGE TO A GREAT ORCHESTRA PUT DOWN THE BATON AND GET OUT IF YOU DON'T LEAVE ON YOUR OWN, YOU WILL BE REMOVED—PERMANENTLY!

In fact, all three weren't exactly alike. The wording differed, though only slightly. The "on your own" in the last sentence was missing from one note, and the first sentence didn't have an exclamation point in another. Maria had lightly penciled the numbers 1, 2, and 3 on the backs of each to indicate the order in which they were received. The envelopes were of a similar ordinary stock, each hand-printed to Milan Stevens at an address in the East Seventies. "His apartment?" I asked.

Maria nodded. "Yes, he and I have lived there since we came to this country, a little over two years ago."

"Miss Radovich, before we talk more about these notes, tell me about your uncle, and yourself. First, you said on the phone that he and Mr. Wolfe knew each other in Montenegro."

She eased back into the chair and nodded. "Yes, my uncle—his real name is Stefanovic, Milos Stefanovic. We are from Yugoslavia. I was born in Belgrade, but my uncle is a Montenegrin. That's a place on the Adriatic. But of course I don't have to tell you that—I'm sure you know all about it from Mr. Wolfe.

"My uncle's been a musician and conductor all over Europe—Italy, Austria, Germany. He was conducting in London last, before we came here. But long ago, he did some fighting in Montenegro. I know little of it, but I think he was involved in an independence movement. He doesn't like to talk about that at all, and he never mentioned Mr. Wolfe to me until one time when his picture was in the papers. It was something to do with a murder or a suicide—I think maybe your picture was there too?"

I nodded. That would have been when Orrie died. "What did your uncle say about Mr. Wolfe?"

"I gather they had lost touch over the years. But he didn't seem at all interested in getting in touch with Mr. Wolfe. At the time I said, 'How wonderful that such an old friend is right here. What a surprise! You'll call him, of course?' But Uncle Milos said no, that was part of the past. And I got the idea from the way he acted that they must have had some kind of difference. But that was so long ago!"

"If you sensed your uncle was unfriendly toward Mr. Wolfe, what made you call?"

"After he told me about knowing Mr. Wolfe back in

Montenegro, Uncle Milos kept looking at the picture in the paper and nodding his head. He said to me, 'He had the finest mind I have ever known. I wish I could say the same for his disposition.'"

I held back a smile. "But you got the impression that your uncle and Mr. Wolfe were close at one time?"

"Absolutely," Maria said. "Uncle Milos told me they had been through some great difficulty together. He even showed me this picture from an old scrapbook." She reached again into her bag and handed me a gray-toned photograph mounted on cardboard and ragged around the edges.

They certainly fit my conception of a band of guerrillas, although none looked to be out of his teens. There were nine in all, posed in front of a high stone wall, four kneeling in front and five standing behind them. Some were wearing long overcoats, others had on woolen shirts, and two wore what I think of as World War I helmets. I spotted Wolfe instantly, of course. He was second from the left in the back row, with his hands behind his back and a bandolier slung over one shoulder. His hair was darker then, and he weighed at least one hundred pounds less, but the face was remarkably similar to the one I had looked at across the dinner table last night. And his glare had the same intensity, coming at me from a faded picture, that it does in the office when he thinks I'm badgering him.

To Wolfe's right in the photo was Marko Vukcic, holding a rifle loosely at his side. "Which one's your uncle?" I asked Maria.

She leaned close enough so I could smell her perfume and pointed to one of the kneelers in front. He was dark-haired and intense like most of the others, but he appeared smaller than most of them. None of the nine, though, looked as if he were trying to win a congeniality contest. If they were as tough as they appeared, I'm glad I wasn't fighting against them.

"This picture was taken up in the mountains," Maria said. "Uncle Milos only showed it to me to point out Mr. Wolfe, but he wouldn't talk any more about the other men or what they were doing."

"Not going to a picnic," I said. "I'd like to hang onto this for a while. Now, what about you, Miss Radovich?

How does it happen you're living with a great-uncle?"

She told me about how her mother, a widow, had died when she was a child in Yugoslavia, and that Stefanovic, her mother's uncle, had legally adopted her. Divorced and without children, he was happy to have the companionship of a nine-year-old. Maria said he gave her all the love of a parent, albeit a strict one, taking her with him as he moved around Europe to increasingly better and more prestigious conducting jobs. At some time before moving to England, he had changed his name to Stevens—she couldn't remember exactly when. It was while they were living in London that he was picked as the new conductor, or music director if you prefer, of the New York Symphony. Maria, who by that time was twenty-three, made the move with him, and she was now a dancer with a small troupe in New York.

"Mr. Goodwin," she said, leaning forward and tensing again, "my uncle has worked hard all his life to get the kind of position and recognition he has today. Now somebody is trying to take it away from him." Her hand gripped my forearm.

"Why not just go to the police?" I asked with a shrug.

"I suggested that to Uncle Milos, and he became very angry. He said it would leak out to the newspapers and cause a scandal at the symphony, that the publicity would be harmful to him and the orchestra. He says these notes are from a crazy person, or maybe someone playing a prank. I was with him when he opened the first one, or I might not know about any of this. He read it and said something that means 'stupid' in Serbo-Croatian, then crumpled the note and threw it in the wastebasket. But he hardly spoke the rest of the evening.

"I waited until he left the room to get the note from the basket. It was then that I said we should call the police. He became upset and said it was probably a prankster, or maybe a season-ticket holder who didn't like the music the orchestra had been playing."

"How long until the next note?" I asked.

"I started watching the mail after that. Six days later, we got another envelope printed just like the first one. I didn't open it—I never open my uncle's mail. But again I found the crumpled note in the wastebasket next to his desk in the library. This time I didn't mention it to him, and he said nothing about it to me, but again he seemed distressed.

"The third note came yesterday, six days after the second, and again I found it in the wastebasket. Uncle Milos doesn't know that I've seen the last two notes, or that I've saved all three."

"Miss Radovich, does your uncle have any enemies you know of, anyone who would gain by his leaving the symphony?"

"The music director of a large orchestra always has his detractors." She took a deep breath. "There are always people who think it can be done better. Some are jealous, others just take pleasure in scoffing at talented people. My uncle does not discuss his work very much at home, but I do know, from him and from others, that he has opposition even within the orchestra. But notes like this, I can't believe—"

"*Someone* is writing them, Miss Radovich. I'd like to hear more about your uncle's opposition, but Mr. Wolfe will be down in just a few minutes, and it's best if you're not here when he comes in. He may get interested in your problem, but you'll have to let me be the one to try getting him interested."

For the third time, Maria dove into her bag. She fished out a wad of bills and thrust it at me. "There's five hundred dollars here," she said. "That is just for agreeing to try to find out who's writing the notes. I can pay another forty-five hundred dollars if you discover the person and get him to stop." Five grand was a long way below what Wolfe usually got as a fee, but I figured that for Maria Radovich, it was probably big bucks. I started to return the money, then I drew back and smiled.

"Fair enough," I said. "If I can get Nero Wolfe to move, we keep this. Otherwise, it goes back to you. Now we've got to get you out of here. You'll be hearing from me soon—one way or the other." I wrote her a receipt for the money, keeping a carbon, and hustled her out to the hall and on with her coat.

My watch said ten fifty-eight as she went down the steps to the street. I rushed back to the office, put the money and receipt in the safe, and arranged Wolfe's morning mail in a pile on his blotter. Included in the stack was one item the carrier hadn't delivered: a faded fifty-year-old photograph.

2

I just had time to get my paper in the typewriter and start on yesterday's dictation when I heard the elevator coming down from the plant rooms. "Good morning, Archie, did you sleep well?" he asked as he walked across to his desk, arranged a raceme of orchids in the vase, then settled his bulk into the only chair he likes and rang for beer.

"Yes sir," I answered, looking up. Despite his size, and we're talking about a seventh of a ton here, I've never gotten used to how efficient Wolfe is when he moves. Somehow, you keep thinking he's going to trip or do something clumsy when he goes around behind his desk, but he never does. Everything is smooth, even graceful— if you can use that word with someone so large. Then there are his clothes. Fat people get a rap for being sloppy, but not Nero Wolfe. Today, as usual, he was wearing a three-piece suit, this one a tan tweed, with a fresh yellow shirt and a brown silk tie with narrow yellow stripes. His wavy hair, still brown but with a healthy dose of gray mixed in, was carefully brushed. He'd never admit it to me or anybody else, but Nero Wolfe spent his share of time in front of the mirror every morning, and that included shaving with a straight razor, something I quit trying years ago when I got tired of the sight of my own blood.

I kept sneaking glances at Wolfe while he riffled through the stack of mail. The photograph was about half-way down, but he took his time getting there, stopping as I knew he would to peruse a seed catalog. I typed on.

"Archie!" It was a high-grade bellow, the first one he'd uncorked in months.

I looked up, feigning surprise.

"Where did this come from?" he asked, jabbing at the picture.

"What's that, sir?" I raised one eyebrow, which always gets him because he can't do it.

"You know very well. How did this get here? What envelope was it in?"

"Oh, *that*. Well, let me think . . . yes, of course, I almost forgot. It was brought by a young woman, nice-looking, too. She thought you might be interested in helping her with a problem."

Wolfe glowered, then leaned forward and studied the photograph. "They must all be dead by now . . . Two were killed by firing squads, one died in a foolhardy duel, another drowned in the Adriatic. And Marko . . ."

"They're not *all* dead," I put in. "You aren't, not legally anyway, although you've been putting on a good imitation for a couple of years. And there's at least one other living man in that picture."

Wolfe went back to the photograph, this time for more than a minute. "*Stefanovic.*" He pronounced it far differently than I would have. "I have no knowledge of his death."

"You win a case of salt-water taffy," I said. "Not only is he still breathing, but he lives right here in New York. And what's more, he's famous. Of course he's changed his name since you knew him."

Wolfe shot me another glower. His index finger was tracing circles on the arm of the chair, the only outward indication that he was furious. I knew more than he did about something and was forcing him to ask questions, which made it even worse.

"Archie, I have suffered your contumacy for longer than I care to think about." He pursed his lips. "Confound it, report!"

"Yes, sir," I said, maintaining a somber expression. Then I unloaded everything verbatim, from Maria's phone call to the money. When I got to the part about the three notes, I opened the safe and pulled them out, but he refused to give them a glance. During my whole report, he sat with his eyes closed, fingers interlaced on his center mound. He interrupted twice to ask questions. When I was through, he sat in silence, eyes still closed.

After about five minutes, I said, "Are you asleep, or just waiting for me to call in a portrait painter so he can capture your favorite pose?"

"Archie, shut up!" That made it two bellows in one day. I was trying to think up something smart to say that would bring on a third and set a record, but Fritz came in and announced lunch.

Wolfe has a rule, never broken, that business is not to be discussed during meals, and it had been an easy rule to keep for the last two years, since there wasn't any business. That day, though, my mind was on other things and I barely tasted Fritz's superb sweetbreads. Wolfe, however, consumed three helpings at his normal, unhurried pace, while holding forth on the reasons why third parties have been unsuccessful in American elections.

We finally went back to the office for coffee. During lunch, I decided I'd pushed Wolfe enough and would leave the next move to him. We sat in silence for several minutes, and I was beginning to revise my strategy when he got up and went to the bookshelf. He pulled down the big atlas, lugged it back to his desk, and opened it. He looked at a page, then turned back to the photograph, fingering it gently.

"Archie?" He drew in a bushel of air, then let it out slowly.

"Yes, sir?"

"You know Montenegro, at least superficially."

"Yes, sir."

"You also know—I have told you—that in my youth there, I was impetuous and headstrong, and that I sometimes showed a pronounced lack of judgment."

"So you have said."

"A half-century ago in Montenegro, Milos Stefanovic and I were relatively close friends, although I never shared his consuming interest in music. We fought together, along with Marko and others in the photograph, for a cause in which we strongly believed. On one occasion in Cetinje, Stefanovic saved my life. And then, for reasons that are now irrelevant, he and I parted, not without rancor. I haven't seen him since that time, and I probably haven't thought about him for twenty years, at least. I mention this by way of telling you that we are faced with an extraordinary circumstance."

"Yes, sir." Although Wolfe's upstairs horsepower is far greater than mine, I've been around long enough to know when he's rationalizing. I stifled a smile.

"I am duty-bound to see this woman." He spread his hands in what for him is a dramatic gesture of helplessness. "I have no choice. Tell her to be here at three o'clock. Also, it's been a long time since Mr. Cohen has joined us for dinner. Call and invite him for tonight. And tell him we will be serving that cognac he enjoys so much."

I was delighted, of course, that Wolfe had agreed to see Maria. But his wanting Lon Cohen to come for dinner was a bonus. Lon works for the *Gazette*, where he has an office two doors from the publisher's on the twentieth floor. He doesn't have a title I'm aware of, but I can't remember a major story in New York that he didn't know more about than ever appeared in the *Gazette*, or anyplace else, for that matter. Lon and I play in the same weekly poker game, but he only comes to dinner at Wolfe's a couple of times a year, and it's almost always when Wolfe wants information. This is all right with Lon, because he's gotten a fat file of exclusive stories from us through the years, not to mention some three-star meals.

As it turned out, Lon was available, although he wanted to know what was up. I told him he'd just have to wait, and that there was some Remisier to warm his tummy after dinner. He said for that he'd sell any state secrets he had lying around the office. And Maria could make it at three. "Does this mean Mr. Wolfe will take the case?" she asked over the phone breathlessly.

"Who knows?" I answered. "But at least he'll see you, and that alone is progress."

I went to the kitchen to tell Fritz there would be a guest for dinner. "Archie, things are happening today, I can tell. Is he going back to work?"

Fritz always fusses when Wolfe is in one of his periodic relapses. He acts like we're on the brink of bankruptcy at all times and thinks that if Wolfe isn't constantly performing feats of detection, there won't be enough money to pay his salary or, more important, the food bills. Needless to say, the last two years of inactivity by Wolfe had left Fritz with a permanently long puss, and I more than once caught him in the kitchen wringing his hands, looking heavenward, and muttering things in

French. "Archie, he needs to work," Fritz would say. "He enjoys his food more then. Work sharpens his appetite." I always replied that his appetite seemed plenty sharp to me, but he just shook his head mournfully.

This time, though, I delighted to report that prospects were improving. "Keep your carving knives crossed," I told him, "and say a prayer to Brillat-Savarin."

"I'll do more than that," he said. "Tonight, you and Mr. Wolfe and Mr. Cohen will have a dinner to remember." Whistling, he turned to his work, and I whistled a bit myself on the way back to the office.